PATRICIA WENTWORTH
DANGER CALLING

PATRICIA WENTWORTH was born Dora Amy Elles in India in 1877 (not 1878 as has sometimes been stated). She was first educated privately in India, and later at Blackheath School for Girls. Her first husband was George Dillon, with whom she had her only child, a daughter. She also had two stepsons from her first marriage, one of whom died in the Somme during World War I.

Her first novel was published in 1910, but it wasn't until the 1920's that she embarked on her long career as a writer of mysteries. Her most famous creation was Miss Maud Silver, who appeared in 32 novels, though there were a further 33 full-length mysteries not featuring Miss Silver—the entire run of these is now reissued by Dean Street Press.

Patricia Wentworth died in 1961. She is recognized today as one of the pre-eminent exponents of the classic British golden age mystery novel.

By Patricia Wentworth

The Benbow Smith Mysteries
Fool Errant
Danger Calling
Walk with Care
Down Under

The Frank Garrett Mysteries
Dead or Alive
Rolling Stone

The Ernest Lamb Mysteries
The Blind Side
Who Pays the Piper?
Pursuit of a Parcel

Standalones
The Astonishing Adventure of Jane Smith
The Red Lacquer Case
The Annam Jewel
The Black Cabinet
The Dower House Mystery
The Amazing Chance
Hue and Cry
Anna Belinda
Will-O'-the-Wisp
Beggar's Choice
The Coldstone
Kingdom Lost
Nothing Venture
Red Shadow
Outrageous Fortune
Touch and Go
Fear by Night
Red Stefan
Blindfold
Hole and Corner
Mr. Zero
Run!
Weekend with Death
Silence in Court

PATRICIA WENTWORTH

DANGER CALLING

With an introduction by
Curtis Evans

DEAN STREET PRESS

Published by Dean Street Press 2016

Copyright © 1931 Patricia Wentworth

Introduction copyright © 2016 Curtis Evans

All Rights Reserved

The right of Patricia Wentworth to be identified as the Author of the Work has been asserted by her estate in accordance with the Copyright, Designs and Patents Act 1988.

Cover by DSP

First published in 1931 by Hodder & Stoughton

ISBN 978 1 911095 47 7

www.deanstreetpress.co.uk

Introduction

BRITISH AUTHOR Patricia Wentworth published her first novel, a gripping tale of desperate love during the French Revolution entitled *A Marriage under the Terror*, a little over a century ago, in 1910. The book won first prize in the Melrose Novel Competition and was a popular success in both the United States and the United Kingdom. Over the next five years Wentworth published five additional novels, the majority of them historical fiction, the best-known of which today is *The Devil's Wind* (1912), another sweeping period romance, this one set during the Sepoy Mutiny (1857-58) in India, a region with which the author, as we shall see, had extensive familiarity. Like *A Marriage under the Terror*, *The Devil's Wind* received much praise from reviewers for its sheer storytelling élan. One notice, for example, pronounced the novel "an achievement of some magnitude" on account of "the extraordinary vividness...the reality of the atmosphere...the scenes that shift and move with the swiftness of a moving picture...." (*The Bookman*, August 1912) With her knack for spinning a yarn, it perhaps should come as no surprise that Patricia Wentworth during the early years of the Golden Age of mystery fiction (roughly from 1920 into the 1940s) launched upon her own mystery-writing career, a course charted most successfully for nearly four decades by the prolific author, right up to the year of her death in 1961.

Considering that Patricia Wentworth belongs to the select company of Golden Age mystery writers with books which have remained in print in every decade for nearly a century now (the centenary of Agatha Christie's first mystery, *The Mysterious Affair at Styles*, is in 2020; the centenary of Wentworth's first mystery, *The Astonishing Adventure of Jane Smith*, follows merely three years later, in 2023), relatively little is known about the author herself. It appears, for example, that even the widely given year of Wentworth's birth, 1878, is incorrect. Yet it is sufficiently clear that Wentworth lived a varied and intriguing life that provided her ample inspiration for a writing career devoted to imaginative fiction.

It is usually stated that Patricia Wentworth was born Dora Amy Elles on 10 November 1878 in Mussoorie, India, during the heyday of the British Raj; however, her Indian birth and baptismal record states that she in fact was born on 15 October 1877 and was baptized on 26 November of that same year in Gwalior. Whatever doubts surround her actual birth year, however, unquestionably the future author came from a prominent Anglo-Indian military family. Her father, Edmond Roche Elles, a son of Malcolm Jamieson Elles, a Porto, Portugal wine merchant originally from Ardrossan, Scotland, entered the British Royal Artillery in 1867, a decade before Wentworth's birth, and first saw service in India during the Lushai Expedition of 1871-72. The next year Elles in India wed Clara Gertrude Rothney, daughter of Brigadier-General Octavius Edward Rothney, commander of the Gwalior District, and Maria (Dempster) Rothney, daughter of a surgeon in the Bengal Medical Service. Four children were born of the union of Edmond and Clara Elles, Wentworth being the only daughter.

Before his retirement from the army in 1908, Edmond Elles rose to the rank of lieutenant-general and was awarded the KCB (Knight Commander of the Order of Bath), as was the case with his elder brother, Wentworth's uncle, Lieutenant-General Sir William Kidston Elles, of the Bengal Command. Edmond Elles also served as Military Member to the Council of the Governor-General of India from 1901 to 1905. Two of Wentworth's brothers, Malcolm Rothney Elles and Edmond Claude Elles, served in the Indian Army as well, though both of them died young (Malcolm in 1906 drowned in the Ganges Canal while attempting to rescue his orderly, who had fallen into the water), while her youngest brother, Hugh Jamieson Elles, achieved great distinction in the British Army. During the First World War he catapulted, at the relatively youthful age of 37, to the rank of brigadier-general and the command of the British Tank Corps, at the Battle of Cambrai personally leading the advance of more than 350 tanks against the German line. Years later Hugh Elles also played a major role in British civil defense during the Second World War. In the event of a German invasion of Great Britain, something which seemed all too possible in 1940, he was tasked with leading the defense of southwestern England. Like Sir Edmond and Sir William, Hugh Elles attained the rank of lieutenant-general and was awarded the KCB.

Although she was born in India, Patricia Wentworth spent much of her childhood in England. In 1881 she with her mother and two younger brothers was at Tunbridge Wells, Kent, on what appears to have been a rather extended visit in her ancestral country; while a decade later the same family group resided at Blackheath, London at Lennox House, domicile of Wentworth's widowed maternal grandmother, Maria Rothney. (Her eldest brother, Malcolm, was in Bristol attending Clifton College.) During her years at Lennox House, Wentworth attended Blackheath High School for Girls, then only recently founded as "one of the first schools in the country to give girls a proper education" (*The London Encyclopaedia*, 3rd ed., p. 74). Lennox House was an ample Victorian villa with a great glassed-in conservatory running all along the back and a substantial garden--most happily, one presumes, for Wentworth, who resided there not only with her grandmother, mother and two brothers, but also five aunts (Maria Rothney's unmarried daughters, aged 26 to 42), one adult first cousin once removed and nine first cousins, adolescents like Wentworth herself, from no less than three different families (one Barrow, three Masons and five Dempsters); their parents, like Wentworth's father, presumably were living many miles away in various far-flung British dominions. Three servants--a cook, parlourmaid and housemaid--were tasked with serving this full score of individuals.

Sometime after graduating from Blackheath High School in the mid-1890s, Wentworth returned to India, where in a local British newspaper she is said to have published her first fiction. In 1901 the 23-year-old Wentworth married widower George Fredrick Horace Dillon, a 41-year-old lieutenant-colonel in the Indian Army with three sons from his prior marriage. Two years later Wentworth gave birth to her only child, a daughter named Clare Roche Dillon. (In some sources it is erroneously stated that Clare was the offspring of Wentworth's second marriage.) However in 1906, after just five years of marriage, George Dillon died suddenly on a sea voyage, leaving Wentworth with sole responsibly for her three teenaged stepsons and baby daughter. A very short span of years, 1904 to 1907, saw the deaths of Wentworth's husband, mother, grandmother and brothers Malcolm and Edmond, removing much of her support network. In 1908, however, her father, who was now sixty years old, retired from the army and returned to England, settling at Guildford, Surrey with an older unmarried sister named Dora (for whom his daughter presumably had been named).

Wentworth joined this household as well, along with her daughter and her youngest stepson. Here in Surrey Wentworth, presumably with the goal of making herself financially independent for the first time in her life (she was now in her early thirties), wrote the novel that changed the course of her life, *A Marriage under the Terror*, for the first time we know of utilizing her famous *nom de plume*.

The burst of creative energy that resulted in Wentworth's publication of six novels in six years suddenly halted after the appearance of *Queen Anne Is Dead* in 1915. It seems not unlikely that the Great War impinged in various ways on her writing. One tragic episode was the death on the western front of one of her stepsons, George Charles Tracey Dillon. Mining in Colorado when war was declared, young Dillon worked his passage from Galveston, Texas to Bristol, England as a shipboard muleteer (mule-tender) and joined the Gloucestershire Regiment. In 1916 he died at the Somme at the age of 29 (about the age of Wentworth's two brothers when they had passed away in India).

A couple of years after the conflict's cessation in 1918, a happy event occurred in Wentworth's life when at Frimley, Surrey she wed George Oliver Turnbull, up to this time a lifelong bachelor who like the author's first husband was a lieutenant-colonel in the Indian Army. Like his bride now forty-two years old, George Turnbull as a younger man had distinguished himself for his athletic prowess, playing forward for eight years for the Scottish rugby team and while a student at the Royal Military Academy winning the medal awarded the best athlete of his term. It seems not unlikely that Turnbull played a role in his wife's turn toward writing mystery fiction, for he is said to have strongly supported Wentworth's career, even assisting her in preparing manuscripts for publication. In 1936 the couple in Camberley, Surrey built Heatherglade House, a large two-story structure on substantial grounds, where they resided until Wentworth's death a quarter of a century later. (George Turnbull survived his wife by nearly a decade, passing away in 1970 at the age of 92.) This highly successful middle-aged companionate marriage contrasts sharply with the more youthful yet rocky union of Agatha and Archie Christie, which was three years away from sundering when Wentworth published *The Astonishing Adventure of Jane Smith* (1923), the first of her sixty-five mystery novels.

Although Patricia Wentworth became best-known for her cozy tales of the criminal investigations of consulting detective Miss Maud Silver, one of the mystery genre's most prominent spinster sleuths, in truth the Miss Silver tales account for just under half of Wentworth's 65 mystery novels. Miss Silver did not make her debut until 1928 and she did not come to predominate in Wentworth's fictional criminous output until the 1940s. Between 1923 and 1945 Wentworth published 33 mystery novels without Miss Silver, a handsome and substantial legacy in and of itself to vintage crime fiction fans. Many of these books are standalone tales of mystery, but nine of them have series characters. Debuting in the novel *Fool Errant* in 1929, a year after Miss Silver first appeared in print, was the enigmatic, nautically-named *eminence grise* Benbow Collingwood Horatio Smith, owner of a most expressively opinionated parrot named Ananias (and quite a colorful character in his own right). Benbow Smith went on to appear in three additional Wentworth mysteries: *Danger Calling* (1931), *Walk with Care* (1933) and *Down Under* (1937). Working in tandem with Smith in the investigation of sinister affairs threatening the security of Great Britain in *Danger Calling* and *Walk with Care* is Frank Garrett, Head of Intelligence for the Foreign Office, who also appears solo in *Dead or Alive* (1936) and *Rolling Stone* (1940) and collaborates with additional series characters, Scotland Yard's Inspector Ernest Lamb and Sergeant Frank Abbott, in *Pursuit of a Parcel* (1942). Inspector Lamb and Sergeant Abbott headlined a further pair of mysteries, *The Blind Side* (1939) and *Who Pays the Piper?* (1940), before they became absorbed, beginning with *Miss Silver Deals with Death* (1943), into the burgeoning Miss Silver canon. Lamb would make his farewell appearance in 1955 in *The Listening Eye*, while Abbott would take his final bow in mystery fiction with Wentworth's last published novel, *The Girl in the Cellar* (1961), which went into print the year of the author's death at the age of 83.

The remaining two dozen Wentworth mysteries, from the fantastical *The Astonishing Adventure of Jane Smith* in 1923 to the intense legal drama *Silence in Court* in 1945, are, like the author's series novels, highly imaginative and entertaining tales of mystery and adventure, told by a writer gifted with a consummate flair for storytelling. As one confirmed Patricia Wentworth mystery fiction addict, American

Golden Age mystery writer Todd Downing, admiringly declared in the 1930s, "There's something about Miss Wentworth's yarns that is contagious." This attractive new series of Patricia Wentworth reissues by Dean Street Press provides modern fans of vintage mystery a splendid opportunity to catch the Wentworth fever.

Curtis Evans

Chapter One

It has been said that life would be intolerable if we could know what was waiting for us round the next corner. Sometimes, of course, one is sure that one does know. On that Monday morning, coming back from a last bachelor week-end with the Raynes, Lindsay Trevor was sure.

This was Monday, and on Saturday he was going to be married to Marian Rayne. They would spend a honeymoon month in Italy, and when they returned they would have a flat in town and live happily ever after. He had not the least idea when he got into the train at Guildford that he was stepping off the path that he had so pleasantly mapped out. He bought a paper, closed the carriage door, and settled himself into a corner seat.

He was still unfolding his paper, when the door was wrenched nervously open and Miss Alethea Witherington got in with two bags, a basket, and a dog, and an attaché case, and some parcels. The parcels dropped, the basket caught Lindsay on the ankle, and the dog yapped. Lindsay supposed that it was a dog. It was very small and fluffy, and it wore a pale blue collar with three gilt bells, and was attached by a blue lead to a bony middle-aged lady with an enthusiastic eye and odd clothes. She settled herself in the opposite corner, and just before the train started a tall man with a stoop drifted in and sat down with his back to the engine. He at once produced a pair of horn-rimmed spectacles and began to read a shabby book which he pulled out of his pocket.

The train moved out of Guildford station, and Miss Alethea Witherington began to talk cooingly to the little fluffy creature on her lap.

"Didums like a puff-puff—didums then? Didums like to travel with 'ums mother, a precious?"

Lindsay looked over the top of his paper and caught her eye.

"I hope you don't object to dogs," she said at once.

He murmured something polite and went back to the golfing news.

Miss Witherington continued to talk to Didums. Perhaps if she went on talking, the young man would put down his paper and see what an exceptionally beautiful and intelligent creature Didums was. It was the chief object of her life to collect admirers, not for herself, but for Didums. The old gentleman was no good at all. Old gentlemen hardly ever liked animals—in railway carriages they sometimes approached rudeness; but young men liked dogs. This was a pleasant-looking young man, quite a gentleman—such a nice grey suit, and really pleasant features, without being handsome. Everyone couldn't be handsome, but this young man was decidedly pleasant looking and quite a gentleman.

She talked on. Was Didums warm? Was Didums cold? Was Didums hungry? Was he a clever, clever, *clever* boy? She had the sort of penetrating whisper which comes through everything.

Lindsay gave up trying to read, and merely kept the paper up because he felt certain that if he lowered it, he would be inveigled into a conversation about Didums. He envied the man in the far corner, who read his book with an air of classic calm. He himself was naturally impatient, and the woman was getting on his nerves. She was asking Didums again if he was hungry, after which there was a storm of yaps and an overpowering smell of banana. A paper bag crackled, and Didums was seized with a joyous frenzy.

"Sit then!" said Miss Witherington. "Sit up! No—not on Mother's knee! Oh, *no*, a precious—sitting up good and clever on the seat like a grown-up boy!"

Lindsay took another look round the paper. The creature was balancing its inches of fluff, waving its minute paws, and goggling brightly at the banana which Mother was peeling.

"Trust now!" she said. She pinched off a bit in her fingers and stuck it on the fluffy nose. "Trust!"

Lindsay withdrew. He could see that she was simply dying to gather an audience. There was an Ancient Mariner look about that enthusiastic eye, and quite definitely he declined the part of the wedding guest.

Miss Witherington continued to hope. After all, he had glanced once—and was it possible to glance at Didums once and not wish to glance again? Miss Witherington did not think so—not in the case of a young man who was quite a gentleman and so pleasant looking. Now that she had had another peep at him, he had quite a look of Lady Lorrimer's grandson—the one who had taken a scholarship and was such a comfort to her; not the one who got into debt at Oxford and so very nearly made a most unfortunate marriage.

Didums performed his whole repertory of tricks to the back of *The Times*. Miss Witherington no longer whispered, but the same penetrating quality informed her louder tones. The last trick was the best. Surely no one could be unmoved by the sight of Didums dying for his country.

"Die for your country, a precious! Die for your country, a clever, clever, *clever* boy!"

Didums died very realistically with one glistening eye on the last bit of banana. *The Times* was not lowered. No applause came from behind it. And then the train ran into Woking station and stopped.

Miss Witherington's colour had risen. She was revising her opinion of the young man opposite—an insensible person, and not really like that charming Mr Lorrimer at all. She gathered up the slighted Didums, and his basket with the pale blue lining, and the attaché case, and the paper bag full of bananas, and another bag full of biscuits, and precipitated herself out of the train and on to the neck of the stout red-faced woman, who was Ida Clement and her dearest friend. Ida loved Didums and had invited him specially to spend the day.

She embraced Mrs Clement more warmly than usual, and did not notice that she had dropped her paper bags until Lindsay picked them up for her. He picked up the basket too, and retrieved the parcels, which she had forgotten, and was snapped at by Didums for his pains. Ultimately he got back into his seat, a porter slammed the door, and the train began to move.

The train drew out of the station. The man in the corner turned a page and read on with that air of being in another century. Lindsay was wondering whether he so much as knew that there had been a dog in the carriage, when he laid his book down upon his knee, pushed up his spectacles till they rested on his forehead, and said, in a gentle cultured voice,

"How would you like to die for your country?"

Chapter Two

LINDSAY TREVOR looked across the carriage with a sort of startled amusement. How would you like to die for your country? What did one say to a total stranger who asked you a question like that?—a distinguished looking stranger, who gazed, not at him but past him at the window which framed a section of railway embankment? He might have been admiring the view, but it did not seem very likely. Lindsay began to wonder whether he was committed to making the rest of the journey with a lunatic.

As the thought passed through his mind, the distinguished stranger smiled very slightly and shifted his gaze. It rested now upon the cushioned back of the seat a little to the right of Lindsay's head. He spoke dreamily:

"Yes—you would naturally think so. But"—here for a moment he looked straight into Lindsay's eyes—"I am afraid I am quite responsible for my actions."

Lindsay experienced a curious shock of surprise. The smile was gentle, whimsical, and the eyes were as steady and sane as the multiplication table.

"I beg your pardon," he said, "but you asked me a question."

"Undoubtedly."

"And may I ask why?" said Lindsay Trevor.

The stranger took out a white silk handkerchief and another pair of spectacles, which he began to polish in an absent-minded manner.

"Yes," he said—"yes. Why does one ask anyone anything?"

"I suppose because one wants to know."

He breathed on the right-hand lens and rubbed it.

"You see, that is my point—I want to know. But if I ask you what I want to know, you jump to the conclusion that I am mad—a little madder, that is, than the vast mad majority. You see"—he stopped polishing—"I really have a reason for asking you whether you would die for your country."

He was not mad. It was curious that Lindsay was able to feel sure of this. He was an impressive person—and he was not mad. Lindsay began to have a vague idea that at some time he had seen him before. The pale classic features and thick grey hair, and the air of gentle abstraction, produced some far-away response of memory. He had the impression that here was someone he ought to be able to recognize, and yet he could not believe that they had ever met.

He leaned forward a little, his interest deepening.

"That is your question, sir—but I asked one too."

"Yes," he said—"yes."

"I asked you—advisedly—whether you would die for your country."

"And I asked you why you should ask me such a question."

He nodded slowly twice. Then he put his handkerchief on the seat beside him, laid the second pair of glasses on the top of it, and took out a very old Russia leather pocket-book. He extracted a card, a letter, and a photograph, and then laid the case down on the seat between him and the handkerchief. The initials lay uppermost—Gothic letters in tarnished silver—B. C. H. S. With the photograph in his hand, he leaned forward and proffered it to Lindsay.

Lindsay stared at it. The face was as familiar as his own—four years at Harrow, two years of the war. He had the duplicate of this photograph in an album at the flat.

"Jack Smith!" he exclaimed.

"Yes—John Warrington Smith—a nephew of mine."

Looking vaguely past Lindsay, he handed him the card which he had taken out of his pocket-book.

Lindsay took it with a good deal of curiosity. The lettering was old-fashioned, and the names corresponding to the four initials on the case were sufficiently remarkable. The card was inscribed:

MR BENBOW COLLINGWOOD HORATIO SMITH.

Light broke upon Lindsay Trevor. He had shared a study with Jack Smith, and it was in a frame on that study wall that he had seen Mr Smith's rather striking features. Some kind of a vague idea emerged that Jack Smith's uncle was rather a big bug in his way—some connection with the Foreign Office—with public events of the first magnitude. He had written a book—yes, that emerged quite clearly—a book in which he had not only forecast the war, but also its social and economic consequences. He rummaged for the title...*The European Problem*— yes, that was it—published somewhere about 1910. Only last week Hamilton Raeburn was quoting from it, and Egerton...no, he couldn't recall what Egerton had said; but whatever it was, it helped to make a background for Mr Benbow Collingwood Horatio Smith.

Mr Smith had by now unfolded the letter which he had taken out of his pocket and put on the second pair of glasses he had been polishing. With the first pair riding above them on his high white brow, he spoke, gazing sometimes at the space above Lindsay's head, and sometimes, with an effect of not really seeing it, at the paper in his hand.

"If I had to recognize you from a description, this would, I think, be a good one—and yet a description is at the best a mere catalogue."

He read: "Lindsay Trevor. Height medium—say five foot nine and a half. Slight build. Light brown hair. Light eyebrows and lashes. Eyes grey to hazel. Distinguishing features none. Marks and scars none."

He glanced up.

"I have a memorandum here. *Confirm this.*"

He continued to read from the letter: "Voice of medium timbre. Strong facial resemblance to—er—I think that's all."

Lindsay felt a vigorous curiosity. The description was an accurate one. But why describe him? He was neither a celebrity nor an absconding criminal. The unfinished sentence was decidedly intriguing. If he bore a strong facial resemblance to some unspecified person, he not unnaturally desired to know who that person was, and why Mr Smith should have stopped short of the name.

Mr Smith did not seem to be going to impart any more information. He folded the letter and put it away in the pocket-book with the initials. Then he held out his hand for his own card and his nephew's photograph.

"A little puzzling," he said. "But then you haven't answered my question."

All at once there was something immensely serious in the air. Lindsay could not have described it. He had a moment of confused thought such as is apt to follow upon a shock. In the confusion was a mingling of curiosity, excitement, and apprehension, with a hard-running undercurrent of something which threatened to take him off his feet and out of his depth. He did not know what this something was.

Mr Smith was putting away his pocket-book. Lindsay made a movement and spoke.

"I've heard of you, sir. Jack and I were at school together—I expect you know that. Why did you ask me that question? Were you serious?"

"Oh, entirely—entirely." He did not look at Lindsay. "I am a very serious person, and any question I ask is undoubtedly a serious affair." He paused, and added in a perfectly casual manner, "It might be serious for you."

"I suppose it would be—if I died."

It was a laughable thing to say, but Lindsay did not feel like laughing. He felt that current catch him by the feet.

"Yes—yes," said Mr Smith. And then, after a silence, "You have not answered my question."

A serious question, seriously asked—would he, Lindsay Trevor, like to die for his country? Theoretically, every decent citizen is prepared to do so—a good many of them did it in the war—Lindsay had taken his chance with the rest for two years...

It was a long time ago. A junior partner in a publishing firm isn't really in the running for laurel wreaths. He said so.

Mr Smith nodded.

"Publishing...just so...an adventurous business."

"Not always."

"If I had to read some of the books you publish, I should be inclined to welcome death!" said Mr Smith.

Lindsay wondered more than ever what he was driving at.

"What are you asking me to do?"

"Oh—a job." He folded his hands on his book and looked up. They were beautiful hands, very white and carefully kept. They looked strong too. "Yes, decidedly a job—for, if we take the definition given in the Oxford Dictionary, a job is—' a piece of work, especially one done for hire or profit'—the labourer being worthy of his hire, and the profits accruing to the state. The second definition would, I think, have to be inverted. The dictionary gives it as a transaction in which duty is sacrificed to private advantage'; where-as—" he paused, removed the upper of the two pairs of spectacles he was wearing, and balancing them between his thumb and forefinger, continued—"in your case it is your private advantage which you are being asked to sacrifice. The word duty has a highfalutin sound, but—well, there it is."

Lindsay was watching him closely. He was being played, as an angler plays a fish. The question was, would he allow himself to be played, or would he break the line and make off? He could, naturally, at any time. The fact was, he did not want to. The whole business had a lure, and in other circumstances he would probably have jumped at it. As it was—

"You're offering me a job of some sort—a dangerous job?"

"Well—" said Mr Smith in non-committal tones.

All at once the line snapped.

"I'm afraid, sir, that I have got a previous engagement."

Mr Smith swung his spectacles by the bridge.

"Engagement?" he asked.

"Yes, sir." Lindsay hesitated, and then put himself out of temptation's way. "I'm being married next week, sir."

The spectacles swung on Mr Smith's finger. He gazed at them earnestly. After a moment he spoke:

"Ah—yes—married. That is rather a pity—but I suppose you will not think so. May I congratulate the lady?"

"You may congratulate me," said Lindsay.

"Ah yes—of course," said Mr Smith.

He put the spectacles away in his waistcoat pocket, picked up the shabby book which he had been reading, and leaning back in his corner, retreated into the classic past. Lindsay could no more have addressed him than he could have addressed the emperor Marcus Aurelius with whom Mr Smith was engaged.

He too sat back in his corner. It was astonishing how hard temptation had tugged at him. A job—a dangerous job. Why? It was just as if the clock had been set back twelve years. His mind filled suddenly with pictures of his two years' work under Garrett in the Secret Service. The pictures came with such a rush that they ran one into another, quivering, blending, breaking; but each broken bit was astonishingly alive.

Lindsay sat and wondered at himself. If it hadn't been for Marian…

The train slid into Waterloo station. Mr Smith dropped his shabby brown book into his pocket and drifted out of the carriage in the same way that he had drifted in. On the platform he turned, however, and put out his hand, not in conventional farewell, but in a gesture vague yet arresting.

"If you change your mind—" he murmured.

"I only wish I could."

The words had spoken themselves. Lindsay had certainly not meant to say them, and he was aware of something like contrition. But Mr Smith had already turned and was making his way down the platform, a tall figure with a certain air of old-world distinction.

Lindsay Trevor watched him go. He had not meant what he had said; it had just slipped out. He put the whole thing from his mind and tried to realize that by this time next week he and Marian would have been married for nearly two days. It did not seem possible, He went on trying to make it seem possible.

Chapter Three

THE LETTER came next day.

Lindsay woke up to the sound of Poole drawing up the blind. He must have been sleeping more soundly than usual, for, as a rule, if the knock at the door did not rouse him, the firm manner in which Poole put down the tray with his early cup of tea did. The tray was already by his side, and, propped against the edge of it, a letter from Marian Rayne. He hated reading letters in bed, but it was Poole's habit to pick out Miss Rayne's letters and bring them in with the tea. He could, of course, have told Poole not to do this; but he was aware that if he did so, he would drop tremendously in his estimation. Sometimes he felt as if living up to Poole was rather a strain. He ran the flat and all that was in it, and there were times when Lindsay suspected that he ran Lindsay Trevor, and times when he wondered how Poole and Marian were going to get on together.

Poole was the perfect servant, but like all perfect servants he had very strong views as to how this perfection should be maintained. He had saved Lindsay's life twice in the last year of the war, and had looked upon him, respectfully but quite firmly, as his own property ever since.

When he had pulled up the blind, he turned from the window, displaying a pale clean-shaven face, sandy hair rather thin on the top, short sandy lashes, grey eyes, and a rather wooden cast of countenance. He told Lindsay the time and withdrew. In exactly a quarter of an hour Lindsay would hear him turning on the bath water.

Meanwhile Lindsay took a look at the weather, and thought what a beastly day it was—one of those unconvinced sort of fogs that are havering about whether they will turn to rain or settle down into a real peasouper. He thought December was a pretty good month to be getting out of England, and wondered where they would fetch up for Christmas. They hadn't been able to make up their minds about that.

Then he yawned, stretched, sat up, and reached for Marian Rayne's letter. It was very light and thin. She usually wrote as she talked, just running on and on. This envelope couldn't possibly hold more than a single sheet. He felt a little cheated as he switched on his reading-lamp and opened the letter. There was only one sheet, and on that sheet there were only a few blotted lines:

"Lin, I can't marry you. It's no use—I *can't*. If you love me the least little bit, don't try and make me change my mind. I can't do it.

"MARIAN."

He read the words, and then he read them again. He read them very slowly. He read them for the third time. Everything seemed to have come to a full stop.

He went on reading the letter, but he couldn't make himself feel that it had anything to do with Lindsay Trevor. It was like something read in a book. Afterwards it reminded him of trying to read Dutch—if you know English and German, the words all look perfectly clear and plain, and yet you can't make a page of it mean anything. He couldn't make Marian's letter mean anything.

He put it down and drank his tea. Then he took the letter up and began to read it all over again. Marian wasn't going to marry him; he had hold of the words. But she didn't say why. She only said, "Lin, I can't marry you." Why? She didn't say why; she just said, "I can't marry you—I *can't*."

He found that the hand in which he was holding the letter had started to shake a good deal. He tried holding it with the other hand, but it wasn't any better, so he put the letter down. There is nothing that makes you feel more of a fool than to see your own hand shaking like a bit of rag in the wind.

Then all at once the thing got through to where he could feel it. Marian—Marian wasn't going to marry him. It had got right through like fire that has been smouldering in a garment and suddenly reaches the flesh.

Lindsay sat there with the letter in his hand and the words of it burning themselves slowly into his consciousness—slowly, deeply, surely. The moments slid into minutes, very long minutes. And then, when realization was full, he forced himself to face it.

It was a relief to find that he could think quite clearly. The feeling of shock and pain seemed to be quite separate from his thinking. He looked again at the letter. Marian was not going to marry him. She gave no reason, and he knew of none—he knew of *none*. Something surged up in him at the word. There are words that touch the springs of agony. No reason—none—*none*. Other words pressed in through the breach made by this surging something—No more—never. He beat them back, closed down the breach, and turned ordered thought upon the catastrophe.

He had spent the week-end with the Raynes—the house very full, and so not much time alone with Marian; but no quarrel, no coldness— or none of which he had been aware. Marian was pale. He saw her for a moment like that, looking in, as it were, upon the havoc she had made—watching it; a little pale, a little pensive; black hair just pushed from her forehead, black lashes just drooping over grey-green eyes. The impression was startlingly distinct. He went resolutely back to the week-end. She was pale. Mr Rayne had joked about it—"Too many dressmakers!" he said. "Why does a girl want ten times as many dresses as usual just because she's going to get married? She can't wear more than one of them at a time—can she?"

It shocked him horribly to realize that he was looking back to the week-end of only two days ago as if it were something far away in the past. He was separated from it by a dim gulf. It was far—it was endlessly far away. It was like a country which one has left behind one long ago.

He got out of bed and put Marian's letter away in a dispatch-box. As he turned the key, the worst of the stunned feeling went. The fighting thing in him got up, raging. If she thought she could just chuck him over like that without a word—well, he would show her she couldn't. Half a dozen lines on a blotted sheet…He would show her. If she'd got a reason, she was damned well going to give him the reason. And, if she hadn't got a reason—if she hadn't got a reason…His thoughts seemed to run slower. If she hadn't got a reason, wasn't he well rid of a woman who would break a man's life for a whim?

He said it, and tried to mean it; but he couldn't—not at once—not quite at once. This was Tuesday. They were going to have been married on Saturday…"I can't marry you, Lin—I *can't*."

He heard the bath water running.

Chapter Four

IN A PLAY the curtain comes down on a situation. In real life there is no curtain to come down; everything goes on; there is no darkened stage, no retreat to the dressing-room where one may refit for another part. Marian Rayne was not going to marry Lindsay Trevor—but the bath water was running.

It was as much a part of the scheme of things that he should have his bath, shave, dress, and go through the routine of an endless, empty day, as it was that the earth should turn upon its axis. The earth turned because of some compelling force.

It turned in fact because it had to. Lindsay would go on for the same reason. He thought with a kind of bitter resentment that he was not the first man who would have given almost anything to be able to blot out the immediate future, and by many millions he would not be the last. People talk and write about blotting out the past; but after some shattering blow it is the next intolerable minutes—hours—days—weeks which one would give the world and all to blot out.

Lindsay went through his accustomed routine. He bathed, shaved, dressed, and went into his sitting-room, where he put up *The Times* between himself and Poole and did what he could to make an inordinate amount of bacon look as if some of it had been eaten.

With a perfectly wooden face, Poole presently removed the mangled remains, returning immediately with two boiled eggs. He did not say anything. He put the eggs down and stood there with his eyes fixed on the back sheet of *The Times*. Lindsay could feel Poole's determination that he should eat those eggs positively burning a hole in the paper. It was very difficult to deceive Poole. In this case it really was not worth while to try.

He pushed back his chair and got up, speaking abruptly, his voice a little louder than usual because it was an effort to speak at all.

"I've had bad news, Poole. I'll tell you about it presently. Take all this away and clear out. I want to telephone."

Poole asked no questions. When he was gone, Lindsay went to the telephone and gave the Raynes' number, turning a singularly obstinate profile to the room as he did so. Everything in him was now bent upon the determination to see Marian. Anger, resentment, and outraged pride clamoured for a hearing. He told himself that he had not any idea of asking her to change her mind. No, he put it more strongly—he had no desire to make her change her mind. A change of mind, a swing of the pendulum—no, thank you! She had smashed their affair, and that was all there was to it. It was smashed, and neither of them could put it together again. The old jingle of Humpty Dumpty ran in his head: "All the King's horses and all the King's men couldn't put Humpty Dumpty together again;" and on top of that, quite irrelevantly: "You can't make an omelette without breaking eggs." The words flickered on the surface of his mind, as such things do when the thoughts below cannot be faced. Lindsay was not ready for those thoughts yet.

Marian had smashed their marriage, and there was no mending it. But he was going to know the reason why. She owed him that. She had got to face the music—she had got to stand up to him and give him a reason for what she had done.

He got a servant at the other end of the line, and, after about two minutes, Mr Rayne, rather breathless. Lindsay wondered if he was breathless because he had been hauled in a hurry from the stables, or because he felt embarrassed at having to talk to him.

He said, "Hullo!" and then, "Is it you, Lindsay?"

Lindsay said, "Yes—Lindsay Trevor. Can I speak to Marian, please?"

"I don't think you can."

"I think I must."

Lindsay could hear him clearing his throat. It seemed curious to hear Rayne clearing his throat thirty-five miles away and yet not to be able to get hold of Marian.

"This is awkward—very awkward indeed." Rayne was certainly embarrassed.

"I've got to see her," said Lindsay.

Rayne cleared his throat again.

"It's very awkward. It's—it's damned awkward. Had you any suspicion?"

"No," said Lindsay Trevor. "You weren't prepared in any way?"

He said, "No," again.

"It was an absolute thunderbolt to her aunt and myself—an absolute thunderbolt. It's—it's—it's incredibly awkward."

"I want to see Marian."

Rayne cleared his throat.

"She won't see you."

The woman at the exchange intervened. She had one of those bright voices.

"Thrrree minutes, please."

"I'll have another three," said Lindsay sharply.

He was afraid Rayne would jump at any opportunity of getting away from his end of the telephone. He made up his mind what he was going to do. He said,

"Are you there? Can you give Marian a message? I think she ought to see me. I shall come down this afternoon. Will you tell her that?"

He rang off quickly. Then he rang up old Hamilton Raeburn and asked him if he need turn up at the office. Raeburn was fatherly and jocose—said they didn't expect to get any work out of him this week, called him "my boy," and finished up with, "My respects to Miss Marian." He was one of the people who would have to be told. He wasn't going to tell anyone until he had seen Marian, but then they would all have to be told—"The marriage arranged between Mr Lindsay Trevor of the well known publishing firm of Hamilton Raeburn, and Miss Marian Rayne, niece and adopted daughter of Mr William Rayne of Rayneford, Surrey, will not take place."

Lindsay hung up the receiver. He had spoken on an impulse when he had told Rayne that he would come I down that afternoon. He was wondering why he had put off to the afternoon what he might do now. It came to him that if he waited till the afternoon, h: might find that he had waited too long. If Marian didn't want to see him, he had given her plenty of time to pack up and go away. At the thought of arriving at Rayneford only to be told that he had had his journey for nothing, a sort of cold rage took hold of him.

He called Poole, told him he was going out of town for the day, and took a taxi to Waterloo. All the way down to Guildford he was going over things in his mind, going over the last three months with a determination to find some reason for what Marian had done. There must be a reason, and if there was a reason, he meant to know what it was.

He went back to the beginning. Three months before Bertie Raeburn had dragged him to a dance at the Raynes'. He could remember himself asking, "Who are the Raynes?" And Bertie: "Rolling, my dear chap—absolutely. One of the kings of commerce—throne just vacated—rural retreat running to about a thousand acres—pretty niece—chance for you—go in and win!" Lindsay had laughed and retorted, "Go in and win yourself!" It seemed a long time ago. He looked back with some curiosity and some amazement. Three months ago he would have said that he was the last person in the world to take an unconsidered plunge into matrimony; yet within a month of his first meeting with Marian he had proposed to her, and she had accepted him. During that month they had met perhaps half a dozen times. They had danced together in town, and he had spent a week-end at Rayneford. How much does any man really know of a girl whom he has met six times? Nothing—less than nothing. Yet he had asked Marian to marry him. She had clear eyes and a pretty smile. Her voice was sweet—and sweeter when she spoke to him. He discovered that he had been lonely all his life.

During the two months of their engagement they had met continually. Marian was a good deal in town with convenient cousins who were always pleased to put her up—kind, dull, elderly people whom Lindsay hardly knew. Actually he knew very little of either her relations or her friends. Those whom he met at Rayneford were not very much in his line. He knew the Raynes as little as any of them. Rayne bored him. He had made his money in steel, and since his retirement had gone crazy over racing. He had an idea that he was going to win the Derby in 1931, and he talked of very little else. Mrs Rayne was the most colourless woman he had ever met—an amiable, drab woman, with a Pekinese. He had wondered often how Marian came to be Marian. She stood out from her surroundings like bright water in a dull place. It didn't do to think about that.

He came down to the last week. Marian had been up in town. They had dined and danced together. Everything had been all right. She seemed happy. It felt like a very long time ago.

He came to the week-end. A biggish house-party. Wedding presents pouring in, and endless letters to write. They had had very little time alone. She was pale, but when they said good-bye…

Lindsay steadied himself. She had come down late. He had had his train to catch. They had a moment in the library, a bare moment. He had kissed her, and she had kissed him back…He found that he could not think dispassionately of that moment. It came into his mind to wonder whether she had known that she was kissing him good-bye. It came into his mind and stayed there.

The train ran into Guildford station. The fat old man who had shared the compartment with Lindsay began to fidget with his suit-case and fumble at the carriage door. Lindsay let him get out first. There was no hurry. He had the blank feeling that there was no hurry about this errand of his. He had not now to count the lagging minutes until he could see Marian.

It was at that moment that he saw her. He had not quite reached the door. He looked sideways through the window and saw her walking down the platform. She walked as if she were walking in her sleep, her head high, her eyes wide open. She was pale. She wore a fur coat and a small black hat like a cap with wings. A porter walked behind her carrying a couple of suitcases.

Lindsay drew back quickly and shut the door.

His first feeling was one of bitter anger. She was trying to cheat him. An equally bitter triumph followed the anger. She was going to discover that he was not so very easy to cheat.

The train was a corridor train to Portsmouth. She was doubtless on her way to the Isle of Wight. He knew that the Raynes had relations on the island. He sat back in his corner and waited for the train to move. As they ran out of the tunnel, he got up and walked along the corridor. He had no plan. He had no idea what he should do if he found Marian in a carriage full of people. Travelling first class, the chances were that she would be alone.

She was in the third compartment he came to. It was labelled "Ladies only," and she was the only lady in it. He opened the door, stepped in, and shut it behind him.

She did not look round. She was sitting by the window looking out. Her hat and the high collar of her coat hid all her face. She did not turn her head.

Lindsay sat down in the opposite corner. He had meant to speak at once, but he could not; something took him by the throat. It was only a little over forty-eight hours since they had said good-bye. He sat there almost touching her, and she was as far away as the other side of the world.

He did not know how long it was before either of them moved. It seemed like a long time. He wondered why she did not turn. He wondered if it was because she had been crying. He felt that he ought to speak, to let her know that he was there, but for the life of him he could not do it. He just sat there.

Then, with a whirr and a rush, a train met and began to pass them. The noise and the impact of the driven air startled Marian Rayne. She drew back from the window, and saw Lindsay Trevor.

It must have been a shock. She had been very far away, and then when she turned, there was Lindsay so close to her that if she had moved her hand in a foolish seeking gesture, it must have touched his. She looked at him, and could not take her eyes away.

If she was shocked, so was he. It was plain that she had not slept; but it was not fatigue that had marked her face like that. The clear creamy skin with its light powdering of golden freckles looked like parchment, The freckles seemed to have darkened on it. Her eyes had wept until they could weep no more. The colour had gone out of them, and the starry look. There were marks under them like bruises. She must have been weeping all through the hours of a long night.

Lindsay was so shocked that he forgot his anger. He said her name—he did not know how. Her face did not change. She looked at him as if she were too tired to speak. Then she said, in a flat, extinguished voice,

"Why did you come?"

The train which had been passing them was gone. A cold, wet, wintry light shone on her. She put her elbow on the sill and screened her face from it with her ungloved left hand. He saw that she had taken off his ring.

That hardened him. It was all very well to say, why had he come; but he had come, and he meant to get what he had come for.

"Did you think I wouldn't come?" he said.

"I hoped you wouldn't." Her voice was so low that he had to guess at the words.

That hardened him still more.

"Naturally," he said. "But you can't break off our engagement four days before the wedding without giving me some reason for it."

He thought she said, "I can't." Her lips moved. He thought they made those words. There wasn't any sound.

He was angry by now. He wanted to hurt her, to make her speak. He said,

"I suppose you realize what will be said?"

There was another faint movement that said "No."

"Well, people will say that one of us has made some unpleasant discovery. Your friends will believe that you have found out something about me, and I'm afraid that mine—" he stopped. After all, he could not say it. She was so pale.

Yet she spoke at once:

"It doesn't matter."

"Perhaps not." Nothing really seemed to matter just then. "I just thought you'd better consider the point. But that's not what I came down here for. I'm not here to persuade you, or talk you over, or anything of that sort. You needn't be afraid. You've broken our engagement—it's smashed. All I want is to know why you've done it. You've got to give me a reason. Do you see?"

She shut her eyes for a moment.

I can't.

"You've got to. I'm not disputing your decision, but I've got to know why you made it."

She sat there. She didn't move, she didn't speak.

"You'd better tell me. It will save trouble if you tell me at once."

Her eyelids closed down over her eyes again. She leaned on her hand. That dumb obstinacy of hers was rousing the brute in him.

"Has anyone slandered me? I think I've a right to know that."

She opened her eyes rather suddenly. They were dark and startled.

"Oh—no—no!"

That was something.

"You got engaged to me of your own free will?"

She nodded, still with that startled look in her eyes.

"Then I have offended—disappointed—or—perhaps bored you?"

She said "No on a breaking whisper, and when I she had said it, the tears began to run down her face. They changed his mood.

"Marian—for God's sake! What is it? You look—" He could not say how she looked. He groped for words, and could not find them.

"For God's sake!" he said; and then, "Marian—what is it? Some—trouble?"

She said, "Yes," as if it was a relief, and leaned on her hand and wept.

"Can't you tell me what it is?"

She shook her head.

"Not now," she-said. "Not—yet—"

He waited until he could steady his voice.

"There's someone—else?"

She didn't answer that.

"Marian—is there—someone?"

She lifted her head and pushed back the hair from her wet cheek.

"Oh yes—*someone*, she said. There was something wild in her voice. She hid her face again with a sob.

"There's someone—you care for?"

Her head had dropped on her arm. She spoke in a muffled voice.

"Oh, please go! I've told you—there's someone. I can't—marry you. Won't you go away? I can't—there's someone I love—that's why I can't marry you. Oh, please, *please* go!"

He leaned across and put a hand on her shoulder, turning her so that she had to look at him.

"You care for this man—really?"

She looked up at him.

"I've told you."

"You might have told me before."

There was a silence. He could not bear her piteous eyes.

"Does he care for you?" he said sharply.

She said, "*Please* go!"

"Are you going to marry him?" His voice sounded strangely.

She said, "No—never." She said it quite gently and quietly. And then, "Please go, Lin." Lindsay went.

Chapter Five

ALL THAT CAN be said of the days that followed is that, having dragged out their interminable hours, they did in the end pass and join themselves with other dead days. Strong emotion at its height has movement, colour, depth; but when the tide, ebbing, leaves one high and dry amidst the wreckage it has achieved, there comes the sordid business of picking up the bits and getting things straight again.

There was an announcement in the papers. "The marriage arranged...will not take place." People wrote and condoled. And Poole spent all his spare time packing up wedding presents.

Hamilton Raeburn suggested that Lindsay should take a fortnight, or more if he wanted it, and go off abroad. He was fond of Lindsay and went out of his way to be kind. Lindsay found his kindness a little oppressive. He wanted work at this juncture, not time on his hands. A solitary honeymoon lent itself rather too easily to ribald jesting. On the other hand, if he went away and came back again, perhaps people would stop treating him in the hushed, unnatural manner which made him feel like smashing the furniture.

He told Hamilton Raeburn he would think it over, and sat down to finish the proofs of his second book. Raeburn thought it a distinct advance on *Golden Apples*, and though at this moment Lindsay didn't care whether it was published or not, he thought that later on his interest would probably revive. Anyhow, Raeburn wanted to get it out early in March, and he had promised him the proofs.

It was on Thursday afternoon that the letter came. Poole brought it in and put it down on the table. There was a registered packet as well as the letter.

Lindsay opened the packet first. It was either a wedding present, which would have to be sent back, or—The 'or' met the case. Marian Rayne had sent him her engagement ring. It rolled out of the box and lay tipped up against the edge of his paper. Marian had a fancy for jade, and he had managed to pick up a really good bit. The green translucence, with its setting of tiny diamonds, caught the light and made it lovely.

He wondered what one did with a returned engagement ring, and he wished that she had not sent it back. After a while he locked it away in his dispatch-box and opened the letter.

It was from Mr Benbow Collingwood Horatio Smith. It began formally:

"Dear Mr Trevor—"

He read it through to the "Yours sincerely" and the signature, "Benbow Smith." Then he read it again. Mr Smith wrote, in a beautiful clear hand:

> "It has occurred to me that our conversation in the train might be resumed. If you can call at my house at nine o'clock this evening, we could discuss the matter in detail. It would be better not to ring me up on the telephone, and I should be glad if you would destroy this note as soon as you have read it."

As he finished reading the letter for the second time, he experienced an extraordinary change of mood. He was not one of those mercurial people who is up on the heights one moment and down in the depths the next, but at this moment he experienced one of the sharpest changes of mood that he could ever remember. He could not really account for it, though he supposed the memory of having been stirred to a sense of excitement and adventure during that conversation in the train played its part. However that might be, there came over him a passionate impatience of his present situation, and an equally passionate desire to escape from it.

He burnt the letter and sat down to his proofs again.

At nine o'clock precisely he rang Mr Smith's front door bell. He waited for the door to open with conflicting feelings. It was odd that Mr Smith should have written to him. An odd letter—a formal, disjointed, mysterious letter: "Dear Mr Trevor...burn this...it would be better not to telephone." He must know of the broken engagement. He had said, "If you change your mind—" and Lindsay had said, "I wish I could."

The door opened, and a neat elderly man-servant let him in. He took hat, coat, and scarf in a methodical, silent way. Then, with a measured ritual tread, he preceded Lindsay to the first door on the right, threw it open, and stood aside to let him pass in. Lindsay did not give his name, and the servant did not ask it. It was all rather hushed and impressive. There was therefore something incongruous in the peal of laughter which greeted him. It was coarse, side-shaking laughter of a vulgar, rollicking kind:

"Ha—ha—ha—ha! Oh, Lor! Ha—ha—I'll bust my sides! Oh, Lor, I will! Oh mussy, mussy me!" And then more peals of laughter, in the midst of which he heard Mr Smith say in his gentle cultured tones,

"Good evening, Mr Trevor."

Lindsay looked up the long book-lined room. It was soberly, handsomely furnished. There was some mahogany panelling above the mantelpiece and between the books. The carpet was Persian, the chairs a man's chairs, deep, capacious, and comfortably shabby. A large table with claw feet held papers and periodicals. The lighting was in the ceiling. At the far end a grey and rose-coloured parrot on a tall perch flapped his wings and continued to laugh.

Mr Smith, after shaking hands, turned and reproved him.

"Be quiet, Ananias! That is not the way to greet a guest."

Ananias said "Ha!" very loudly, spread his wings to their full extent, and fixed the guest with a menacing eye.

"Now, Ananias," said his master warningly.

"Awk!" said Ananias. He ended the word with a hissing escape of breath.

Mr Smith drifted over to him and scratched him behind the ear; but the parrot retreated to the opposite of his perch, where he began to perform an elaborate toilet, spreading out his left wing and turning his back on the room.

Mr Smith walked aimlessly back again. After straying past the table, he returned to it and stood there fingering a magazine. Then,

"I am glad you have come," he said.

He did not look at Lindsay, and his voice was quite expressionless. All at once he turned and moved to where the two largest chairs had been drawn in to the fire.

"Sit down," he said, "and tell me why."

Lindsay took this to be a continuation of his last remark, and answered it as such.

"Because you asked me."

He nodded, sitting there rather upright. Without his glasses, his features had a fine Greek look, and his whole air was one of extreme distinction. He joined his fingers at the tips and gazed at a point above Lindsay's head.

"In the train the other day," he said, "I ventured to give you a description of yourself. If you will forgive the impertinence, I should like to add to the description a brief, a very brief, sketch of your career."

Lindsay wondered what he was driving at.

He said, "I'm afraid it doesn't amount to much," and then felt that he had better have held his tongue.

At the sound of his master's voice the parrot turned half round, but as soon as Lindsay began to speak he clapped his wings, rose on his toes, and screamed loudly and unmelodiously:

"Three jolly admirals, all of a row—

Collingwood, Nelson, and bold Benbow!"

Mr Smith got up languidly, went across, cuffed him, and returned without any change of countenance. As he sank into his chair, he resumed the conversation as if there had been no break in it.

"You will correct me if I am inaccurate—and there are one or two points which I find a little obscure—but the main outline is, I fancy, correct. You were at Harrow with my nephew Jack. You were, even then, an orphan with no near relatives. You were sixteen when the war broke out, and you served for rather over two years before the armistice, and for another two years after it. I am not quite clear as to why you resigned your commission. It was, I believe, a permanent and not a temporary one?"

"I wanted to take my degree. I had a very favourable opening offered to me by Hamilton Raeburn on condition that I did so. He was an old friend of my father's."

"Yes," he said—"yes. Life in the Secret Service did not attract you?"

Lindsay was a little startled.

He said, "No"; and then added, "Not as a permanency."

"In 1918," said Mr Smith in his gentle voice, "you were taken prisoner. You escaped in company with Colonel Garrett. He reported on you afterwards as possessing ideal qualifications for the Secret Service."

"That was only because I could speak the language. My guardian used to send me to spend all my holidays with some family abroad."

"Colonel Garrett considered that you had other qualifications. He is a good judge. He asked for you specially, and you worked under him for two years after the armistice."

"It's a long time ago."

"Your languages are rusty?"

He could not truthfully say that they were. He therefore said nothing. Mr Smith dropped suddenly into German.

"My reason for asking you to come here to-night is a serious one."

"Yes, I suppose so." Lindsay answered him in the same language.

Mr Smith continued:

"I would like to test your languages. You will find to-day's *Times* on the table. Will you make a running translation of the first leading article?"

"Into German?"

"Yes—yes, I think so—German first."

Lindsay brought the paper over and began. Mr Smith looked at the ceiling. When Lindsay had read about a third of a column, he stopped him.

"Now French, if you please."

Lindsay repeated the same passage. It was really perfectly easy.

"Italian," said the languid voice when he had reached the same place again.

"I could not pass as an Italian."

He proceeded to prove this by rather a halting translation.

"Spanish?" said Mr Smith.

"The merest smattering."

"Anything else?"

"I can understand and read Russian, and I can talk enough to get along. I couldn't pass as a Russian in Russia."

"But you could pass as a German in Germany?"

"Well, I have done so."

"When your life depended upon it—yes. Could you pass as a Frenchman in France?"

"Not as an educated Frenchman. I can do a southern dialect that will pass in the north, and I think I could pass as a Breton in the south. It's—it's been a sort of hobby of mine."

"Yes," said Mr Smith—"a very useful hobby." He relapsed into silence.

Lindsay wondered where all this was leading to. He had had some exciting times with Garrett. The thought of stepping out of his present circumstances into the byways of adventure had its lure. This on the surface. But beneath the surface he was aware of currents that ran strongly. That there was something desperately serious in question became momentarily plainer.

Ananias broke the silence. He began in a piercing yet cautious whisper:

"What shall we do with the drunken sailor,
What shall we do with the drunken sailor,
What shall we do with the drunken sailor,
So early in the morning?"

Each line was a little louder than the last.

Mr Smith looked over his shoulder and said, "No—*no*, Ananias!"

Then he spoke to Lindsay.

"When I asked you if you would like to die for your country, I was serious."

"That is not the usual way of baiting the trap, sir," said Lindsay with a laugh.

"Danger is not always such a bad bait."

"What do you want me to do, sir?"

"A little difficult to answer that comprehensively at this stage of the proceedings."

"And why me? Any experience I have had is ten years old and out of date. I am a peaceful publisher. What's wrong with the men who are up to date in the game?"

"Most of them are too well known," said Mr Smith. "This"—he looked straight at Lindsay for a moment, and his eyes were not dreamy any more—"this is a very big thing." He let the words fall slowly and heavily.

"What is it?" said Lindsay.

Mr Smith said, "Presently," and looked at his own hands.

In a rapid whisper, Ananias recited:

"Put him in the long-boat until he's sober,
Put him in the long-boat until he's sober,
Put him in the long-boat until he's sober—"

"No, Ananias!"

Ananias said "Awk!" and turned his back.

"Take—" said Mr Smith in a dreamy voice—"take a hypothetical case. There are suspicious circumstances I—things small in themselves but cumulative. In the ordinary course of official routine A is detailed to make investigations and to report. He reports that he has not found out anything. Then he reports that he is on the brink of finding out something. Then he does not I report at all."

"Why?"

"The department asks why. It gets no answer—from A. A good many months afterwards a rumour trickles in to the effect that A's wife, who is known to have been much attached to him, has gone out to Peru and married again out there. Her husband is said to be extremely well-to-do. His hair is black, whereas A's hair was a lightish brown—but for a well-to-do man the price of a good hair-dye is not prohibitive."

With his back to the room, Ananias whispered malignantly:

"Pull out the plug and wet him all over!"

"So much for A," said Lindsay.

Mr Smith was lying back, his head against the worn crimson leather, an arm stretched full length on either arm of his chair.

"Yes," he said—"yes. And that brings us to B—a man of a different type—not quite so clever as A, but more solid. At first he is up against a stone wall, and he is very discouraged. Later he forms the opinion that there is nothing to find but a mare's nest—he writes and says so. And then he disappears." He paused. "He did not go to Peru—he went into the river."

"But why—if he had found nothing?"

"The department asked that question too. B was not married, but he had a girl. They asked her why, and she gave them a reason. B came to see her on the evening of the day that he disappeared. He had been going to take her to the pictures, but he looked in to say that he wouldn't be able to go. She was angry and disappointed, and to pacify her he said, 'If you only think why I couldn't come, you'd be as pleased as I am. Why, if I pull this off, we shall be able to marry right away. It will be the most tremendous feather in my cap'."

"Tie him to the taffrail when she's yard-arm under!"

shrieked Ananias with vindictive suddenness.

Mr Smith said, "Hush!"

Ananias did not hush. He rose on his toes and poured out a flood of Spanish oaths. Then, as Mr Smith made a movement to rise, he stopped in midstream and plunged again into his toilet.

"I don't know why I keep a parrot," said Mr Smith. "He never forgets anything he has ever learned—which is a pity. Well, that was what happened to B. C came back to the department and said I he couldn't find out anything. I don't think he was telling the truth. The matter was then put into D's hands." He paused.

Lindsay said nothing.

Ananias combed his feathers.

Mr Smith said nothing.

Lindsay had the feeling that it was Mr Smith's J silence, and that it was up to him to break it.

He did break it at last, rather unexpectedly.

"The question is—do I tell you about D's case, or do not?"

"That is for you to say."

"Not at all. That is quite a mistake on your part, because D's case is irrelevant unless—" He paused again.

"Unless?"

"Oh, unless you are E," said Mr Smith in his dreamiest voice.

Chapter Six

AN IMPORTANT choice has probably seldom been put to anyone in a less important manner. The man who had put it so casually leaned back in his chair and gazed abstractedly at the ceiling. Lindsay felt a certain impatience.

"I want to know a good deal more before I say yes or no to that," he said.

Mr Smith maintained his abstracted gaze at the ceiling for what seemed like quite a long time. When he spoke, he had abandoned his letters of the alphabet.

"Ideas are very disturbing things—ideas and ideals. All that the human race has ever desired is to be left alone. The explorer, the missionary, the discoverer, the inventor, the man of science, the seer disturb this comfortable lethargy. They introduce ideas—and there is nothing so disturbing as ideas. Their exponents, after an appropriate martyrdom, are accommodated with handsome tombs—there is an impression that they are safer dead. You cannot, however, burn an idea at the stake, nor can you immure it in a tomb—it continues to seek for expression. Each new expression rouses the old antagonism of animal ignorance, laziness, and hate. We have arrived at a time when the of an advancing age are expressing themselves in such protests against the violent folly and ruin of the Kellogg Pact, The League of Nations, and the Court of International Justice." His voice ceased. It had been slow and gentle throughout. It was more like hearing a man think than hearing him speak.

He raised himself slightly in his chair and turned his eyes upon Lindsay. After a moment he looked away.

"These things are effects, not causes. They are the expression of the enlightened thought of the world, But everyone does not wish for light in his house, Darkness suits dark things. Light is being focussed upon some of these dark things. Do you think they will all vanish without a struggle, without any resistance? I am speaking to you to-night of a phase of this resistance."

Lindsay sat still and thought about that. Mr Smith, let him think. He had certainly roused his interest. Lindsay did not know quite what he had expected, but the horizon had widened in the last few minutes.

"It's not a national business then?" he said at last.

"International," said Mr Smith; and then, "Does that lessen your interest?"

Lindsay shook his head.

Mr Smith began to talk of the world situation. He touched upon the interlocking difficulties and problems of each nation. He was extraordinarily sure and lucid, He talked for some time. At the end he said,

"That's where we are. And on the surface every responsible man in the public life of every nation in the world, with perhaps one exception, is pledged to peace and progress and all that peace and progress stand for. There is not a single prominent man in this country, or in a dozen other countries, who would dare to stand up to-day and denounce the activities of peace. But they are not all whole-hearted—they say things in private which they no longer say on a public platform."

He stopped and made a slight gesture with his right hand, raising it and then letting it fall again.

"That does not take us very much farther—does it? That is my difficulty—I cannot take you much farther, because the next step takes us into the dark, and we don't know what may be happening in the dark. We don't know—and we want to know. We believe that things are moving in the darkness—gathering themselves together, organizing—and we want to know what is going on."

"Awk!" said Ananias very loudly. Then, on a rapid scream, "If you want to know the time, ask a policeman!"

Mr Smith leaned forward, picked up a lump of coal with a pair of brass tongs, and put it on the fire. When he had laid down the tongs, he said,

"I have been a little high-falutin—Hush, Ananias!"

"Ask a p'liceman!" shrieked Ananias. "Ask a p'liceman! Ask a p'liceman!" Then, at a second "Hush!" he descended to a low mutter.

"There is something up, and we want to know what it is," said Mr Smith in quite a brisk voice. "Well now—are you E? That is the immediate question."

Lindsay meant to say yes. He had virtually said yes by coming here to-night. But he had a cautious streak in him. He thought that he would not say yes just yet.

There was a pause, during which he could hear him saying the word "p'liceman" over and over mumbling undertone. He thought it came very pat on Mr Benbow Smith's last question—"Are you E—p'liceman—p'liceman—p'liceman—are you E—are you—p'liceman—p'liceman."

"Well?" said Mr Smith. "What about it? I can tell you a little more when you've really said yes."

Lindsay laughed. He could not help it.

"Didn't I say yes when I came here?"

"Then it is yes?"

Lindsay nodded.

"Then we may proceed," said Mr Smith.

He was still leaning forward and looking into the fire, which had sunk to a red glow about the new lump of coal.

"Let us come back to D—I think we were talking about D? D is a man who has done occasional jobs for the department. When C threw in his hand, D was in Paris. He wrote giving quite a useful piece of information. He finished up by saying that he knew C had been shadowing a certain person, and suggested that he might take on the job. He had, it seemed, made this person's acquaintance, and considered that he might turn it to account. After some hesitation he was told that he could report to the department.

"That was about two months ago. He reported nothing of any real interest. Three weeks ago something very interesting happened. He was offered the post of secretary to the person he was watching. He was, you must understand, playing the role of the young man without a job—hard up, in the modern luxurious manner. The man who offered him the job fairly pushed it at him. He wrote and asked if he was to accept. He was told to do so. Ten days ago he was sent to England on his employer's business, and met with a motor accident. His injuries were of them slightest, but he appeared to be on the edge of a very serious nervous breakdown. We had taken care to put a special nurse on to the case. Her report was a disquieting one. The man was in a perfect panic of fear. He woke screaming in the night, and proffered as an apology that he thought they had got him. He talked in his sleep. You shall see the notes the nurse made—she had instructions to write everything down. The conclusion we came to was that D had been got at; but we don't know whether he was got at before his engagement as secretary or afterwards."

He turned and moved his left hand in a gesture that invited Lindsay's attention.

"You see the importance of this. If he was got at first, the appointment would have been offered in order to make use of him to mislead the department. If, on the other hand, he wasn't got at until afterwards, they seem to have been taking a considerable risk, and the motive must have been a strong one."

Lindsay said, "Yes, I see."

"D, of course, denies having been got at. He really denies it too vehemently. He is, I am sure, in fear of his life. He knows something that he is afraid of knowing—he would un-know it if he could—he sweats if you look at him. In fact he has the jumps, and would go on his knees to anyone who would pick him out of the mess he has got into and drop him down in, let us say, Australia."

There did not seem to be anything for Lindsay to say.

"So much for D," said Mr Smith. "We want you to take his place."

Lindsay waited.

"To take his place," Mr Smith repeated. "To step shoes, and wear his clothes, and be the intelligent who has been got at."

The sheer impossibility of the thing hit Lindsay between the eyes.

"You don't mean—"

"Well, I fancy I do," said Mr Smith.

"But—"

"A little family history is indicated, I think. You had a very narrow escape of being expelled when you were at Harrow."

Lindsay stared at him.

"I suppose Jack told you."

Mr Smith made a movement of assent.

"You were seen by one of the masters having supper at a night-club during term, and the matter was brought to the headmaster's notice. You denied it. The master was prepared to swear to you. The Head cast about him for an explanation, and, fortunately for you, he found one. Your cousin, Trevor Fothering, was asked to leave."

Lindsay felt himself flushing. The thing had always galled him. That little beast Froth—

"It was stupid of him," said Mr Smith, "to keep a brown wig and a make-up box where they were bound to be discovered in the event of a search being made."

"We're not really alike," said Lindsay. "Barfoot was an ass!"

"There is a considerable facial resemblance," said Mr Smith. "The fact that his hair is red blinds one to it at first sight, but there is certainly a strong facial resemblance."

He had said that in the train. Lindsay had wondered what he meant. Now he wondered again. What was he driving at? And where were they getting to?

Mr Smith told him in one short sentence.

"D is Trevor Fothering."

Lindsay must have been prepared for it; but it was a shock. He had hardly seen Froth since that time at Harrow. He was a poisonous little beast then. His father was only a second cousin, so no one could say that the relationship was a near one-the more distant the better as far as Lindsay was concerned.

So D was Froth, and he was to take his place as somebody's secretary. The thing appeared to him to be most patently absurd. His mind got to work like a tape-machine and began to pour out reasons why it was not only absurd but impossible.

He got out of his chair.

"The thing is a sheer impossibility."

"Not at all," said Mr Smith. "Your cousin, Trevor Fothering, is undoubtedly D."

"I didn't mean that. I mean it's impossible for me *to take his place*."

Mr Smith repeated, "Not at all," in a gentle conversational voice.

"He has been three weeks with this man as secretary. How could I possibly pass for him?"

"The likeness is strong."

"He has red hair."

"Henna," said Mr Smith placidly. It is easily applied and certain in its effect."

Lindsay pushed that away.

"Have you considered the question of handwriting?" He thought he had him there.

"Oh, naturally. But he has been using a typewriter. I suppose you can type. You would have to copy his signature."

Life has its surprises. Lindsay had certainly never imagined that he would live to forge Froth's signature.

"Oh, I can type," he said. "But—hang it all, sir, the thing is ridiculous. I might pass as Froth across a room or in a crowd—I suppose I must take your word for it that I could do that—but as for impersonating him in a house full of people with whom he's been living for three weeks, it simply isn't within the bounds of possibility."

Mr Smith gazed into the fire.

"Oh, I think it is. You see you haven't got the facts quite right. Fothering met his—er—employer first in Paris, and then at Monte Carlo. He took on the secretaryship three weeks ago at Monte Carlo. His employer went away almost immediately—next day, I believe—leaving him to cope with arrears of correspondence. He came back for one day, and went away again for five. The day after his return he sent Fothering to England with instructions to go down to his place in Surrey and wait for him there. It was whilst he was motoring down there that he met with the accident, and he has been in a London nursing home ever since. Now where is the impossibility? He has had a few hurried interviews with his employer. He is now under orders to go down to Rillbourne as soon as he is well enough. No one there—none of the staff, that is—has ever seen him. If he seems changed in any way, the accident can be called in to account for it. Your voices, I may say, are extraordinarily alike."

Lindsay's old dislike fairly flared.

Mr Smith put another lump of coal on the fire, then drew out a white silk handkerchief and dusted his hands.

"I am afraid you will have to put up with the family likeness," he said.

There was something in his voice that startled Lindsay. Mr Smith had not looked at him. He seemed to know what was going on in his mind. A few hundred years ago and he could imagine this faculty sending Mr Smith to the stake, with Ananias on his shoulder. He felt that Ananias would make a very good familiar.

Mr Smith put the handkerchief back into his pocket and stood up. He leaned a shoulder against the mantelshelf. He did not look at Lindsay.

"Well?" he said.

Lindsay got up too.

"If you think it can be done, I'll do it."

A long thin hand lay for a moment on his shoulder, and a very fleeting but most charming smile changed Mr Smith's face. Lindsay had burnt his boats, and instead of regretting it he felt exhilarated. To have to think, plan, act, and live on the edge of danger would be a godsend.

"Oh, it can be done," said Mr Smith, with so much quiet certainty that the difficulties did not seem worth bothering about.

All the same there were a good many things Lindsay wanted to know. To start with, if he was going to be a secretary, he wanted to know whose secretary he was going to be.

Ananias had been looking over his shoulder. He turned now, spread his wings a little, and craned his head forward as if he was listening intently for what Lindsay was going to say.

"You haven't told me who Froth's employer is."

"No," said Mr Smith—"no, I haven't. I dare say you will know him by name—most people do. Restow—Algerius Restow."

"The devil!" said Ananias in a low hoarse whisper. He flapped his wings and continued on a rapidly rising note, "Devil! Diable! Diablo! Diavolo! *Der Teufel!*" With the last word he went back to a creepy whisper.

"Perhaps," said Mr Smith. "Ananias is sometimes apt. On the other hand, perhaps not."

Restow…Like everyone else, Lindsay had heard of Restow. There could not possibly be anyone in the newspaper-reading world who had not heard of Algerius Restow—his enormous wealth, his control of the Restow-Adamson trust, his art collection, his erratic philanthropy, his spectacular ruin some dozen years ago, his equally spectacular recovery. His matrimonial affairs had been, and still were, the subject of innumerable paragraphs.

"Restow!" he said.

"Do you know him?"

Lindsay shook his head.

"I saw him play polo at Hurlingham two years ago. They say he's too heavy now. He was getting fat then."

He was really talking to give his surprise time to settle. *Restow— Restow…*If Restow…That might be a big business. Benbow Smith seemed to know what he was thinking.

"You understand why I look for a motive when it is Restow who engages Fothering as a secretary—Froth, you call him—a very good nickname. On the other hand, he is a man of whims, a modern Haroun-al-Raschid, who might at any time bring in a beggar to dine with him or pick up a secretary at a gaming-table. He is, of course, a formidable person. If he chose to make himself the rallying point for an organized resistance to such world necessities as peace, disarmament, and fiscal understanding, he would be very formidable. He is, you understand, a true international—that is a politer word than mongrel. He has some roots in every country, some drops of every nation's blood, some understanding that would enable him to play successfully upon each nation's susceptibilities."

"What does he call himself?" said Lindsay. "English?"

"I believe he was born in England, so he may claim a British nationality. One grandfather was American, the other French. The American was married to a German, and the French grandfather to an Irish woman. Amongst his great-grandparents there figure, I believe, a Levantine Greek, a Turk, a Balkan princess, a Dutch planter, and a Spanish grandee—the descent from the latter illegitimate of course. I don't know what country will claim him ultimately. If he succeeds in plunging the world into another war, they may none of them be very anxious to own him." He paused, and then went on in his gentle, dreamy manner.

"It is a singular commentary on our civilization that there is no law to restrain a man from planning such a thing. If you and I conspire together to bring a single Brown, Müller, or Leblanc to a violent death, the law has a gallows or a guillotine most conveniently ready for us; but you may conspire with perfect impunity to precipitate a war in which a million or so of Browns, Leblancs, and Müllers will kill each other."

He paused again.

"And that is where the weakness of our position comes in," he said. "Restow may be doing this thing, and yet be keeping comfortably on the respectable side of the law. On the other hand"—he made a very slight gesture—"he may not. People who have a great deal of wealth and a great deal of power get careless. Also we might be able to bring public opinion to bear. As I read it, he would look for support to four classes of people—politicians and public men; business men with an axe to grind; discontented minorities in the countries which have changed their system of government; and the avowed enemies of society as at present constituted. The politicians hope to shift the balance of power to their own advantage. The business men are for profiteering. The minorities are tired of being underdogs. And the Communists want to smash everyone. Besides these four classes, there is the, criminal underworld, which is hard hit by international agreements which limit their activities. Of these classes the first two are intensely susceptible to public opinion, and if they withdraw, the bottom falls out. Do you see why you are going to be Restow's secretary?"

Lindsay walked the length of the room and back. He saw. What he did not see was how it was going to be done. Yet he was quite sure that under a gentle, almost imperceptible pressure from Mr Smith it would be done. He pushed what had been said away into the back of his mind and concentrated on the details.

He came back to the hearth.

"May I ask a few questions?"

"Yes," said Mr Smith.

"Well then, I am Restow's secretary—that's settled. What happens to Froth? It won't do to have two of us knocking about."

"Froth," said Mr Smith, "is—er—arranged for. He disappears."

"May I ask now?"

Mr Smith waved his hands.

"A private yacht as far as Madeira—a liner to the Cape—a different one on to Australia. He disappears. He is I may say, passionately anxious to disappear."

"That disposes of Froth. But what about me? What is Lindsay Trevor supposed to be doing when I've dyed my hair red and am typing Restow's letters?"

Mr Smith smiled pleasantly.

"Oh, you'll be dead," he said.

"Dead?"

"You will remember that I asked you whether you would like to die for your country."

Chapter Seven

It was late when Lindsay came back into his flat and saw the proofs which he had been correcting in a neat pile on his writing-table. It was strange to see them lying just as he had left them. It seemed so long ago.

It was three nights since he had slept, but to-night no sooner had he put out the light than he plunged headlong into sleep. It was sleep, not unconsciousness.

His first step in the dark took him into a rioting tangle of adventure. He strode from dream to dream, and with each new dream he forgot the last. After what seemed like a lapse of time so great that he could not measure it, he was riding an elephant down the main staircase of Buckingham Palace, whilst the King and Queen, the Lord Mayor, three Aldermen, and the Archbishop of Canterbury sat on graded golden thrones in the hall below, watching the performance with a good deal of human interest. The elephant was fully caparisoned, but he himself was attired in no more than a pair of bathing drawers. They had reached the hall, and he was trying to make the elephant bow to Royalty, when Mr Smith's parrot Ananias came flapping slowly down from some unseen height. He had a red wig in his claws, and he was swearing horribly in Spanish. The Archbishop of Canterbury said, "Eight o'clock."

Lindsay opened his eyes—and it wasn't the Archbishop; it was Poole.

Of course it is very indiscreet to write down what anyone has dreamed nowadays, because anything that does not mean something bad is an indication of something still worse, and so on down to the bottomless pit. However, this is what Lindsay dreamed.

He spent an extremely busy day. His untimely decease was to take place on Monday, and, this being Saturday, there was a good deal to do, and it was only once or twice that he had time to remember that this was to have been his wedding day. He told Poole that he was going abroad on Monday morning. He also told him to catch the next reporter who came to ask for the whole story of why his engagement had been broken off, and to tell him that Mr Trevor was flying to Algiers with his friend Mr Peel Anderson, and that they were leaving Croydon aerodrome at eight a.m. on Monday, weather permitting. He got three reporters in the course of the morning, which seemed quite good for a start. There would be nice little paragraphs in quite a number of papers, all leading up to, "Shocking Flying Accident," "Fatality to Bridegroom," and "Death of Author-Publisher."

So far, so good; but he was feeling distinctly unhappy about Poole. Those paragraphs were going to hit Poole hard. At first sight Lindsay had been unable to see why this spectacular decease should be necessary. It seemed as if it would be so much simpler just to change places with Froth. Whilst Lindsay Trevor became Trevor Fothering and Restow's secretary, what was there to prevent Trevor Fothering from pushing off to Madeira as Lindsay Trevor? It wouldn't be the first time he had worn a brown wig. This simple plan was, however, unworkable by reason of the state of Froth's nerves. He had apparently got the wind up to such an extent that he could not be relied upon.

Mr Smith's idea was to dye Froth's hair brown, call him William Jones, and let him sink unnoticed into the general mass of Joneses. In a way this was an undoubted relief to Lindsay. He did not particularly care about posing as Froth, but the idea of Froth going all round the world as Lindsay Trevor fairly put his back up. He rang up Hamilton Raeburn and asked if he could take a month's leave. He did not write a lot of letters, because he thought that least said was soonest mended. The thought of Poole worried him a good deal. It was going to hit him hard, and Lindsay would have liked to take him into his confidence. As he could not get Mr Smith's consent to this, he had to make the best of a bad job.

He told Poole that he would be away for about a month. He wanted to tell him what to do in case he failed to return, but could not get it out with that solemn, reproachful eye upon him; so in the end he put twenty five-pound notes into an envelope with a few lines to say that he wanted Poole to have them in case of anything happening. He left it at that, but not very happily.

His private affairs would probably get into the most horrible mess, but that couldn't be helped. He hoped that he would not find his flat let to somebody else and most of his furniture sold if and when it suited Mr Benbow Collingwood Horatio Smith for him to come to life again.

Peel Anderson came round on Sunday. Lindsay had been thinking it would be awkward if he did not know him by sight when he arrived at Croydon. He was a quiet, pleasant fellow, and he had had his instructions, for whilst Poole was still in the room he alluded very naturally to a mythical last meeting.

When Poole had gone away and shut the door, he kept up this pose of the old acquaintance. Lindsay gathered that they had met six years ago at winter sports and had foregathered at intervals ever since. There was some good corroborative detail. Lindsay met him half way, and when Poole came in with drinks he was provided with enough to satisfy the reporters, who would certainly be coming round to pick up anything they could on Tuesday.

With Lindsay it went against the grain, for he would have trusted Poole with anything.

Chapter Eight

MONDAY GOT UP in a fog. Lindsay looked at the blurred outline of the houses opposite and wondered if Peel Anderson would start, but when he reached Croydon it was clearer and the Channel report gave visibility as fair.

Poole had insisted on coming to see him off. He looked more wooden than usual. He held on to Lindsay's suit-case till the last moment. Lindsay could very well have done without his presence. He had to make a fuss about being strapped in, lose his temper, and make a fool of himself. Poole made him self-conscious. In the end Lindsay of course gave way.

They pushed off, and he carried with him an uncomfortable feeling that Poole must have thought he was making an ass of himself. It was about eight years since he had flown. To be candid, he had always disliked it extremely, and could have wished that a flying accident were not so much the simplest and most convincing way of killing him off.

Mr Smith's plan was simple in the extreme. Peel Anderson would discard him at an agreed spot. Subsequently—for publication—while passing over the Channel he would look round and find his passenger gone. It would be conjectured that he had unstrapped himself and come to grief. Lindsay hoped that it would pass as an accident; he did not want to be a suicide if it could be avoided. But that was one of the things that had to be chanced.

They came out of fog into mist, and out of mist into haze. Presently there was just a white coverlet lying close down over the countryside with trees and church spires sticking up out of it. Peel Anderson was steering for a place where he had made a forced landing a few months before. The sun was out, and the sky blue overhead as they came down in a wide meadow where the last of the mist lay on the grass like rime.

Lindsay stood and watched the plane rise and take the air again. A high, thin sunlight caught the wings, the roaring beat in his ears and droned away. He watched till what had been an aeroplane was a distant bird, a speck of flying dust, and then just nothing at all.

He turned and walked across three fields, and came to the road. The whole thing had gone very well. He had left his leather coat behind, and presently Peel Anderson would drop it into the sea. Instead, he had over his arm the Burberry provided for him to change into. He put it on, drew a muffler up round his chin, climbed through a hedge, and walked down the road at a brisk pace. He was glad enough to walk, for there is nothing quite so cold as fog. He walked for four miles and hardly saw a soul. A car or two went by, and he passed a man ploughing; he looked as small as a doll in the middle of the immense brown empty field.

Lindsay soon got warm, and just as he could see by a straggle of cottages and a church spire that he was coming to a village, a car ran out of it going dead slow. It passed Lindsay by about half a dozen yards and then stopped. He turned round and went back.

"I wonder if you can tell me the time," he said.

The driver was a youngish man with a bright, hard eye and a tight mouth. He said,

"You've made quite good time;" and then, "Would you care about a lift?"

This was according to plan, and Lindsay had his answer ready.

"To Notting Hill?"

"Righto!" said the driver; after which Lindsay got in at the back and slammed the door.

The car was a saloon. He leaned back in the corner. So that was that. He had stopped being Lindsay Trevor, but he had not yet begun to be Trevor Fothering. It felt queer to be nobody. A couple of lines of Matthew Arnold's floated through his head:

"Two worlds—one dead, the other powerless to be born."

He felt rather like that.

The man who drove the car had not got that tight mouth for nothing. He did not utter a single word during the whole run. After passing Notting Hill station he turned off to the left and presently stopped at a neat, inconspicuous house in an inconspicuous street. He did not speak then, but as soon as Lindsay was out of the car he turned and drove away.

Lindsay rang the bell. He was to ask for Miss Agnes, and when the door opened he guessed at once that it was she who had opened it. She had grey hair and grey eyes, and a tall buxom figure in a rather old-fashioned grey dress. She looked like somebody's nicest aunt, and when Lindsay said, "I was to ask for Miss Agnes," she smiled one of the pleasantest smiles that he had ever seen. He found her a very pleasant person.

After producing bacon and hot coffee, she showed him to a comfortable room with a fire, and said she was afraid it would be rather dull, but she thought he had better stay there.

About an hour later she fetched him upstairs to the bathroom and dyed his hair in the most efficient manner. She used a double henna shampoo, left it on for half an hour, and then rinsed it in soda to set the colour. It came out a flaring ginger, which she compared with a clipping of Trevor Fothering's hair, to her satisfaction and Lindsay's disgust. She did his eyebrows too, and altered their shape very slightly. By tweezing out some of the hairs she gave them an upward twist.

Lindsay looked at himself in the glass and felt that she had been almost too successful. He would not have believed that anything could have so robbed him of his own identity. He certainly wasn't himself any more, and he was quite willing to take her word for it that this was what Froth looked like now.

Miss Agnes appeared to be very much pleased with her handiwork.

"But you must remember to let your lower lip hang down a little on the left. And you mustn't look too cheerful—not at first at all events. When everyone is quite used to you, you won't need to be so particular, but at first you will have to remember all the time. You mustn't look too intelligent, you know. Mr Fothering is not a very intelligent person. He can be sharp, but he is not intelligent."

Lindsay laughed.

"You must keep your voice high," said Miss Agnes, turning on the cold tap to rinse out the bath. "And remember your cousin only knows the amount of French that a boy brings away from his public school. He doesn't know *any* German, or *any* other language at all."

Lindsay spent the rest of the day in this odd niche between his two worlds getting used to a codfish mouth and carroty hair. At half past seven he and Miss Agnes sallied out together on foot. He wore the Burberry, a soft hat rammed well down, and a scarf pulled well up. The evening was damp and misty. It was warmer. By and by the mist would probably turn to rain.

Lindsay bought a paper, and stood for a moment under a street lamp to find the headlines he was looking for. They stared him in the face:

SHOCKING AIR FATALITY. DEATH OF PROMISING
YOUNG AUTHOR. BRIDEGROOM WHO WAS TO HAVE
BEEN MARRIED ON SATURDAY.

He ran his eye down the column. Peel Anderson seemed to have played up all right. His statement was according to plan. He had looked back in mid Channel and had been horrified to find his passenger gone. Mr Trevor had objected to being strapped in, and had only given way under protest. He was afraid etc. etc. He had seen Mr Trevor after passing the coast-line. He had not noticed whether he was strapped in then—and so forth and so on.

"I don't think you'd better stand under the light," said Miss Agnes.

They proceeded on their way and presently arrived at the nursing home which had been sheltering Trevor Fothering for the last ten days. They were expected, for Mr Fothering's nurse opened the door at the first touch of the knocker. She had bright hair, a blue dress that matched her eyes, and an air of clean efficiency. She put them in a little room on the right, took Lindsay's Burberry, scarf and hat, and went out again, shutting the door. She had not spoken a word.

They heard her run upstairs, and in two or three minutes footsteps came down again—the steps of more than one person. When she heard them, Miss Agnes got up, took Lindsay's hand in a nice strong clasp, said "Good luck!" and went out. Through the open door he caught a glimpse of his late Burberry—just that and nothing more. His intelligence supplied him with the information that Froth was inside it. No, not Froth—William Jones—William. Jones who was going to Madeira. From now on he himself was Froth. His new world had been born, and it lay around him to explore.

He heard the front door shut on Miss Agnes and William Jones. Then his door opened and the nurse beckoned him. She did not wait for him, but ran lightly up the stairs and into a room on the left of the landing.

Lindsay followed her into what was quite evidently Trevor Fothering's empty room. Afterwards he thought that was the oddest moment in the whole change over. There were all Froth's things lying about—a suit-case half packed on the chair at the foot of the bed; an open drawer, with letters and cigarettes; some loose coins on the dressing-table; his brushes—sponge—pyjamas. Lindsay had, as it were, to assimilate all this, to be able to think of these things as his own. And Lord—how it went against the grain!

He had forgotten to shut the door, and the nurse came over and pushed it to. Then she took a good look at him from not more than a yard away. Lindsay returned the compliment. She was undeniably pretty, and was undeniably capable; but somehow he did not think he would have wanted to be nursed by her if he were really ill.

"Well," she said, "she's made a pretty good job of you."

"Do you think I'll do?"

"Yes, you'll do all right. If I hadn't just seen him go out of the door, I might have been taken in myself. You needn't be afraid—you'll put it across all right. Of course, to anyone who knew him well, there'd be the sort of difference that you can't put into words. What I mean is, I should think you weren't really alike in your characters."

"And what makes you think that?"

She laughed.

"Well, I can't imagine anyone picking him out for the sort of job you've got in hand—he hasn't the nerve."

"Nerve or not, it was his job," said Lindsay—"so I suppose someone did pick him for it."

She laughed again.

"He picked himself. Didn't they tell you? He told me all about it. When the last man threw up the job, *he* was in Paris, and he'd scraped some acquaintance with Restow. Well, he wrote on his own to the department, told them something he'd picked up, and offered to supply them with information. He'd done an odd job or two before, but nothing big. He knew the man who had just thrown the case over, and he fished for it—at least that's what he told me."

Lindsay was thinking that he ought to have met Trevor Fothering and picked his brains. He had said so to Miss Agnes, but she would not hear of it. He said so now to the nurse.

"Much too great a risk," she said.

"I don't see why."

"He doesn't know about you. He doesn't know, and he isn't to know."

Lindsay was a little startled.

"What does he know?"

"Only that he's being got out of the country. He's in such a blue funk that's all that interests him."

"Do you know why he is in a blue funk?" he asked quickly.

"No, I don't. He'd talk quite freely up to a point, and then he'd shut up like a clam."

"He didn't say anything?"

"He liked talking about himself, and he liked talking about Restow up to a point, but he wouldn't go beyond it. We shouldn't know there was anything to know if he hadn't talked in his sleep." She hesitated for a second and then added, "I made notes. I suppose you've seen them?"

He had the notes in his pocket. Presently, when he was alone, he sat on the edge of the bed and read them over again.

"Midnight. F—muttering. Words here and there: 'Restow—francs.' Muttering: 'I can't!' Muttering: "No—no—no!' Screamed and woke. Held my wrist and kept on saying 'I thought they'd got me!' I said, 'Who?' He said, 'Is that you, nurse? Give me something to drink.' Dozed. Woke again screaming. Said the same thing: 'I thought they'd got me!' I asked, 'Why should they want to get you?' He said, 'I know too much. They don't trust me. I wish—' Stopped. Presently dozed. Later, muttering again: 'If she knows—she doesn't know—she doesn't know anything I *swear* she doesn't—no!' Louder: 'No!' Screaming: 'No!'

Muttering again: 'If you touch her—I haven't—I tell you I haven't—I'll do anything.' Muttering."

It wasn't very illuminating. He felt that he wanted to know who "She" was, and he thought that on the whole the disjointed sentences pointed to Froth having been got at. It looked as if "she," whoever she might be, had been used to put the screw on him.

Lindsay learnt the notes by heart and destroyed them. He could not very well take them with him to Restow's house.

He was not, after all, to go down to Rillbourne. One of the letters in the drawer was from Restow, telling his secretary to meet him at his town house. It wasn't quite clear when Restow himself expected to arrive. The letter was typed, and signed with some thick black markings rather like cuneiform which did duty for "Algerius Restow". Lindsay wondered what they had been written with—perhaps the butt end of the pen.

He slept in Froth's bed, and did not dream at all. In the morning he put on Froth's clothes—his own would go back to Miss Agnes—and in the evening he got into a taxi with Froth's luggage and drove to No 1 Blenheim Square. He could have wished that he had been going to Rillbourne—he could not have said why. It was farther off; but that wasn't exactly a reason.

He sat in the taxi, and would have given anything in the world to be out of the adventure. The whole thing was the purest madness. Within twenty-four hours he would be exposed as an impostor and, his identity once out, the laughing-stock of London. Like a jigging squib the thought racketed through his mind—"Oh, printer's ink! What an advertisement for my book!"

The squib went out in a stench of sulphur. He would certainly never be able to show his face again. A desert island in the Caribbean and anonymity for life loomed towards him from the darkling future. He had colder feet than he had ever had before in his life.

When the taxi stopped he got out, beheld magnificent steps flanked by crouching lions, and, ascending, pressed a bell in the centre of a marble flower. Before he had time to draw his hand back the door opened and a couple of footmen appeared.

Lindsay remembered suddenly that he was not Lindsay at all but Froth—*Froth*! He had carroty hair and a codfish mouth.

He must keep his voice high.

He was Restow's secretary.

He was Froth.

All these thoughts appeared simultaneously and with perfect distinctness.

He pitched his voice high and said,

"I am Mr Restow's secretary, Mr Fothering. Has Mr Restow arrived?"

As soon as he had spoken, the worst moment was over. What to him was a plunge into adventure was to Restow's household a mere unnoticed addition to its numbers. He heard that Restow had not arrived yet. His luggage was lifted out and brought in. He passed through a vestibule into Restow's surprising hall.

Chapter Nine

LINDSAY STARED about him incredulously. The hall was enormous; it did not seem as if a single house could contain it. And then he remembered that this was not a single house. Innumerable paragraphs had informed the public five years ago of Restow's sensational purchase of a whole block of houses.

Lindsay searched his mind for details. Here and there one bobbed up to the surface. A fabulous sum of money had been spent. Restow had imported Italian workmen, had made a camp for them at Rillbourne, and run them up and down in a fleet of motor buses. Lindsay remembered the raging row that had broken out in the Labour press, and Restow's extraordinary gesture in reply—for every pound paid to the Italians he would spend another in laying out a public park in Ledlington and endowing almshouses there.

Fragmentary echoes of the conflict beat against Lindsay's mind as he looked about him. Lines of marble pillars rose from a marble floor to meet a golden roof. From the capitals gilded heads of dragons stared down with blazing electric eyes. Some of the eyes were red, and some were violet, and orange. All the marble was green—deep, smooth, polished green—floor, pillars and walls. High up on the wall was a frieze of rolling golden dragons intermixed with monstrous peacocks. The peacocks had golden feet and golden crests, and spreading tails in which every eye was a brilliant point of light. All the light in the hall came from these flaring tails and from the dragons' eyes.

The hall seemed to grow larger as he looked at it. A wide double staircase of the same green marble rose from the far end. It had a massive gilded balustrade and newel posts wrought into golden nymphs. Lindsay found himself momentarily expecting the arrival of the *corps-de-ballet.* If this was not the Arabian Nights, it was the Russian Ballet. He felt that at any moment Karsavina might float down the stairs whilst a hundred damsels or so posed between the pillars. His imagination boggled at peopling this hall with ordinary human beings.

One of the footmen had passed him in the direction of the stair. Lindsay was just about to follow, when the door from the vestibule was thrown open. The footman stopped, turned, came back. Lindsay, who had begun to move, stopped and turned, and through the open doors, large, fur-coated and vigorous, strode Algerius Restow. Lindsay was irresistibly reminded of a mammoth. The huge bulk ("Good Lord! I should think he *was* too fat for polo!"), the height, the bull shoulders, the hairy coat, the little shrewd pig eyes with their restless questing look, the heavy jaw with its effect of jutting molars, the sheer brute power, the swinging stride with which he came into that amazing hall of his—all made up the unforgettable impression of something immense, portentous, pre-historic.

Restow advanced upon him, stripping his fur coat and flinging it to a footman. He spoke as he came, and his voice was the voice of quite a different person, soft and slightly husky.

"Well, Fothering—all right again?"

It was something to have been hailed as Fothering. Restow's enormous hand came down on his shoulder as he said, "All right again?"

"Oh yes—quite." Lindsay hoped his voice was high enough.

The hand on his shoulder gripped him, spun him round. The little pig eyes fixed themselves on his face.

"You look a bit dicky—how shall I say—off the colour." He spoke with a strong accent, but it was impossible to tell what the accent was. "Tell me now—you had not any bones smashed? Oh no"—as Lindsay shook his head—"I remember—no bone-smash, no dislocation, no cut, or gash, or scratch to spoil my Fothering's beauty." He took his hand off Lindsay's shoulder to make a schoolboy gesture, while his mouth stretched into a wide smile. "That would be a thing to weep over—*nicht?* And we have not to weep—*ach!* It is only a shock, a nerve—the fine susceptibilities of my Fothering jangled like sweet bells in a tune—or out of a tune...Now—which? I have read it somewhere and I don't know which." He beat his brow, unwound an immensely long scarf of crimson silk from about his neck, and flung it passionately over his left "I do *not* know which!" he reiterated. "Bells jangled in a tune—or out of a tune? Which is it, my Fothering—which?"

Lindsay felt perfectly certain that Froth had never read Hamlet or heard of sweet bells jangled out of tune. He hung his mouth down on one side and said,

"I don't know."

Restow had him by the lapel in a moment. He had a great pale hand with black hairs on it. The blunt fingers jerked at Lindsay's coat.

"What is the good of a secretary who does not know? *Hein?* You have a most inferior education. It is your public schools which teach nothing, not even how to tell lies. And that is why the English politician makes his score. He looks down his English nose and he tells the truth—aha—yes!—but secretly—but as if he is ashamed of it—oh yes, and as if he is practising all those concealments which the other politicians think that he is practising. It is a great art to tell the truth in such a way that everyone must think you are telling a lie. *Hein?*"

He let go just as Lindsay was wondering if his lapel would bear the strain.

"*Bon!*" he said. "*Bon!* Your nerves are recovering—I see that for myself. And for your education—it is not past praying for. You shall go and pray for it with my good Drayton in my good library. It is a very good library, and it has all the works of Mr William Shakespeare, and you shall read in them until you find my jangled bells—because, though I am an ignoramus, I know they come from Shakespeare. For myself, I had no time to be educated—I had to fight day and night and every hour to keep myself from starving." He made an expansive gesture. "I have starved in all the capitals of Europe. And that"—his voice deepened and swelled—"that, my Fothering, is a very liberal education."

Lindsay followed a footman to his room. The marble stairs led to the first floor, on which the principal rooms were situated. He himself was shot up in a lift to the third floor, and found himself very comfortable, with a suite comprising bedroom, sitting-room and bathroom. The windows looked out at the back over what had been a courtyard. It was glazed in now to the height of the second floor with opaque glass tiles which allowed him to learn nothing of what was beneath. The house lay in a square on the four sides of this glazed-in court. Lindsay wondered how long it would take him to learn his way about it.

He thought about Restow. He had passed muster—yes, even with Restow's hand shaking him. The man had the strength of a bull. He would be a bad enemy. But he wouldn't be dull—life under Restow's roof was not going to be dull.

He turned from the window with a laugh.

Chapter Ten

HE WAS NOT, he found, expected to dine with Restow; his meals would be served in his own sitting-room. This was a great relief, but he wondered how Froth would have liked it. Never very fond of his own society, Froth—

When he had dined, he asked the way to the library. Whether Restow's recommendation was seriously meant or not, it provided him with a perfectly good excuse for finding his way there. He emerged from a lift screened by a gilded grating at the point where a corridor left the green marble hall. It turned at right angles and brought him through a massive carved doorway into a vast hushed room with more books in it than he had ever seen in one place before.

He had been wandering round looking at a book here and there for perhaps ten minutes, when a shadow crossed the page which he was turning. He looked over his shoulder, and very nearly collided with a thin man in shabby black. He was tall as well as thin, and what with his height and his thinness and the forward stoop which had brought him so near, Lindsay was irresistibly reminded of a bird of prey. The man had been hovering, positively hovering. He had not heard him come. He was glad that the book in his hand was one at which Froth might have been glancing.

He stepped back, subdued a sharp feeling of annoyance, and said, "Mr Drayton—"

The man inclined his head. He had untidy grey hair and dull eyes. His right forefinger was splashed with ink and deeply stained with nicotine.

Lindsay produced a laugh.

"Mr Restow told me to come and read Shakespeare. He wants me to look up a quotation."

Drayton blinked his eyes. He looked more like a bird of prey than ever. He had the long sinewy neck too, and a feathering of hair behind his ears longer than the untidy rest of it. He moved down the room and indicated a shelf.

"You will find most of the editions there, but I would recommend the moderns for reading." He ran the stained fingers along the backs of the books. "Any of these." Then in the same voice, a singularly dreary and monotonous one, "Have you quite got over your accident?"

Lindsay's pulse jumped. Did Drayton know Froth? Ought he to have known Drayton? Had he betrayed the fact that he didn't know Drayton? He wasn't sure. He said,

"Oh yes, thanks."

Drayton went on speaking. A desperately dreary fellow.

"It was a shock—"

"Yes, it was a bit."

The man had an odd way of putting things. He was still fingering the books. His nails were none too clean.

"A shock—a fright. It wouldn't do to have another."

What was the man getting at? Was he getting at something? Lindsay pulled out one of the big bound Shakespeares.

"Oh, it was nothing really," he said.

Mr Drayton continued to talk in his creaking voice.

"One never knows how a shock will affect one. It should make one more careful—for another time."

Lindsay opened the cover of the book he was holding and shut it again. If Mr Drayton meant anything by these rather odd remarks, Lindsay thought that Froth would be liable to show signs of nervousness. The clapping book cover might do duty for a guilty start.

"For another time," repeated Mr Drayton.

Lindsay fumbled with the book. Froth was most undoubtedly being warned.

"Er—yes," he said, and was pleased to observe that his voice wavered.

Mr Drayton began to move away.

"A good memory is a very good thing," he said.

"Oh, undoubtedly," murmured Lindsay. He wondered what he was being invited to remember.

Mr Drayton looked over his shoulder. Just so had Lindsay seen a vulture turn its head.

"If the right things are remembered," said the creaking voice.

"Er—of course."

Mr Drayton moved further away. He turned again with that forward stoop that gave him the air of hovering.

"It is as dangerous to remember what you ought to forget as it is to forget what you ought to remember."

He walked away, reached a part of the wall covered with books, and opened a masked door. It swung inwards, showing volumes set sideways on wooden shelves. There was a room beyond. The corner of a writing-table showed, and a leather chair.

Drayton turned on the threshold, pulling at the door to close it.

"Don't remember the wrong things, Fothering," he said, and shut the door rather quickly.

Lindsay looked at the backs of the books that masked it. Froth had undoubtedly been got at. He, as Froth, was being warned by Drayton. There were things he was not to remember, and there were things he was not to forget. He saw the razor edge of danger stretching before him. He had to walk upon that edge without falling off it on the one side or on the other, and he had to walk it in the dark.

When and where had Froth encountered Drayton? *Had* he encountered him? Lindsay thought he had. Froth had crossed from France and gone straight to Rillbourne. *Had* he? He was on his way to Rillbourne when he had his smash. That much was certain. But had he stayed in town on his way? Had he stayed here?

Lindsay turned away frowning, and saw Algerius Restow, huge in evening dress, watching him with a dozen yards of Persian carpet between them. The little grey eyes brooded on him. The forehead above them frowned deeply.

"That was Drayton who went away?"

Lindsay said, "Yes."

"Why?" said Restow.

"I don't know."

"I open my door—he shuts his. I enter—he departs. I ask why—and you say that you do not know."

"But I don't know."

Restow advanced upon him, took him by the shoulder, swung him round.

"You are changed—you are not yourself! What is it? If you suffer, you should be in your nursing home. I will not have a secretary to suffer here under my nose when London is full to the brim of hospitals. Go to your hospital if you suffer!"

"But I don't."

"You are only stupid—*hein?* If there were hospitals where stupidity could be cured, would they not be packed to the roof?" He let go of Lindsay with a push. "Perhaps not! Stupidity is the fashion, after all—the cotton wool which prevents the clever, brittle, dangerous ones from breaking one another into bits. You are not a man, my Fothering—you are packing. You are cotton wool, and you shall pad me all round so that I do not break myself—and others—but I do not care so much about the others. Drayton is one of the clever ones. Some day he will break himself if he does not look about him for some nice safe cotton wool."

He began to laugh, and Lindsay drew breath again. He had had a bad moment. He breathed deep, and watched Restow laughing, with his eyes gone away into crinkles of fat and the black hair which he wore *en brosse* quivering all across his scalp.

"Have you seen my house?" he asked suddenly when he had stopped laughing.

Lindsay hoped that it was safe to say, "Not all of it."

"Drayton did not show it to you?"

"It's a very large house," said Lindsay.

Restow began to tell him that it was five houses thrown into one. He took him out through the long passage and into the glazed-in courtyard, which was a swimming-pool with artificial rocks, and palms and tropical plants on either side of an irregular path skirting the water.

"You do not like bathing, and that is a pity."

Lindsay felt that he simply could not bear to waste that pool.

"Anyone would like bathing in a place like this," he said.

"But you do not swim."

Hang it all, Froth could swim—did swim when they were at school together—and it wasn't the sort of thing you forgot.

"Oh, I swim in a sort of a way," he said.

They left the courtyard by another door. There was a gymnasium and a Turkish bath, a bowling alley and a covered tennis court. Restow walked him through them, talking rapidly with his queer mixed accent. He had been everywhere in the world and had his head well stored with odd layers of knowledge, one burying the other until some sudden explosion of interest hurled a mixture of battered fragments to the surface.

They emerged at last into the green marble hall and mounted the stair. Immediately opposite the head of it tall double doors of carved and gilded wood led into the ball-room. Restow took him through it. The mirror-lined walls reflected his gesticulations.

They passed by another door into a room that was all gold. Walls, floor, and ceiling were of some gold mosaic which reminded Lindsay of St Mark's in Venice. Gold curtains veiled the windows; a thick gold brocade moulded the chairs and couches; and, for sole relief, two long runners of deep-piled emerald green crossed the hard polish of the golden floor. It was a dreadful room. The Empress Theodora might have felt at home in it, or the lady whose head the Sultan cut off before he married Scheherzade.

"A nice room—*hein?*" said Restow. "A beautiful room? A room for a beautiful woman—*nicht?*" He flung out his arm in an expansive gesture. "Where is she? Where is she? Here is the room—but where is the woman? You ask me, and if I could tell you, I would tell you. But I cannot tell you. There is nothing but a portrait. Prepare now, and you shall see the portrait of the most beautiful woman in the world!"

He advanced with a rush and flung open what Lindsay had taken to be the two gilded halves of an arched door. They fell back, emerald green on the inner side, and disclosed a picture. With a flamboyant wave of the hand Restow stood aside.

Lindsay remained face to face with a vividly handsome woman. A short tunic of emerald gauze left her magnificent arms and legs quite bare. Chains of emeralds dripped from throat and wrists and were twined in the sweeping waves of hair which fell about her to the knee. It was as black as pitch—dull soft masses of it, tossed back to leave one shoulder bare. Above the other, and parting the flowing hair, there peered the head of an enormous snake. The greyish yellow coils crossed the woman's body twice, and the tail was twined about her feet. Out of the shadows on her right a panther leaned, its head raised to meet her hand. The woman's eyes looked out across the room, dominating it.

Lindsay stared, and heard Restow's voice behind him:

"What a woman! *Hein?*"

Lindsay turned, and saw that he was passing a handkerchief across his brow. The hand that held it shook visibly.

"Ah! What a woman!" said Restow.

Lindsay discerned that he was being given a cue.

"Who is she?" he asked.

"Who is she? The most beautiful woman in the world! That you can see for yourself—*nicht?* And the bravest, and the cleverest, and"—he drew himself up and thumped his chest—"my wife, I tell you—mine!" He thumped again. "For me—out of all the millions in the world! In India three hundred and fifty millions. In China eight hundred millions. In America a hundred and twenty millions. In Europe, in England—more millions. In Australia, in Japan, in South America—more again. And out of all those millions I alone"—he beat furiously on his breast with a huge clenched fist—"I myself alone have the incredible, the stupendous good fortune to be the husband of Gloria Paravicini!"

Lindsay began to have flashes of memory. Restow had married a—a barefoot girl out of a travelling circus?—a famous lion tamer's daughter?—a *dompteuse* of international celebrity? He said,

"I congratulate you."

Restow drew in his breath with the effect of a sob.

"No—no—*no!* A thousand times no! For all those millions who have never had her—they can bear it, because they do not know what they have lost. But for me, the one incredibly sought out by fortune, to have and to lose her—what can you say to that?" He waved his hand with the crumpled handkerchief in it. "Do you say 'I congratulate you?' Or do you say with some damfool poet, that it is better to love and to lose than never to get anybody to love you at all? I have not got that right—but no matter, it is a damfool thing to say and not worth getting right, so why does it matter?"

Lindsay had not the slightest idea of what to offer in the way of condolence.

"I tell you," said Restow, once more mopping his brow, "I tell you that to lose a woman like that is something—*something!*" He rushed at the doors and flung them to. "I cannot look—I have not the courage! I do not come here alone, because I am afraid of what I might do—but sometimes I must look at her, and I must speak, or I shall go mad!"

"If it does you good—"

"Nothing does me good!" said Restow.

"Perhaps time—"

"What is time? I tell you, Fothering, the first time she left me it was for a week, and every minute of that week was like three hundred years. Then she came back. Then again we quarrelled. Brute—beast—insensate fool to quarrel with such a woman! This time it is a month before she returns—and the third time six months—and then a year. And now she has already divorced me for the second time. What do you say to that?"

Lindsay hadn't anything to say. To suggest that there might be luck in third numbers was beyond his audacity.

"In a word," said Restow, "I cannot live with her, and I cannot live without her. I am Mahomet's coffin—and it is a dismal sort of married life that has a coffin for its symbol." He rammed the handkerchief down into his pocket. "Enough! We will not talk of it any more. Some day, if she continues to divorce me, I shall marry again—a quiet, dull, kind, gentle, docile nonentity." He marked each adjective by beating with one hand upon the palm of the other. "She will have golden hair. She will have blue eyes, big as saucers and blue as skim milk. She will have many children, all docile as little dogs. She will faint if she sees a mouse. And if she displeases me, I shall beat her." He threw back his head and laughed, showing strong, crowded teeth. "Aha! Aha! To-night I write to Gloria to tell of this plan! Aha, my Fothering! We will see!"

Chapter Eleven

Lindsay spent the greater part of the evening listening whilst Restow declaimed the story of his married life. He had fallen in love at first sight—"With one beat of the heart, with one *coup d'oeil*. As Shakespeare says, he don't know the first thing about love—no, by Jing—who didn't fall in love at first sight—though, as you are about to remark, he didn't put it just like that. How does he say it—*hein?*"

Lindsay gave up the unequal struggle. After all, even Froth might be supposed to know a quotation or two.

"'He never loved who loved not at first sight,'" he murmured.

"That's the goods!" said Restow. "You have it in one—you hit the bull! No, the bull's eye—*nicht?* And that is how Gloria Paravicini hit me—right in the eye—biff!"

He leaned forward in his chair—they had come to rest in a more human apartment where there were real chairs meant to sit on. He leaned forward, a hairy hand on either knee.

"It was a travelling circus, and you are to imagine a flare of kerosene lamps, and a smell of wet canvas, and lamp-oil, and wild beasts, and many people all hot and wet, because outside the rain comes down like thunder that never stops. And in the middle of all this"—his little eyes glowed—"I see Gloria! And how do I see her—*hein?* Can you tell me that? You cannot. I will tell you. She stands there with her black hair hanging, her beautiful black hair, and that snake—Typhoon, she calls him—a beast straight from Satan, coiled all about her—six coils, for I counted them. It has only to tighten the coils and she is crushed. It lays its head upon her shoulder, and its tongue goes to and fro, *flic-flic,* like evil lightning, and its eyes are full of wickedness. And on one side of Gloria there is a lion, and on the other there is a lioness, and she makes those beasts stand up on either side and rest their paws against her shoulders. And they are afraid of the snake. I see them turn their heads this way and that, I hear them groan, and growl, and grumble to themselves. And the snake looks at them and moves its tongue, and thinks of all the evil that has ever been done in the world."

He banged suddenly with one fist on his knee.

"One of the times she left me, it was because the painter of that picture put a panther into it instead of a lion—he said the lion was too large—and Gloria went into one of her magnificent passions and said that it was done between us to humiliate her. Women are extremely various, as the Latin proverb says, and it is a fool who fights them."

Lindsay got away to his rooms in the end. He was safer than he had thought to be. Restow's preoccupation with his own affairs made his secretary a mere distant point on the horizon. It would simply never enter Restow's head to think about him except as a speck, a distant unremarkable speck.

He took off his coat, raised his arms above his head, and stretched. At any rate the first evening was over. He stretched again. This time something crackled. He investigated the crackle, traced it to a waistcoat pocket, and drew out a crumpled bill and a note folded small. The bill was for socks. The note—

He began to unfold it. He had read the words "I must see you," when in the dressing-mirror before him, he saw the door of the room swing open.

The mirror was before him and the door behind. The swing of the door passed in the mirror like a shadow passing in water. His eyes were on the note, yet he saw the shadow move, and knew what it was. An old trick served him; the note went up his sleeve, and he swung round with the bill in his hand, to see Drayton standing in the doorway, a hand on either jamb, his head stooped forward and his eyes intent. He stood there for a moment, then stepped inside and closed the door.

Lindsay waited for him to speak. He considered that he might without indiscretion appear astonished. He raised his eyebrows and looked a question.

Drayton spoke harshly.

"We were interrupted—and I have things to say to you."

"Won't you sit down?" said Lindsay.

Drayton shook his head.

"You must have anticipated that I should have things to say to you."

Lindsay shrugged his shoulders. It had been a trick of Froth's.

"What do you want to say?" he asked.

Drayton came a step nearer.

"Don't you know?"

"Well—I suppose *you* do."

What a cold, dull stare the fellow had. The heavy lids gave only a glimpse of it. The half hidden eyes were like the eyes of a lizard—a lizard, or a snake.

Drayton spoke with a sudden forward thrust of the head.

"Have you talked? That is what I have come to ask you. Have you talked—or have you remembered to be very, very careful?"

Lindsay turned away. He was still holding the bill. He laid it down on the dressing-table before he answered.

"Of course I've been careful."

"Careful all the time? Careful with everyone? Very, very careful?" Drayton made a grating guttural of every 'r'.

"Of course!"

"Look at me!" said Drayton. "Don't stand turned away, or I shall know that you are lying. Now—answer! Whom did you see whilst you were in that nursing home? Think carefully—very, very carefully."

"I didn't see anyone."

"No nurse—no doctor?"

Lindsay shrugged again.

"Oh, if you count nurses and doctors—"

"I count everyone. Isn't a doctor a man? And isn't a nurse a woman, which is ten times worse? Did you talk to these people? Did you tell them anything? What did you tell them?"

Lindsay's brain worked like lightning. Someone had been making inquiries. Someone knew that he had talked, cried out in his sleep. He had better put an innocent face on it and tell the truth.

"I didn't tell them anything. I had a nightmare and screamed out—"

Drayton came nearer.

"And what did you say? Be careful, Fothering!"

"I don't know—I can't remember. Not anything to matter. The nurse said I screamed out that someone was after me."

Drayton smiled. It was a horrible thing to see him smile. The lips drew away and showed blackened teeth. The cold, dull stare was fixed on Lindsay's face.

"Someone—*someone?* Or was it something?"

A crawling shudder ran down the back of Lindsay's neck. He had no idea why these words of Drayton's should make him shudder, but they did. A flash of anger followed.

"What do you want, Drayton?" he said.

Drayton seemed to hang above him for a moment; even with his stoop he was the taller by a head. Then he drew back.

"I want to be satisfied of your—discretion."

Lindsay jerked a shoulder.

"How can I satisfy you?"

"I shall tell you that. But first—you adhere to the story that you have told nothing?"

"Absolutely."

"Then why did you meet Elsie Manning?"

"When?" said Lindsay boldly.

"Are you going to deny it? You were followed. Did you think that I should take no precautions? You left this house at two o'clock to go to Rillbourne. You had your luggage with you in the car, and you drove yourself. You thought that was very clever. You stopped the car in Cannington Square and parked it there. Then you met Miss Manning at the corner of Leaham Road. You walked up and down with her, talking all the time. You were with her for half an hour. After that you left her, got into the car, and continued your journey to Rillbourne, which you never reached. You ran into a lorry on the Great West Road and were taken to hospital. The same evening you were transferred to a private nursing home. You can see that it is no use lying to me. You talked for half an hour to Elsie Manning. I want to know what you said."

Lindsay allowed himself to snigger. Froth had had a most irritating snigger.

"My good Drayton, what does one say to a girl?"

"What did you say to Miss Manning?"

"Let me see—" said Lindsay. "I must be very careful to be accurate—mustn't I? I think I said, 'Hullo!' but I won't swear to it. And then—well, I may have said I was pleased to see her, but I won't swear to that either."

Drayton's look became more intense. He said quite slowly,

"Do not talk like a fool! What did you say to Miss Manning?"

Lindsay looked back at him steadily.

"In the sense that you mean—nothing."

In a way he was burning his boats. Froth would probably have knuckled down to Drayton—Lindsay didn't know. All he knew was that, having been accepted as Froth, he must henceforth play the game his own way.

"You mean that?" said Drayton.

"Yes, I mean it," said Lindsay. "After all, why should I tell her anything?"

Drayton went on looking at him. He had the most unnerving stare. It shifted at last.

"Why indeed?" said Drayton. "As you say. It would be dangerous. To her. Very dangerous. And to you. So dangerous that one might almost say it would be fatal." He used only half his voice and delivered each short sentence as if it were an isolated remark, then after a pause followed it with another.

"I've told her nothing," said Lindsay with a touch of impatience.

Drayton walked to the door, but turned before he reached it.

"I trust no one," he said. "Remember that. I want you to realize that. If you talk to the girl—if you give away—if you have given away so much as one whisper about the little, the very little, that you know, she will be removed. You will not hurt us—we have our safeguards. You will sign her death warrant and your own." He opened the door, moved slowly across the threshold, and turned again. "You will have your orders in a day or two," he said and shut the door.

Lindsay remained where he was for a minute or two. He had a feeling that the door might open again and disclose Drayton hovering. He waited. The door did not open. He crossed to it and turned the key. Then he took the note out of his sleeve and read it.

There was no beginning. The handwriting was rather pretty. It slanted downwards across a sheet of cheap paper stamped with the initial E.

"I must see you. Why won't you let me come to the home? I can't see why I shouldn't come and see you. Who's to know anyhow? If you are really coming out on Monday, will you meet me without fail on Tuesday at the same place as last time? I can be there by a quarter past six."

"E.M."

Chapter Twelve

LINDSAY SAT DOWN next day to Restow's arrears of correspondence. His job was certainly going to be no sinecure. He wondered how long Froth would have managed to hold it. Restow, from his own table, would fling him a couple of words to build a letter on—"Say no. Say yes. He asks too much." Or, "Tell him I am once bit and one hundred times shy."

When Lindsay came to a French letter, he remembered that he had only schoolboy French, and asked Restow to vet his stumbling translation. Restow was caustic about public schools.

"The more they charge, the less they teach! By Jing! I never had one sou, one nickel, one dime paid for my schooling—not one, I tell you—and I know more in my little finger than you with all your brain—if you have one! Many people do as well without. Are you one of them?"

Lindsay thought he might look a little offended.

"I don't know about that," he said, and Restow roared with laughter.

During the lunch hour Lindsay was left to his own devices. He read his own obituary and an account of his fatal accident in half a dozen different papers, and turned cold all down his spine at the discovery that three of them had photographs of the brilliant young author, Mr Lindsay Trevor. Some guardian angel must have been watching over the reproduction. In one paper he was a blurred figure in a group, and in the other two the round-faced boy he had been twelve years before. The obituary notices all spoke kindly of *Golden Apples,* and mentioned his second book now in the press.

He went on writing letters until five, when Restow told him to knock off.

"Half past nine to five until you polish off the arrears—the rest of the time you may dance, or drink, or play any fool you like just so long as you do not play it up on me. I do not know what your head is like, but if you come to type my letters with a shaky hand and an eye that blears and is looking for the next drink, we shall have a quarrel—and when I quarrel, my Fothering, what is left of the other one is not worth the trouble of picking up—here a little bit and there a little bit as Solomon says. So I give you my advice to climb on a water waggon and stay there."

Lindsay left the house at half past five. He had to keep an appointment with E.M., who was Elsie Manning. She was expecting him to meet her at the same place as last time, and she would be there at a quarter past six. If it had not been for Drayton, he would not have had the remotest idea where, in all London, she would be waiting for him. According to Drayton, Froth had met Elsie Manning at the corner of Leaham Road. Lindsay had therefore to get to Leaham Road by a quarter past six, and to be quite certain that he got there without being followed.

He strolled easily across the square and along the rather narrow street which leads out of it on the north side. A couple of turnings, one to the right and one to the left, brought him down to a wide road brightly lighted and full of traffic. He was quite certain that he was being followed, not so much because of anything he had noticed as because he made sure that Drayton would be keeping him under observation.

He went into a stationer's, bought an evening paper, and stood just inside the door turning over the sheets with one eye on the street. He made nothing of that, and presently took a side turning, then another, sprinted a hundred yards as noiselessly as possible, turned again, and ran up the first steps he saw.

The nearest lamp was a comfortable distance away. He stood on the top step as if about to ring the bell and watched the corner round which he had come. He watched it for five minutes. Nobody passed through the lighted space about the lamp-post.

Lindsay ran down the steps, sprinted again to the end of the road, and then made his way back to the thoroughfare, where he took a bus. He changed buses twice, keeping a sharp look-out. In the end he came into Cannington Square.

He was now quite sure that he was not being followed. His mind, relieved on this score, found another to deal with. If someone had been following him, only to be shaken off, would this someone have given up, or would he, with Drayton's knowledge at his disposal, have taken a chance on Cannington Square and Leaham Road? Lindsay squared his shoulders. There was the risk, and it had to be taken.

The evening was turning to fog; Cannington Square was opaque with it, each lamp a yellow point in a nimbus like a yellow cocoon. He had to search for the opening of Leaham Road, and finding it, was confronted by a new fear. He did not know who Elsie Manning was, or what her relations with Froth were, but it was at least likely that they were of a sentimental kind. It wasn't going to be easy to pass as Froth with a girl who, for all he knew, was in love with Froth. It seemed extraordinary to think of a girl being in love with Froth; but girls did fall in love with the most extraordinary fellows. No, it wasn't going to be easy, and the fog—the fog was going to make it pretty well impossible.

He stood still on the kerb at the corner. He had no likeness to Froth except the surface likeness which lies in the colour of the hair, the shape of the features, the build and height. The fog, thickening and deepening the January night, was going to rob him of all this likeness and leave him just a chance-met stranger to a girl whose every perception must refuse to take him for Froth.

He must make the best of it and trust to luck. He removed his hat by way of giving the red hair its full value, and moved into the misty circle of light about the corner lamp. If he were being spied upon, he was giving himself away. He thought of that and chanced it. He stepped into the light, waited, and hoped that he would not have to wait long. A church clock somewhere away on his left struck the quarter.

He did not have to wait at all. Someone came running to him out of the fog, catching at him, pressing against him, and saying in a little panting voice,

"O-oh—you've come! I'm so glad! Are you all right again? O-oh—I was so afraid you wouldn't come! Are you really quite all right?" She shook him lightly, a hand on either arm. "Why don't you say something? You're nearly as depressing as the fog."

There was an intimacy about her touch, her manner. The lamp-light, yellow and diffused, seemed to hang like a veil between them. He had an impression of warm colour and bright eyes. He disengaged himself, put a hand through her arm, and walked her out of the yellow light into a deep, dark, comforting patch of fog.

"Why—Trevor!" said the girl in a tone of astonishment.

Lindsay brought his voice down to a whisper.

"We can't stay here."

"Where shall we go?" She was whispering too.

"I don't know. Ssh!"

She pressed closer to him. She felt very little and soft—little, and young, and soft.

They stood leaning together, and from across the way a solitary footfall sounded through the fog. There was something terrifying about it. It had the quality of a sound heard on the edge of sleep. The girl was trembling up against him on tiptoe. He felt her lips at his ear, her warm panting breath tickled his neck.

"I'm frightened."

"Run!" said Lindsay, whispering sharply. With the word, he caught her arm in a compelling grip and ran with her back across the corner of Cannington Square and down the narrow turning which leads into Fosdyke Row.

Elsie Manning ran well. They turned out of Fosdyke Row on the right, ran up Green Street, turned again, and found themselves in a street of dark old houses set back behind gloomy squares of garden full of fog. Lindsay stopped running, but still held her arm.

They stood listening in a profound silence. From one end to another of the long dark street nothing stirred. The windows kept their lights shut in like secrets. Not a door opened, not a footfall sounded, not a car went by. The place might never have emerged from the century in which it had been built. It seemed a good place to talk.

The girl drew in her breath with a trembling laughing sound.

"You haven't kissed me," she said, and put up her face in the dark.

Lindsay bent his head and kissed the tip of a soft little nose. An extraordinary sense of guilt touched him, and then withdrew. The little nose slid away and two warm, soft lips touched his. As he kissed them, they kissed him back. Then, with a gasp, Elsie Manning slipped from him.

"Who are you?" she said.

Lindsay said her name under his breath:

"Elsie—"

Her voice throbbed and shook, though she kept it low.

"Oh—who *are* you?"

"Elsie—"

She came close again, beating down on him like a startled bird. He could not see her, but he had that picture of her—a bird with bright, startled eyes, beating itself against glass. There was the feeling of an impalpable barrier between them. Her hands caught at his arm and shook it.

"Who are you? Who *are* you? Where's Trevor? What have you done with Trevor? You *must* tell me!"

It was no good. He knew when he was beat. He had been a fool to kiss her; but it would have been all the same if he had refused her kiss. If she and Trevor were on kissing terms, the hand was lost before he had played a card.

She was still shaking him and demanding Froth, when he said, "Miss Manning—" And at once her hands were gone from his arm. She had sprung back, pushing him away. He guessed at a wild, frightened gesture suddenly checked. Somewhere in the darkness close to him she was standing quite still, waiting.

"Miss Manning—"

He heard her catch her breath. He could not see her, but he had the feeling that she had come a little nearer. When she spoke, he knew it for certain. A whisper that was just the return of that caught breath came to him through the fog:

"Who are you?"

"Why do you think I'm not Trevor?"

He heard her foot tap the pavement.

"Don't be stupid! Tell me who you are. If you don't—" Her voice stopped short.

"Well? If I don't?"

"I shall scream."

Lindsay laughed.

"But why?"

"You wouldn't like me to—that's why. Why did we run away? Who did we run away from? If I scream, they'll hear me."

Lindsay had been playing for time. He wanted her to talk, to give him some impression of the girl who met Froth. He was getting his impression, but it wasn't quite what he expected. Courage, presence of mind, quickness of thought, and intuition—he had that impression of her, and the memory of her soft little nose and warm soft lips.

"I hope you won't scream," said Lindsay in his own natural voice.

"Then tell me why—and tell me who you are—quick!"

Lindsay had made up his mind.

"Tell me who you are first."

He heard her foot tap again.

"You know. I'm Elsie Manning."

"Yes, I know that—but it doesn't tell me very much. Who is Elsie Manning?"

He heard her bring her hands together sharply.

"No—no—that's not fair! You know my name, and I don't know yours. It's not fair!"

"If I tell you my name," said Lindsay, "I—well, it sounds melodramatic, but quite frankly I believe I shall be putting my life in your hands."

She pressed up against him suddenly, catching him by the arm. Even then he could not really see her. She clutched him and said breathlessly,

"Is he dead? Please, *please* tell me if he is."

Lindsay found himself patting her arm a little awkwardly.

"But he isn't. I'm most awfully sorry if I frightened you. He's as right as rain."

"Where is he?"

"I can't tell you that. He's all right."

Her hands dropped, but she remained pressed up against him. They spoke in whispers.

"Tell me who you are then."

"I can't tell you that either. This—" He hesitated, and then went on again. "This is a serious business. I can't talk to you about it unless I know how much you know already."

"I see."

She put a hand on his arm again, but did not hold it.

"How did you know he was going to meet me?"

"I've taken over his job. I—found your note."

Her hand dropped again. She said in a steady undertone,

"You'll have to tell me who you are."

Lindsay had just arrived at this conclusion himself.

"I've taken over his job."

"Why?"

"He's broken down. They've got him away. It's a job you want all your nerve for."

"Yes."

Lindsay struck quickly.

"Yes? What do you know about it?"

She receded into the fog.

"I'm asking you that seriously. As I said before, it's a serious business. I want you to tell me if you know just how serious it is."

There was a silence. He had the feeling of their being shut in by it whilst something of enormous importance hung in the balance. It was ridiculous to feel like that. The silence hemmed them in. He could feel that her thoughts were moving in it. She broke it, not with a word, but with a movement that brought her close to him. After a moment she said,

"Yes"; and then, quickly, "I don't know—I know it's serious."

"How do you know?"

"Trevor told me."

The words were what he had been hoping for, but they shocked him into sudden anger with Froth and a sense of her danger.

"Will you tell me exactly what he told you?"

"I can't do that."

Lindsay put out a hand and touched her.

"He told you not to tell anyone?"

He felt her movement of assent.

"We've got a bit tangled up, haven't we?" he said. "I've trusted you, but you're not trusting me. There is no reason why you should, but unless you do—"

She took no notice of his unfinished sentence.

"Why did you trust me?" she said in a little voice like a child's.

"I don't know," said Lindsay, and he laughed. He wondered what she would do if he came out with "Perhaps it was because you've got a soft little nose like a baby."

"Why did you laugh?" she said.

"Because I hadn't got a reason," said Lindsay, and laughed again.

Then suddenly he changed his tone. His hand lay on her shoulder. It was soft and slim under a rough coat. Softness, and youth, and a pretty voice—he knew no more of her than this. And he was putting his life in her hands. What had reason to do with it?

"Miss Manning," he said, "I'm trusting you. Froth is quite safe and out of the country. I'm here, and I've got to carry the job through."

"Why do you call him Froth?"

He laughed.

"Don't you think it's a good name for him?" He heard the faintest gurgle of amusement, and went on, "We were at school together—everyone called him Froth. But that doesn't matter. I want to know what he told you. I've trusted you. Can't you trust me enough to tell me what he told you?"

She stood quiet under his hand.

"Why should I?"

Lindsay's hand fell.

"From my point of view there are plenty of reasons. There's no reason why that should interest you. But from your point of view there *is* a reason. I think you ought to consider it a strong reason. I think what Froth told you is dangerous. I think it will be safer for you if you tell me what it was."

He waited for her answer in an odd suspense. All of a sudden she moved to him and slid her hand under his arm.

"There's someone coming," she whispered.

Lindsay had not heard a sound, but as she spoke, he saw a moving luminous point and caught the faint impact of a stick tapping along the kerb. Someone was coming towards them, feeling his way through the fog with an electric torch. The torch dazzled on the opaque air, the stick tapped nearer. The girl pulled Lindsay off the pavement and set a diagonal course across the road.

They stood on the farther side and watched the faint shine of the torch go past. It served to make the fog visible. They saw it high above them as if they were drowned in the depths of a still yellow river bounded by high black houses which they could not see at all. When there was no light and no more sound, Elsie Manning said,

"Shall I be safe if I tell you?"

"No—I can't promise you that," said Lindsay.

She still had her hand through his arm. It lay there quite motionless.

"But you haven't told me who you are," she said.

"I've told you everything except my name. And you've told me nothing at all, not even your name—I knew that already."

"What do you want to know?" she said.

"Who you are."

"Elsie Manning."

"That tells nothing."

"Ask then."

He felt rather helpless, and had to remind himself that this was not a social encounter.

"Who are your people?"

Her hand moved, a quick, involuntary movement.

"I haven't any."

"What do you do?"

"I earn my living."

"Do you mind if I ask how?"

She laughed in a whisper. It was a pretty sound.

"I'm in a shop—a hat shop. I try on hats, and fat old ladies buy them. That's why I couldn't meet you until a quarter past six."

"Look here," said Lindsay, "we're not getting on. I've got to take a plunge, and I hope you won't be angry. You said 'Ask'."

"Ask then."

"Well—I'm awfully sorry, but are you engaged to Froth or—or anything of that sort? I've simply got to know."

Her hand slipped imperceptibly from his arm.

"Why should I be engaged to him?"

There are probably a hundred reasons why you shouldn't," said Lindsay bluntly. "I want to know whether you are—that's all."

There was a pause. He had again that feeling of their being plunged in deep waters of fog; but this time he felt the undertow. He wished he knew where it was taking them.

Elsie Manning made a sound that was like an impatient sigh.

"I don't know what to do," she said.

"Tell me what you know. Won't you?"

She moved quickly.

"No, I can't. How can I? I don't know you—I haven't even seen you—you're just a black shadow in a fog. How can I tell you things— how can I? Would you—would you advise anyone to tell things like that, important things, dangerous things—Oh, you said that yourself! Would you advise *anyone* to tell things like that to a—a shadow?"

"Well, I don't know that I would, my dear," said Lindsay, and heard her clap her hands again.

"There! You see! How can I? If I could see you, I might know—but not all in an inky fog where you might be *anyone*."

Lindsay was not sure that he had not to be grateful to the fog. He did not think that even in the moment when he had stood bareheaded under the lamp at the corner of Leaham Road it would have been possible for anyone more than three or four yards away to swear to him—and there had certainly not been anyone within three or four yards when Elsie ran into his arms.

"Well, what are we to do?" he said.

"There's the shop." She spoke slowly; the words dragged a little.

"Near here?"

"Quite near." Then after a moment, "There won't be anyone there." And then, "I've got a key." The last short sentence came with a rush, as if she were in a hurry to be rid of it.

Recognition of her courage leapt up in Lindsay like a flame. She didn't know him, she didn't trust him—how could she?—but she was going to risk taking him into a dark empty shop with a fog right up to the windows.

He said, "Aren't you afraid?" and tried to say it lightly.

"I must see you," said Elsie Manning. Then she put a hand on his arm. He turned at her touch, and they went back along the way by which they had come.

Chapter Thirteen

THE SHOP had one unshuttered window. The door gave direct into a narrow room. A lamp just outside made the space seem full of thick, luminous air, out of which the black shapes of two or three hats on wooden stands lifted themselves. They might have been heads on pikes. There was nothing else visible as Lindsay shut the door behind him.

Elsie's hand touched his arm again and drew him across the shop and through a door at the far end. She closed the door, pulled down a switch, and there they were in a rush of light from the unscreened bulb in the ceiling.

The room was tiny, a mere slip cut from the shop. There was a table, a couple of chairs, a sewing-machine, a pile of hat shapes, a pile of cardboard boxes, a litter of ribbons, and rolls of silk and velvet—one of a brilliant cherry crimson. The table was covered with cheap American cloth.

Lindsay took off his hat and stood under the light to be looked at and to look. He was conscious of amusement, interest, and a little compunction. The compunction deepened when he saw how young she was.

Her hand dropped from the switch. She stood against the wall and looked at him. Her eyes were as bright and brown as a bird's. Her hair was all hidden. She wore a tight cap with a black wing that stuck out sideways. Her black coat looked too thin for the weather. The outline of her face was soft. You could not say that she had any features to speak of. Her mouth was painted a pillar-box scarlet, but there was no colour in the pale cheeks. He thought she looked like a little girl who has been dressing up. He wondered how old she was, and wondered why, when she ran to him out of the fog, he had had an impression of colour—bright, glowing colour.

Then all at once it came to him that she was pale because she was frightened. She had brought him to this empty place, and she was frightened. That bright awareness in her eyes was fear. He wondered what she knew. Then it struck him that if he had not been Lindsay Trevor but someone sent by Drayton to find out what she knew, she might have had a very real reason to be afraid.

She was looking at him with those bright, wary eyes. Her painted lips made an absurd splash of colour above a very firm chin. Her hands held one another tightly. One of them was gloved and one of them was bare. She had taken off the right-hand glove to fit her key into the lock. She held the glove crushed up in the grip her hands had taken of each other.

Lindsay saw all this with his first glance. What he thought about it came an instant later. It prompted him to say in his natural voice,

"Please don't be afraid of me—there's no need."

She said, "I'm not." Her chin lifted a little. Her eyes met his, looked deep, and brought something away. The bright, wild look left her own. The scarlet lips relaxed, parted, and trembled into a smile. "That was a lie," she said, "I was most awfully frightened."

"Yes, I knew you were. Will you tell me why?"

She laughed. It was the frankest, most natural sound.

"I was taking a chance. If you'd been one of *them*, I was just making them a present of a really first class opportunity of doing me in." She laughed again. "You see, the rooms over the shop are empty—the people went out last week."

What a thing to tell him! Was she reckless, or...Suppose he had been one of *them*, as she put it.

"Oh, good Lord!" he said, "Don't give things away like that!"

She looked at him impudently.

"Well, you *asked*."

"Do you always do what people ask you?"

"No, I don't. You ought to know that by now."

She came forward as she spoke, pulled out a chair, and sat down, an elbow on the table.

"You might as well sit. I hate people towering over me."

Lindsay sat.

"Seriously," he said, "you—Look here, you won't be offended, will you, but you were doing a very dangerous thing when you brought me here."

Her eyelashes flicked up and down again.

"Things that every girl should know!" she said.

"Yes," said Lindsay. "I wonder whether you do know just how dangerous it was—or might have been if I had been one of *them*."

She leaned her chin on her hand.

"I expect so," she said. She was thinking that she could not have stood for another moment. She supposed her legs wouldn't go on shaking for ever.

Lindsay was smiling at her.

"You're not frightened now?"

She shook her head. It was more of a sideways toss than a shake.

"Why?" he asked.

"Because I'm not. I knew I should know what sort you were if I could have a good look at you. I'd only seen your hair under the street lamp, and you can't tell what a person's like from his hair. You felt all right, but I wanted to see what you looked like, so I had to take a chance and bring you here. Is your hair really red?"

"No—it's out of a bottle—guaranteed fast dye. I'm always expecting it to come off on my towel, but it doesn't. Now tell me—how much like Froth am I? I'd like to know."

"Oh, you're *like*."

"Would you have spotted the difference if you had met me as Froth in the daylight?"

"Oh yes—of course I should."

"How? I'd like to know, you know."

"You're a different person—that's how. If someone else had on my clothes they wouldn't be me."

Lindsay hung his mouth down on one side and altered the pitch of his voice.

"That any better?"

She sat back startled.

"Yes—yes, it is. Oh yes, it is. You did that very well. Do you have to do it all the time? Are you going to tell me who you are? Because it seems to me if you're not going to trust me, we shan't get any farther."

Lindsay had been thinking. He smiled his own natural smile, which was a very pleasant one.

"I'd like to ask you a question or two. You needn't answer if you don't want to. To start with, I want to know what on earth put it into Froth's head to tell you anything. I've never had what you might call an extravagantly high opinion of him, but there are limits."

"Why shouldn't he tell me?" said Elsie Manning with an innocent stare.

"First because it was very dangerous for you, and secondly because it was very dangerous for him."

"Not if I can hold my tongue."

"I suppose," said Lindsay, "the fact was that he was in such a nervy, unbalanced state that he simply couldn't help telling someone, and you happened to be there."

One of the things he had been thinking was that if he could make her angry, she might talk.

The colour had come back to her cheeks—a warm rosy colour, very pleasant to the eye. No angry flush heightened it. She replied calmly, "You're beginning at the wrong end. It wasn't Trevor who started telling things—it was me."

"You!"

She nodded.

"Me."

"What did you tell him?"

"Well, that's just it—what did I tell him? We keep on getting to the point where somebody's got to put their cards on the table."

"Ladies first!" said Lindsay.

She had been watching him all the time, sometimes through a thick screen of lashes, sometimes through bright windows that hid the thoughts behind them. The brightness was just another screen. She looked through it now.

"I'll tell you something."

He said, "Thank you," and to his surprise her colour deepened.

"Wait till you've heard what it is," she said. "I'll tell you something I told Trevor, but you mustn't ask me questions about it."

"I can't promise that."

"I'm not asking you to promise anything. This is what I told Trevor—I wrote it to him. It was about three weeks ago."

"Well?"

"You mayn't think much of it, but here it is. I was crossing the road in—no, I don't think I'll tell you where it was—at least I won't tell you yet."

"Well—you were crossing the road."

She nodded.

"And I saw a man I didn't want to see. As a matter of fact I'd been hoping for eight years that I should never see him again, and there he was on the other side of the road just under a lamp-post. Did I tell you it was in the evening?"

"No, you didn't."

She gave another almost imperceptible nod.

"Well, it was—and dark at that, thank goodness. I could see him, but he couldn't see me." She paused and fixed candid eyes on Lindsay's face. "Do you know what it's like to feel so frightened of someone that the idea of their recognizing you simply shrivels you up?"

"Well, no, I can't say that I do."

"Lucky for you! I just stood where I was and shrivelled. He didn't see me—at least I don't think he did. He went on, and when he'd got well round the corner I thought I'd see where he'd gone to. He was just turning up a side street. I waited, and then I followed him again."

"Why?" said Lindsay.

"You weren't to ask questions. I followed him. The street led into a square. He went up the steps of a house, took a key out of his pocket, and let himself in. I took the number of the house and the name of the square and came away, and when I got home I wrote and told Trevor."

She stopped abruptly, took her elbow off the table, and leaned back with a faint air of triumph about her, and just for a second there was a likeness, a faint, fleeting likeness, to someone. It touched the farthest edge of Lindsay's consciousness, and was gone again. He was left wondering what had touched it. What he had seen, or what he thought he had seen, he could not tell; but there had been something. It was gone now.

He came back to what she had said.

"You wrote and told Trevor?"

"Yes."

"And what did Trevor say?"

"He told me to keep out of the way."

"Only that?"

"He said he was coming over. He told me where to meet him."

"And you met him?"

"Yes—I did."

"Well," said Lindsay, "that doesn't take us very far. Who was the man you followed?"

She shook her head.

"I can't tell you."

"But you told Trevor?"

"Trevor knew."

"And then he told you things."

"No, he didn't—at least—" She paused, lifted her chin, and said with decision, "I shan't tell you that."

Lindsay wondered why she had told him anything. She was afraid of getting Froth into trouble. She was afraid of getting into trouble herself. And she was afraid of this man, whoever he might be. She didn't look as if she would be frightened easily. He wondered why she had told him anything at all. He looked at her, and said what was in his mind.

"You've made me a present of a very small crumb. May I ask what I'm expected to do with it? It's not much use to me as it is."

"The square," she said, "was Blenheim Square."

"Oh, was it?" Had she followed Restow? Was that what she was driving at? "And the house?" he said.

"Number one."

"Do you know whose house it is?"

"It's Mr Restow's house."

"You knew that?"

"I found out."

"And was the man Mr Restow?"

She had been looking down. Now she gave him a momentary view of those bright brown eyes. "I don't know."

"But you knew the man?"

"He wasn't called Restow when I knew him."

"What was he called?"

She said, "I think he's had a lot of names." When she had said it she shivered. Then all at once she leaned forward again, both arms on the table and her hands stretched out towards him. "It isn't his name that matters—it's what he does—it's—it's *him*."

Lindsay felt a little tingle of excitement.

"Well—what is he? Suppose you tell me."

"Can you put him in prison?" Her voice sounded eager.

"We'll see."

She looked at him with the solemn stare of a child who has something very important to say. She said it in a whisper:

"He's a blackmailer."

Chapter Fourteen

THE FOGGY NIGHT had passed into a foggy day, and the foggy day was darkening into a most unpleasantly murky evening. Fog affects business a good deal. From ten in the morning until five in the afternoon only two women had entered Madame Santa's shop, and neither of them had bought anything. One of them inquired the price of Madame's most expensive model, and edged her way towards the door in obvious embarrassment when she heard what it was. She had, as Elsie Manning put it, a bargain basement manner. The other, a drab elderly female, wished to be directed to the nearest Tube station. Altogether a very flat, unprofitable day.

At five o'clock the telephone bell rang. Madame Santa, tall, fair, elegant, and at the moment distinctly out of temper, took up the receiver and changed before the eyes of her girls into a creature of radiant charm.

"Yes, Madam...Oh yes, certainly...Oh yes, I'm sure we can. Any special colours?...Yes, certainly."

The receiver went back with a click.

"Fifteen hats on approval. A Madame Ferrans, recommended by Miss Lester. Miss Manning, you and Miss Wallace can go together. It's no distance—Cannington Place. Yes, put in those three blacks. Medium size, she said. You might try her with the red velvet-it doesn't seem to go. Now those felts. And the model out of the window—we shan't have anyone else in to-night. Miss Wallace, why aren't you putting your things on? Didn't you hear me say that you and Miss Manning were to go?"

"I can't think how you're not frightened of her," said Mabel Wallace as she and Elsie groped their way round the corner into Cannington Square.

Elsie laughed.

"What's there to be frightened about?"

"I don't know. She's so quick."

"Well, you'll never frighten anyone by being quick, my child—will you?"

"Am I very slow?" The fog hid the auburn hair and lovely face. The voice had a droop in it.

"Well, you'll never set the Thames on fire," said Elsie cheerfully. "You're for ornament, not use, ducky. The only thing you've got to worry about is getting fat."

Mabel sighed heavily.

"I wish I didn't *love* cream buns!" she said in a tragic contralto.

Cannington Place runs out of Cannington Square on the south side. Elsie set down the two large cardboard boxes she was carrying and rang the bell of the third house. In a minute the door opened and the maid was asking them into the hall and telling them to wait there. Madame Ferrans had been obliged to go out, but she wouldn't be long. She hadn't expected them so soon. "And if you like to sit down—"

She indicated two hard, shiny chairs with backs profusely and most uncomfortably carved, and left them. The hall was the narrow hall of a London house.

The stairs ran up on the right. Two doors opened on the left. A lamp with a red shade hung from the ceiling. A black and gold mirror reflected it.

The two girls sat and waited. Mabel was very glad to sit—her shoes were too tight. She freed her left heel, and then wondered if she would be able to get the shoe on again in a hurry. She thought she would give it five minutes. And then she hoped she wasn't going to drop asleep. The relief to her feet and the warmth of the hall were making her drowsy. She had sat up late the night before to finish a frock for a dance—a cream lace frock—with yellow roses—her old shoes would have to do— Tom liked her in yellow—Tom—

She woke with a start. The hall door was half open. The cold and the fog struck in and roused her. Two people were coming in, a man and a woman. They were talking. The man had just said something. Funny that she should know that; because she hadn't heard him say it. She had the feeling that a harsh grinding sound had just stopped.

She stood up, startled and confused; and there was Madame Ferrans speaking to her,

"You're from Santa's with the hats?"

Not a bit handsome Madame Ferrans—very foreign looking, very French—smart. She had a cigarette between her fingers, and the smoke hung thickly on the fog that had come into the hall. The man loomed up through it, very tall—very—Mabel couldn't get a word to describe him. She didn't want to describe him, or think about him, or stay anywhere near him.

These were all the impressions of a single bewildered moment. As they passed, she looked instinctively to Elsie for support. And Elsie wasn't there. Her boxes were there. They had each carried two of the big light cartons. And Elsie was gone.

Mabel looked back in bewilderment. The tall man no longer stood there stooping forward through the smoke. He was moving away down the passage. As Madame Ferrans addressed her, he opened the second door on the left and disappeared.

"I have business." The lady had a very decided accent. "You understand? I will not keep you more than I can help, and not in this hall—no—it is cold, foggy, atrocious. Take the boxes. They are light? You can carry them? *Bien!* Then take them up the stair, just so far as you can see. There is my little boudoir, and you shall wait for me there. I will not be long. You have brought me some good hats, I hope? Miss Lester speaks ver' well of your hats."

Mabel picked up two of the boxes in each hand. The string cut her fingers. She walked up a short flight of stairs and in at an open door. She was not a quick thinker. Elsie was gone, and she required to adjust herself to this idea before she could begin to wonder why Elsie had gone, or where, or how. She put on the light in the little room at the top of the stairs and, leaving the door ajar, sat down to wait.

The voice of Madame Ferrans brought her to her feet again.

"Shut the door if you please."

Mabel shut the door.

Elsie Manning had been wide awake on her hard, shiny chair when the click of the latchkey announced Madame Ferrans' return. She stood up, her head turned towards the door, glad that the time of waiting was over. She wanted to get back to her room, to take off her things—to take off her working self, to let herself go, to think. She wanted—

The key clicked, the door began to open, and she heard the voice she had not heard for eight years say,

"I cannot stay."

In a flash the eight years were gone, rolled up and done away to the grating sound of a man's voice. And in the same flash she was across the hall, pushing at the first door she came to, stumbling into a dark room, and leaning on the inner side of the door, her heart thudding against it so hard that she thought its desperate beating must be heard in the hall beyond. For a time she could hear nothing else. Then a woman's voice came through. That was Madame Ferrans speaking to Mabel. What would Mabel say? She didn't hear her say anything, but Madame Ferrans said "Upstairs"—something about upstairs. And then there was a sound of cardboard boxes knocking against each other, and the sound of quick footsteps passing the door and going on down the passage. Another door opened, and shut again. She heard the man's voice—the harsh, grating voice that had rolled back the years.

She came back to herself with a long shudder and stood up straight. Now was her chance. She could open this door and the front door and get away before anyone saw her. The room was quite dark. She felt for the handle. And then, just then, she heard Trevor's name. The harsh voice said, "Trevor Fothering," and her hand dropped to her side.

She was steadying. The first shock was past. She stood there, poised, listening, taking stock of the situation. The house was the ordinary small London house with two rooms on a floor. She was in the front room, and at the back, behind folding doors, there were those two. There must be folding doors or she would not have heard the words so plainly. She wondered whether it would be possible to hear something more, and whether she dare try. Her courage was coming back. She went groping across the room with her hands out, touching a high-backed chair, the sharp corner of what she guessed to be a sideboard, the pole of a standard lamp. Then the door. The tips of her fingers slid across a painted panel that felt smooth and cold, and from behind it came the voice. It said, with harsh emphasis:

"What's behind that door?"

An agony of terror sent her back across the room with outstretched hands, feeling for the door into the hall. And behind her the voices were nearer. They would open the door and switch on the light.

She heard the handle turn, and blundered into something heavy and soft. She had passed the door, because this was a window curtain, a heavy plush window curtain. She was behind it in the half light that came from the street outside, when the electric light clicked on in the room and she heard Madame Ferrans say in her fluent foreign English:

"What did I say? There is no one there. And who you should expect to be there? You fatigue me, my friend. In my house one does not listen at doors. One thinks about one's young man who is a ver' respectable— what you call omnibus conductor. But if you like, I will go and see that Violette—" she laughed—"Vylet; that is how she calls it—is in the kitchen."

"There is another girl. You should have sent her away."

Madame laughed.

"Send away all my beautiful new hats? *Ah mais—*" She was interrupted.

"Lock that door!"

"The key is on the outside."

"Lock it!"

"And my reputation?"

There was no reply to that. Elsie heard the sound of a turning key.

Well, now she was in for it. The door was locked. She couldn't get away if she wanted to. They were going back to the other room. The light clicked off again.

Elsie drew a deep breath of relief. She looked round the edge of the curtain and saw the folding doors half open, and a light in the room beyond—a light, and against the light a man's hand stretched out to emphasize low-spoken words:

"You will do what you are told, and so will he."

She shrank back as if the words had been addressed to herself. She had heard them so often on the other side of that eight years' gap: "You will do as you are told"—and however rebelliously your heart beat, you had done it.

She leaned back against the window, fighting the pictures that came up out of the past. Then she heard Trevor's name again. It was Madame Ferrans who said it.

"This Fot'ering—what is he?"

The man laughed contemptuously.

"A police dog!"

Elsie stopped thinking about the past. Here was matter for the present. She was on the right-hand side of the window. Across the dark room the left side of the folding door stood open eight inches or so. Through it she could see a knee, and the movement of a hand. She crossed the window, as he laughed and spoke. When she slipped from behind the curtain the slant of the door was towards her. She could not see anything now; but she could hear, and she could not be seen.

Madame Ferrans exclaimed in French. Then she repeated his words:

"A police dog? You are sure?"

"Yes, my dear Léonie, I am sure."

"And you will do—what?"

"It is not what I will do—it is what I have done."

"And what have you done?"

"I have put a collar round the dog's neck and offered him a bone."

There was the sound of an impatient movement.

"And you think you can trust him?"

"My dear Léonie, I trust no one. I have a whip as well as a bone. You need not be afraid—Fothering will be safe because it is to his interest to be safe."

There was a pause. Then Madame Ferrans said in a lower voice:

"There are interests and interests, my friend." Then after a moment, "Don't you ask me what I mean by that?"

"It doesn't interest me in the least," said the harsh voice. "Keep to the point. Fothering will do as he is told for his own private reasons, and for his own private interest. He's got my collar round his neck. Also when once he has been used as I shall use him, he will be too deeply dipped himself to give anything away."

"How are you going to use him?" asked Madame curiously.

"That is my business. Now we will transact yours. I told you I could not stay. Here are your instructions. You will return to Paris, and you will see F, J, and N. F is not satisfactory—he is not carrying out his undertaking—his last two articles have been useless. Tell him that he will not receive a second warning. A definitely provocative article must appear in next week's issue. J has been doing well—you can commend him. But say that he can emphasize the Italian question a little more—a crescendo is required. Here are some notes which you will give to N. They are quite rough. He will embody them in the next speech he makes in the Chamber. I suggest that he concentrates on producing some calculated indiscretion which will be repeated in foreign newspapers. Do you follow me? A speech generally antagonistic in tone, with a single sentence sufficiently violent and pithy to be sure of a wide circulation."

Elsie was standing in the dark. Her right hand just touched the edge of the dining-table. She had no idea what all this was about. She was concerned for Trevor and for herself—only Trevor was safe enough—safe out of England. It was the other one who wasn't safe—the one who looked like Trevor, and wasn't Trevor. He wasn't safe. And she herself was in a simply frightful position. The dining-room door was locked on the outside. At any moment they might come in here again. It was madness for her to stand out in the middle of the room like this.

She edged backwards a step at a time and reached the shelter of the curtains. That was all very well, but how was she going to get away? If she dared open the window...She didn't dare. She heard the voices in the next room, but could not have told what they were saying. Her whole thought was concentrated on the question of escape. The voices were like sounds heard from far away; they no longer concerned her. She heard Madame Ferrans laugh once, but she didn't hear what she said. Then the voices stopped. With a click the light in the farther room went out. She heard footsteps, and the slam of the front door. Then a small and most blessed sound—the sound of a turning key. Madame Ferrans had unlocked the dining-room door.

Elsie held her breath in a moment's fear. Suppose she came in...She didn't come in. She was going upstairs. A door opened and shut.

Elsie ran across the room and into the hall with its crimson shaded lamp. As she pulled back the latch of the front door, she caught a glimpse of herself in the mirror on the wall. Her face looked as if it was floating on dark water. It looked white against the dark. The red light shone on it and frightened her.

She got the front door open, and drew a long breath of relief.

Chapter Fifteen

ELSIE MANNING stood on the top step and shut the door softly behind her. Her hands were shaking. She had to control them. If she made the least noise, someone might come. She managed to shut the door without making any noise at all, but the moment she took her hand off it panic came over her and she ran down the steps blindly. There was only one thought in her mind—to get away before *someone* came out of the house and caught her. She had even forgotten for the moment that the man she was afraid of had already left the house. Blind panic knows no past and no future.

She ran down the steps and into the fog. It was much thicker than it had been an hour ago. She ran into it without knowing where she was going. She heard nothing, saw nothing, until suddenly there was a man's hand on her arm. She was never sure afterwards whether she screamed or not. Quite suddenly, in thick fog, to feel yourself caught and held—it was like the most awful moment of the most awful nightmare. And then—how blessed! Jimmy's voice, startled and a little exasperated:

"Hold on, Elsie! Where are you off to? It's only me."

The fog went black. Jimmy Thurloe was not a little alarmed. Elsie, of all girls, to bolt like a rabbit and then go all limp in his arms! Who'd have thought it? And what on earth had she been up to? It was a good thing it was foggy. He had to put both arms round her to hold her up.

"Elsie—I say—come off it!"

She said, "I'm all right," in a far-away voice that he would not have recognized as hers.

He patted her shoulder.

"What's up?"

"I'm all right."

She was still on the edge of the dark. Jimmy's arms were very warm and safe and comforting. She leaned against him, and he went on patting her shoulder.

"What's up, old thing?"

Elsie drew a long breath and came back.

"I—Oh, Jimmy, did you ever see a ghost?"

Jimmy chuckled.

"Met one five minutes ago. No—honest Injun I did. Have you been meeting him too? Anyhow I don't know why you wanted to faint."

"I didn't."

"Jolly good imitation, old thing. *Flopping Extraordinary, by our Miss Manning! Reeling, Writhing, and Fainting in Coils! How to Swoon Gracefully, by one who has done it!*"

Miss Manning extricated herself from Mr Thurloe's arms.

"Display of haughty dignity entirely wasted owing to fog!" said Jimmy cheerfully. "You were very comfortable where you were. Some girls never know when they're well off. However, if you return, all shall be forgiven and forgotten. I might even kiss you—you never know your luck."

"Jimmy, you're a beast!"

"That's better," said Jimmy. "We're ourselves again. Now suppose you tell me what put the wind up you like that."

"Oh, I was a fool."

"I—Yes, sweetheart, I know that. But what about the ghost?"

Elsie thought for a moment.

"I—saw—someone—I used to—be very frightened of lost my head."

"We really are twin souls," said Jimmy earnestly. "If one of us sees a ghost, the other plays up and sees one too."

"What did you see?" She sounded a little breathless. Jimmy couldn't have known—*him*. It wasn't possible—no—that is what one always says when one simply can't bear a thing to be true.

Jimmy put his arm round her shoulders again.

"Hi! Don't wobble like that, my child! The odds are about a million to one against my ghost having anything to do with you."

"Who was it?" said Elsie in a shaky whisper.

"Well, it was a pretty queer sort of start. I went round to your old emporium and drew a blank, but the girl with the marcelled hair—you know, subhuman as far as intelligence goes but quite a good sort—"

"Gladys."

"That's it! Call-me-Gladys!"

"She *didn't*!"

"No, but she's got that sort of expression. If I got to know her well and love her, I should probably call her Tweety—*Ow!* Don't pinch!"

"I can pinch a lot harder than that," said Miss Manning severely.

"I was digressing. Call-me-Gladys was all that is kind and tactful. She told me you'd gone out with some hats, and she told where you'd gone, so I stepped along with the idea of waiting for you—the reward of virtue and all that sort of thing."

"Where's your ghost?"

"We are approaching him. In your delicate state of nerves I couldn't spring a ghost on you suddenly. No look here, I bar pinching!"

"I don't believe you saw a ghost at all."

"Well, I did. I shall write to the Psychical Research Society about it. I was just coming round the corner of the square, when a little puff of wind came down the street and blew away the fog. Just for a moment I could see right across the road."

"What did you see?"

"Well, I saw a ghost."

"Who?"

"A fellow I know quite well. Topping fellow—got killed flying the other day."

"Oh—" It was a breath of pure relief.

"He was standing on the edge of the kerb looking quite ordinary and natural."

"It must have been a likeness."

"M—I don't know. He recognized me just about a second after I recognized him. He turned round and went off, and next minute the fog was as thick as ever again. It was odd, the whole thing. We weren't great friends, but I liked him—a quiet sort of chap."

"What was his name?"

"Lindsay Trevor," said Jimmy.

Elsie Manning said "Oh!" Thoughts swirled suddenly in her head. Lindsay Trevor—Trevor—Trevor Fothering—Trevor. Who had Jimmy seen? She felt a little giddy. *He* had gone by in the fog—the man to whom she never willingly gave a name—the one man in the world who had the power to shake her with fear—*he* had gone by. And somewhere about the same time Jimmy had seen a dead man walking in the fog, and the dead man's name was Lindsay Trevor. She thought she had met Lindsay Trevor too and talked with him. She wasn't sure, but she thought that the man who called himself Trevor Fothering might be Lindsay Trevor. If she saw him again…The recollection of what she had overheard came to her sharply. She *must* see him again.

She came close to Jimmy and whispered,

"Jimmy—don't think me mad. I want to see your ghost."

"My angel child!"

"No—it's serious. Jimmy, it's deadly serious. I can't tell you about it, but I think I know where we might see him. Will you come with me and not ask any questions? Will you?"

"But, my dear old thing—"

"Jimmy, there's no time to argue about it. Will you come?"

"All right—where?"

"Blenheim Square."

Jimmy Thurloe burst out laughing.

"That stronghold of respectability! My child, what a desperate adventure! Lead on!"

Out of the murk behind them came a muffled knocking. Clap, clappity, clap it went, with the sound of large soft surfaces bumping against one another.

"Mabel!" said Elsie in a stage whisper.

Mabel and four hat-boxes emerged from the fog.

"Well, if you aren't the meanest girl I ever knew, going off and leaving me like that—and all these boxes to carry! It's too bad—that's what I call it!" Mabel's ordinarily soft, lazy voice was sharp with offence.

Elsie took two of the boxes, and Jimmy the other two.

"I'm most awfully sorry. Did she keep any of the hats?"

"Three," said Mabel, a little mollified. "Tried them on one after another just like lightning, and paid me cash down."

"You shall have all the commission," said Elsie quickly.

"Oh no, I couldn't, dear. We'll share."

"No—I ran away." She came closer and whispered, "Did anyone ask about me—in the house?"

"No, not a word. Why should they? She took the hats and I came away. I must say I thought you were mean."

"Never mind, ducky—I won't do it again."

It was past six when they reached the shop. Jimmy waited at the corner, and presently Elsie came to him, hurrying.

"That's done, thank goodness! Now for Blenheim Square."

Chapter Sixteen

LONG BEFORE they reached Blenheim Square Elsie was wondering at the impulse that had brought them there. When Jimmy Thurloe had told her he had seen the ghost of Lindsay Trevor, it had been just as if two wires had been brought together, making an electric circuit. She had felt the current run strong. Now it seemed to have gone quite dead. For those first few moments she had felt that it was the easiest thing in the world to come here and wait to see whether Lindsay Trevor's ghost would come to this house where Restow lived, and whether Lindsay Trevor's ghost was taking a new lease of life as Trevor Fothering.

Now that she and Jimmy were actually in the square, the whole thing seemed a tissue of improbabilities. Jimmy had been deceived by a chance likeness; or if he hadn't, the man whom he had seen had had plenty of time to get away. They might just wait fruitlessly for hours.

"You might explain what you're driving at," said Jimmy.

There is a garden in the middle of Blenheim Square. An iron railing almost hidden by an overgrowth of laurustinus bushes guards its amenities. Elsie and Jimmy stood back against the railing and watched the lamp that made the fog luminous in front of Restow's house. The fog was not quite so thick here. The light streaming out into it showed it as a moving mist flowing in a southerly direction on the unseen current of a freshening breeze. Every now and then there was quite a clear space, and they could see the ornate portico and the steps leading up to it.

"I want you to speak to him—if he comes, you know."

"But why on earth?"

"I want you to. I want you to go up to him and say, 'Hullo, Trevor! Lindsay Trevor—isn't it?' You must most particularly say *Lindsay*."

"Can't be done. I'm not—I mean I wasn't on those sort of terms with him."

"What does it matter what sort of terms you were on? You can say his name, I suppose?"

"Not like that, I couldn't. He'd think I'd got a nerve. You see, there's a bit of a gulf between a junior reporter and a partner in a big publishing firm like Hamilton Raeburn."

"Is that what he is?" asked Elsie.

"That's what he was. I told you the poor chap was killed flying. He was just going to be married too."

"If you saw him, he wasn't killed," said Elsie obstinately.

"It must have been a likeness," said Jimmy.

Elsie closed both hands on his arm.

"There's someone coming," she said in a soundless whisper.

That flowing stream of mist had almost ceased to flow. The sound of footsteps came to them from over the way. Then, immediately under the lamp, there emerged from the fog the form of a man with his back towards them, his head and shoulders gigantic like a shadow thrown on a lighted screen. He went up the steps. The door opened. He stood, a tall black silhouette against light streaming from within.

Jimmy, astonished, became aware of Elsie pressed close and small between him and the railings, her face hidden against his coat sleeve, her whole body trembling.

"Old thing—what is it?"

"Has he gone?"

"The old magic lantern show? Rather! Is he a friend of yours?" He felt her shudder and gave her a cheerful squeeze. "He's gone all right."

"No, Jimmy—don't kiss me! There isn't time. If the ghost comes, you must, you really must speak to him. Try his name, and then give him a message from me."

"Hullo! What's this?"

"I've got something very important to say to him. He'd better come straight to Santa's."

"I'm to say that?" said Jimmy rather seriously.

"You're to say, 'Elsie Manning has got something very important to say to you. Will you come straight to Santa's?'"

Jimmy put a hand on her shoulder.

"Look here, you're making my head go round. Did you know Lindsay Trevor?"

"Jimmy, I can't answer any questions."

"Why don't you speak to him yourself?"

This was a tone she had never heard from Jimmy before.

"I *can't*."

"Why?"

"I might be seen." He could only just catch the words. "Jimmy, if you love me—"

"Oh, you're counting on that, are you?"

"*Jimmy!*"

The roughness in his voice shocked her into a realization that the phrase she had used without serious meaning was serious enough to him. They had played together happily for six months or so—danced, dined when either of them had any money, kissed occasionally, all in the way of modern, unsentimental youth. The roughness in Jimmy's voice struck a new note. She pulled away from him impatiently.

"Don't be stupid, Jimmy!" Then, catching at his arm, "He's coming! Jimmy—*please*."

Lindsay Trevor came round the corner of the square. He had lost the man he had been following, and he was hoping that no one had followed him. The whole affair was like the fog—you couldn't see straight in it—you got glimpses, and then had every sense choked. That was a queer encounter with young Thurloe. The fog came in useful there. Of course Thurloe would only think he had been caught by a likeness, but if it hadn't been for the fog…That was the worst of red hair as a disguise—the minute you had to put your hat on, it practically lost its value. Anyhow he was well quit of Thurloe.

He passed under the lamp which lighted Restow's steps and met Jimmy Thurloe face to face. The air was momentarily clearer; what the lamp gave out was light, not luminous fog. Jimmy was only a yard away, staring with all his eyes. Lindsay looked back at him as one looks at any chance-met stranger. He took the first two steps, and heard Jimmy's voice at his elbow:

"I say—Trevor."

Lindsay turned.

"I'm afraid—"

"I'm Thurloe. Aren't you Trevor—Lindsay Trevor?"

"My name's Trevor Fothering." He remembered the trick of the mouth, the pitch of the voice; and as he spoke, he removed his hat and hoped that the light was strong enough to do justice to the red in his hair. He decided that it was. Thurloe was undoubtedly taken aback.

"I—it's a most amazing likeness!"

"Yes," said Lindsay. "We were cousins—but he hadn't got red hair."

Jimmy stood there with one foot on the bottom step.

"It's an amazing likeness! I—I've got a message for you—no, for him—I say, dash it all, I don't know *who* the message is for."

"My cousin was killed in a flying accident a few days ago."

"Yes, I know. But she knew that. Perhaps I'd better give you the message."

"I don't think it can be meant for me," said Lindsay.

He went up another step, but Jimmy followed him.

"I'd better give it you. You ought to know whether it's for you. It's from Elsie Manning."

Lindsay turned back. A message from Elsie Manning would be a message for Trevor Fothering.

"What is the message?"

"She says you're to go to Santa's at once. She's got something very important to say to you."

"Tell her I'll come," said Lindsay.

As he spoke, he came down the steps and without another word walked away into the fog.

Chapter Seventeen

LINDSAY FOUND Santa's shop window densely black. He knocked on the door but nothing happened, tried it and found it fast. He fell to pacing up and down, and in something under five minutes Elsie Manning passed him, walking quickly. He heard her fitting her key in the lock and came up behind her.

Without turning round, she said,

"Don't speak—come right in."

He followed her across the shop and into the inner room where they had talked before. She switched on the light, and the hat shapes and cardboard boxes sprang into view.

Elsie sat down and motioned him to do the same.

"I can't talk to people standing up in the air. I don't know why men always want to stand. I'm on my feet all day, so I take a chair when I can get one."

Lindsay sat down.

"You wanted to see me?"

She pressed her lips together for a moment.

"*Well—*" Then, after a pause, "Will you just listen?"

Lindsay nodded. He wondered what was coming. She looked pale, her brows one frowning line, her mouth unnaturally red. He thought she must be very young indeed.

She began to speak.

"Mabel Wallace and I were sent out with some hats to a Madame Ferrans at 3 Cannington Place—" Lindsay fished out a note-book and pencil. She stopped immediately. "That address isn't one to go leaving about."

"Thanks," said Lindsay—"but you needn't worry. I'd like to take notes, but you shall see me tear them up if you like before I leave this room. Won't you go on?"

She looked at him intently under those frowning brows, then went on speaking:

"Madame Ferrans was out. We had to wait in the hall. Mabel went to sleep. When the front door opened, I heard a man speaking. It was the man I told you about."

"The one you followed to Restow's house?"

She gave a vehement nod.

"Yes, Restow's house—but he didn't call himself Restow eight years ago. I heard his voice, and I bolted into the dining-room."

"Why?"

"Because I'd rather be dead than meet him—that's why."

Lindsay considered this. It suggested a good many questions, but she had better tell her story first.

"There was another room opening out of the dining-room. *He*—that man—went in there. Madame Ferrans sent Mabel upstairs to wait. Then she joined him. I got behind the curtains. I couldn't get away, because Madame Ferrans locked the door on the hall side. The only way out was through the room where they were talking."

"Could you hear what they said?"

"Yes, I could. There were folding doors, and they weren't quite shut. I listened. I thought perhaps you would like to hear what they were talking about."

"Undoubtedly," said Lindsay.

"He told her to go back to Paris. Now why do you suppose she wanted fifteen hats on approval if she was just going back to Paris? Our hats are all right, but they're not Paris models."

"Perhaps she didn't know she was going back to Paris when she sent for the hats."

Elsie nodded.

"Perhaps she didn't—and perhaps she did."

"Tell me what they said."

"She was to go back to Paris, and she was to tell, I think it was F—he didn't say any names, only letters—F and J, and I think N, but I'm not sure."

"They spoke English?"

"Oh yes, English."

"Go on."

"She was to tell F that he hadn't been giving satisfaction—his articles weren't strong enough. No, wait a minute—" She pressed her finger tips against her eyes like a child that is trying hard to remember something. "He said, 'F is not satisfactory—not carrying out his undertaking.' He said, 'He won't receive a second warning. A—a—definitely—provocative—' yes, that was it—'A definitely provocative article must appear next week.' That was all about F. He said J had been doing well, but he was to emphasize the Italian question. Then he said, 'Here are some notes for N.' He said N was to use them for his next speech in the Chamber. He was to make an antagonistic speech with one specially violent sort of sentence that was sure to be repeated in all the foreign newspapers." She dropped her hands in her lap and gave a little sigh of relief. "That was all."

"You didn't hear any more?"

"Not about that. I heard something about you. That is—" She stopped suddenly.

"You heard something about Trevor Fothering, and you don't know who was meant?"

She nodded emphatically.

"You'd better tell me just what you heard."

"I heard Trevor's name—Trevor Fothering—just like that. It was right at the beginning, when I was only thinking about running away, and I thought I'd better hear what they'd got to say about Trevor."

"And what had they got to say?"

"*He* said Trevor was a police dog, and that he had put a collar round his neck and offered him a bone. He said he had a whip as well as a bone. He said, 'Fothering will do as he is told—for his own private reasons and his own private interest.' And he said when he had used you as he was going to use you, you would be too deeply—*dipped* to give anything away. What did he mean by that?" Her colour had risen and her round bright eyes were fixed anxiously on his face.

Lindsay smiled reassuringly.

"Nothing much that I didn't know before."

She went on looking at him.

"Trevor was—a police dog?"

"More or less."

"What did he mean by the collar—and the whip?"

Lindsay looked away.

"What did he mean?" she said.

"Well, I should say he was boasting."

She leaned forward with a sudden impulsive gesture.

"Trevor *wouldn't*. You don't think—Oh, he wouldn't! He must have been pretending. He—"

"My dear," said Lindsay, "if you would tell me just what passed between you and Froth in Leaham Road before his accident, I think it would be a lot safer for both of us."

She shook her head.

I can't.

"Then let's get back to Cannington Place. Did you hear anything else?"

"No. They talked, but I didn't dare listen. I stayed behind the curtain."

"How did you get away?"

"*He* went, and then she unlocked the dining-room door and went up to Mabel, and I simply ran."

Lindsay was thinking hard. "Did she buy any hats?"

"Three."

"Did she ask Mabel any questions?"

Elsie shook her head.

"Not a question. She tried on the hats like lightning one after another, and kept three. What do you make of it?"

"She might have wanted to get a footing here as a customer." He spoke slowly and hesitatingly. "He might want her to come across you—naturally—in the shop—I'm just feeling my way."

Elsie's hand gripped the edge of the table; she leaned forward on it. He saw her knuckles whiten.

"She doesn't know—anything about me," she said.

Lindsay went on watching her.

"Oh, but I think he does."

"He doesn't—he can't."

"Drayton does then."

"Who's Drayton?"

"Restow's librarian."

"How does he know about me?"

"I can't tell you—but he knows that Fothering met you at the corner of Leaham Road on the day he had his accident."

"Oh!" she said with an angry gasp. "He couldn't!"

"Fothering was followed. Drayton could tell me that he walked up and down talking to you for half an hour."

"He said talking to *me*?"

"To Elsie Manning. That"—he smiled suddenly—"that is how I knew your name."

She unclenched her hand and sat back.

"Who is Drayton?" she said under her breath. And then, "If he knows—who told him? Restow?" Her eyes were puzzled and afraid.

"I don't know." It crossed his mind to wonder whether Froth himself had given the show away.

Elsie repeated Restow's name, then asked abruptly,

"What is he like? Very tall? Towering?"

Lindsay nodded.

"You think you know him?"

"Yes—but it's eight years ago."

"And he didn't call himself Restow then?"

"No."

"Will you tell me what he did call himself?"

Elsie pushed back her chair and got up.

"No, I can't tell you that. Will you go?"

He went as far as the door. Then he turned.

"Where does Thurloe come in?"

"Jimmy? Just a friend of mine."

"Same kind of friend as Froth?"

"No."

He came a step nearer.

"I only asked because—Is he likely to talk?"

Elsie laughed unexpectedly.

"About your being a ghost?"

"Oh, he thought I was a ghost, did he?"

She laughed again.

"Lindsay Trevor's ghost. I've never heard of anyone meeting a ghost in a fog. Have you?"

"Fogs are proverbially misleading," said Lindsay.

"This one didn't mislead Jimmy. He recognized you."

Lindsay took a quick decision.

"Miss Manning—it is very important indeed that Thurloe shouldn't talk about a supposed likeness between me and Lindsay Trevor, who is dead. You understand—Lindsay Trevor is dead. If he were alive, it might have very serious consequences for a number of people, including Trevor Fothering."

"Is that true?"

"Perfectly."

She looked at him for a moment.

"You told me the truth about Trevor? He's safe?"

"Safe—and out of the country."

She went past him and through the shop to the outer door. When she had opened it she looked back over her shoulder.

"You can drop the Miss Manning. I'm Elsie to my friends. Good-night, Lindsay Trevor! Jimmy won't talk."

Lindsay walked mechanically into the foggy street. He had received a shock which had taken away his power to think. It was not Elsie Manning's use of his name that had produced this sense of shock; it was quite inevitable that she should guess that he was Lindsay Trevor, and he felt oddly certain that he could trust her not to give him away. No, the thing that had struck him numb and dazed had come and gone like a flash just at the moment when he had answered her question about Froth. She had said, "You told me the truth about Trevor? He is safe?" And he had replied, "Safe—and out of the country." And then, just for a second before she turned and went out through the shop, there was something—a look, a flashing likeness—that left him with this inexplicable sense of shock.

He had reached the corner of the road before he quite knew what he was doing. He stood there for a moment recovering himself. He was just about to go on again, when he heard the sound of running footsteps.

Elsie Manning came up with him, panting a little.

"Come away from the light. You never know who's looking."

He was, for one—looking hard and steadily for a likeness which he didn't believe in. There wasn't any likeness. He told himself he was a fool.

Elsie slipped a hand inside his arm and drew him away from the light.

"I can't stay—Jimmy's waiting."

"Yes. What is it?"

She drew her hand away.

"It might be safer for you—I think you're a pretty good sort—I didn't want to—but it might be safer."

"Are you going to tell me something?" said Lindsay. "Is that it?"

"Yes. I said I wouldn't, and then I thought—"

"Then you thought you would?"

"Yes."

She was breathing quickly. He had a feeling that she might run away without telling him after all.

"What were you going to tell me?" he said, and laid a hand on her arm.

"You asked me what he called himself—when I—knew him?"

"Yes. Are you going to tell me that?"

He felt her arm stiffen under his hand. Then all of a sudden she pulled free.

"Manning," she said, and ran from him into the fog.

Chapter Eighteen

Lindsay stood looking after her. Manning—what did she mean by that? Manning—was Restow Manning? Was Restow Elsie Manning's father?

He went over everything that she had said very carefully. She had seen a man go into Restow's house. It was a man whom she had not seen for eight years. She was obviously terrified of him. She had made inquiries and had found out that the house belonged to Algerius Restow. She had told Froth—now just what had she told Froth? Probably a good deal more than she had told himself. Then exit Froth and enter Lindsay Trevor in his stead. She had told him that the man was a blackmailer. Then to-night there was this story of coming across the man in a house in Cannington Place. Was it Restow who had talked with Madame Ferrans about articles in the Paris press and interpellations in the Chamber? Was it Restow, or was it Drayton? She had asked if he were "towering," and he had said yes, with Restow in his mind. But Drayton was as tall. Was Drayton Manning? For all he knew he might have a dozen aliases. He wondered what Restow was doing eight or nine years ago, and then remembered, or thought he remembered, that the time corresponded with a spectacular crash in his affairs and a temporary disappearance from the limelight.

Lindsay had begun to walk. His thoughts kept him company. It would be much easier for Drayton to be Manning than for Restow. He could make no more of it than that. He roused himself with a jerk. What he had to do at this moment was to find the nearest post office.

He wrote down word for word what Elsie Manning had been able to remember of the conversation between Madame Ferrans and the man who might be Restow, or Drayton, or someone quite unknown. He wrote standing at one of the partitioned desks which the Post Office provides, and hoped that the result was legible. He used paper bought at the stationer's next door, and when he had finished his report he asked for a registered envelope. Whatever else happened, Madame Ferrans would be shadowed, and the identity, at any rate of the gentleman who was to make a violent speech in the Chamber, should not be impossible to establish. With luck, F might also be traced.

He walked to the corner of Blenheim Square and stood looking at the immense block which Restow had converted into his town house. The fog was almost gone from this side of the square, though he had just come out of a street where it was as thick as ever.

He walked back along the side of the block. All this must be part of the house. He was spacing it out in his mind—the depth of the hall, the great central court with its swimming-pool. The house must take in everything down to Blenheim Road. Probably there was an entrance from Blenheim Road. It occurred to him that it might be useful to be free of a second entrance.

He turned the corner, crossed to the other side, and took a look at what must be the back of the immense house. It didn't look like the back of a house at all, but like any row of houses with steps leading up to pillared porches. The last three houses covered about the space required. Each had its own flight of steps, its own door.

As he looked, a taxi drew up before the middle house of the three. Someone got out. With the cab between, Lindsay could not see who it was, but a moment later the taxi made off and a girl walked up the steps and rang the bell.

Lindsay stood on the other side of the road and looked at her. Before the bell could have stopped ringing, the door was opened. The girl stood for a moment, black and slender against the light. Then she moved forward, and the door shut.

Lindsay went on looking at the door. He seemed to have no power to look away, for he thought the door was the back door of Restow's house, and he thought that he had just seen Marian Rayne go through it.

After a very long minute he moved. It was quite, quite impossible. The street was dark; an uncertain lamplight contended with drifting remnants of fog. He had seen the silhouette which is every woman's silhouette—a close cap, a coat with a fur collar—and he must needs call this shadow Marian. A cold anger flooded his mood. He might as well give up his job and have done with it if he was going to see his own thought between him and any chance-met stranger. It was the second time to-day. He had Marian in his thought. It irked him bitterly that his pulses should have leapt and stopped for this mirage of Marian.

He crossed the road. If he were to ring the bell? He tried to debate the point, and found himself unable to clear his mind of the insistent desire to follow the shadow of Marian. He had his foot on the bottom step, when someone passed him. A young man ran up the steps and then, turning, looked down upon him with obvious recognition.

"Forgotten your key, sir?" he said.

Lindsay came up to the same level as far as his feet were concerned; the lad's round rosy face was still well above his own.

"You're—?"

"Robert, sir."

Lindsay recognized one of the younger footmen. The boy had waited on him once or twice; but out of his ridiculous green and gold livery he had a countrified look.

"I don't think I've got a key. I suppose I can get in this way?"

"Oh yes, sir." He was opening the door as he spoke.

Lindsay walked past him into a plain, square hall.

"Which way do I go?"

"Straight through takes you out into the swimming-bath, sir."

Lindsay stopped, turned.

"Robert—"

"Yes, sir."

"A young lady came in here just now. Can you find out where she went?"

"A young lady?"

"Yes."

He waited. Robert seemed a long time gone. A lad who might be useful. He extracted a ten-shilling note and held it ready.

Robert came back rather embarrassed.

"It was one of the maids, sir."

Lindsay shook his head.

"One of the maids wouldn't arrive in a taxi."

"It was Ellen, sir—fourth housemaid she is."

"In a taxi?"

"William let her in, sir. He didn't say anything about a taxi."

"All right," said Lindsay. "Thanks for letting me in, Robert." He put the ten-shilling note into the boy's hand and walked away.

A straight passage led from the hall to the swimming-pool. He would have liked to explore this side of the house. There was a staircase, and other passages going off right and left.

He didn't believe it was Ellen he had seen. Seeing Ellen wouldn't have dug him up by the roots like this. And yet he couldn't have seen Marian Rayne. It was a sheer impossibility.

He skirted the bathing-pool and came to the side of the house with which he was familiar. In the passage that led past the library he hesitated, his mind on Drayton. After a moment he opened the door and went in softly. The big room was in darkness. A dull glow from the recessed fireplace showed where the logs had fallen into red ash. The air was still.

With a hand on the switch he stood, listening intently. He wondered if Drayton was in his room, and as the thought passed through his mind, a pencilled streak of light divided the darkness on the right of the fireplace. Lindsay's hand dropped from the switch. He caught at the door and stepped back into the passage. He could see nothing now of course, for the passage was brightly lighted. The two-inch gap between door and jamb showed him merely darkness. He listened, heard nothing, and was about to move, when he saw the dark gap change to a bright one. The light had been turned on in the library.

On an impulse he pushed open the door and went in.

Drayton's door was ajar, and Drayton himself stood before it looking down the room. At the sight of Lindsay he stretched a hand behind him and shut his door.

Does one shut the door of an empty room like that? Lindsay thought not. He came towards Drayton in as aimless a manner as he could compass.

"I wanted to have a talk to you," he said fretfully.

Drayton stood there, tall, stooping—what was the word Elsie had used?—towering. Lindsay was assailed by a memory of the Leaning Tower of Pisa—Drayton had just that over-balanced look. He said in his harsh, unmodulated voice, "I am engaged."

Lindsay produced Froth's snigger.

"Pleasantly?"

He thought that got home. Imagination boggled at the idea of Drayton changing colour, but just for a second those cold eyes of his became, as it were, fixed. It was not that his expression changed, but Lindsay divined, or thought that he divined, the effort that kept it from changing.

"Well, I thought it would be a good plan if we had a talk," he said.

"When you are required to think, I will tell you."

Lindsay looked blank.

"Oh well—of course—just as you like."

"You may return in half an hour," said Drayton curtly.

Lindsay turned on his heel with a shrug. Less than ever did he believe that it was Ellen he had seen entering the house. Whoever it was, he believed that she was at that moment in Drayton's room. As he went upstairs, he told himself with vehemence that it was not, and could not, be Marian Rayne. But if it were—what madness to follow her! Wasn't she the one person in this world whom he must avoid?

He went up to his room and stared out of his window at the opaque roof of the swimming-pool.

Chapter Nineteen

Half an hour later he was in Drayton's room, with Drayton sitting crouched forward over a big bare writing-table. That was the keynote of the whole room—bareness. There was not a picture, or a photograph. The chairs were cushionless. The window had a plain blind and no curtains. The floor was carpetless except for a hearth-rug. On the writing-table there was no litter of papers; an unmarked blotter held the middle of it; beyond it an inkstand and a tray of pens; a case of writing-paper and envelopes was on the right, and on the left *Bradshaw, Debrett,* and *Who's Who.* The waste-paper basket under the table was empty.

Lindsay found himself with food for thought. Was this tidiness, or caution? It occurred to him that Drayton could not safely leave his correspondence about. There was certainly nothing here to furnish food for servants' gossip.

"You wanted to talk to me," Drayton was saying.

"Er—yes," said Lindsay. He had adopted a nervously jaunty attitude, and sat ankle on knee, making play with an unlighted cigarette.

"Well?" said Drayton.

Lindsay plunged.

"You don't seem to trust me," he said in an injured voice.

"No? How strange! Such a trustworthy person!"

Lindsay tapped his cigarette.

"Oh, *come!*"

Drayton surveyed him coldly. The whole atmosphere was cold.

"So I don't trust you? Perhaps you'd like some mark of confidence. As it happens, I can gratify you. When you've done a job or two for us, we'll have rather more reason to trust you, because if anything goes wrong, it'll be a case of Mr Trevor Fothering first and the rest nowhere." He thrust forward his head suddenly. "First for jug—do you understand that?"

"Oh, I say!" said Lindsay feebly.

"It's what I say," said Drayton. "The sooner you learn that, the better."

"Hang it all—I'm *Restow's* secretary!"

He got a horrible look for this. There was something daunting about the man.

"Do you expect him to move in these matters himself?" said Drayton. "You'll take your orders from me. Restow's the big noise—do you grasp that? And you—you're just one of the specks of dust that he uses because it suits him. You're dust—*dust!* And when you're not wanted any more, he'll just flick you away, and then you won't even be dust." His voice went down into a grinding whisper.

Lindsay supposed that he was being impressed—hypnotized perhaps. He looked away from the fixed cold eyes, and was pleased to feel cool and detached.

Drayton drew back. He sat immensely high in the stiff office chair. He picked up a penholder with a bright new nib and balanced it between finger and thumb as if it were a dart that he was about to throw.

"Do you know Sir John Gladisloe?"

Lindsay fidgeted.

"Not personally. That is—"

"You don't know him. It doesn't really matter whether you do or not."

"I know of him."

"And what do you know?"

"Er—well—he's a big man in steel."

"He is the head of the Gladisloe-Vail steel works. Quite an important person in his—in his way." He repeated the last words and gave a short grim laugh. Lindsay thought it one of the most unpleasant sounds he had ever heard. Then, with harsh directness, Drayton was saying, "You have an appointment with him at nine-forty-five to-night."

Lindsay showed all the surprise he felt.

"I've got—an appointment!"

"With Sir John Gladisloe, at his house in Portesbery Square, at nine-forty-five to-night."

Lindsay said "Why?" and let his mouth hang open in the best Fothering manner. It occurred to him that he must look exactly like a codfish, a dithering redhaired codfish.

Drayton made a darting movement in the air with the pen he was holding. He might have been measuring his distance before launching it at some invisible mark.

"We have had some correspondence with Sir John Gladisloe. We have arrived at the stage of the personal interview. I don't engage in personal interviews myself—I employ deputies. On this occasion you will be the deputy."

"Er—what do you want me to do?"

"Say what I tell you to say—neither more nor less."

"But what am I to say?"

Drayton made another of those darting passes in the air.

"You will be the bearer of an ultimatum. You will not mention any names. You will tell him that, in continuation of the correspondence under dates of December 15th and 21st, and January 2nd and 7th— Write those dates down!"

Lindsay fumbled ineffectively in his pocket.

"I haven't anything to write on." He wondered if Drayton would open one of the drawers of that secretive table to supply him with writing materials.

Drayton did nothing of the sort. He took from his own pocket a half sheet of note-paper and a pencil and pushed them over.

Lindsay wondered whether all the drawers of the table were locked. He wrote down December 15th and 21st, and January 2nd and 7th. Then he read out what he had written.

Drayton nodded.

"You will say that there is to be no further correspondence. He is to begin within the next fortnight to make cuts in the wages of all grades of employees, and he is to be prepared to make further cuts in the case of the first cut being accepted without a strike. Strike conditions are to be induced not later than the first week in February. It is to be understood that the Government's disarmament policy is responsible for the cuts. Will you repeat that."

Lindsay repeated it. He instilled a measure of bewilderment into his voice. What he was actually feeling was a burning flame of triumph. Here was something beyond his most ambitious hopes, not stumbled on, not pieced together, but given whole into his hand. *Timeo Danaos et dona ferentes.* The Latin slid into his mind and out again. Drayton's gifts were very decidedly to be feared. He was to be used as a blackmailer. Elsie Manning's report of what she had overheard was corroborated.

But what was Drayton's security for using him? He had these thoughts clear in his mind whilst he repeated Drayton's instructions.

"Yes," said Drayton—"that's it. Do you hear? That's it—and you won't put anything to it."

Lindsay jerked a shoulder as he had seen Froth do at school when he was being baited.

"Are these Restow's orders?"

Drayton cast his pen down upon the blotting-paper. The nib went into the clean white folds; the holder stood up quivering.

Lindsay jerked again.

"I'd like to have my orders from Restow direct." He caught the look in Drayton's eyes and stopped.

"You'll take your orders from me," said Drayton in the softest tone that Lindsay had heard from him. The softness was by several shades more unpleasant than his usual harsh voice.

"Well, I don't know—"

"Must I remind you of my authority?" said Drayton, still very softly.

Lindsay felt so anxious to be reminded that he ventured a sulky, "I don't know about authority."

"I still hold that cheque—" said Drayton. He paused. "I have only to send it to the right quarter—" He paused again. "I think you would get seven years—" A third pause, longer than before, during which the dull lizard eyes slowly brightened into malignity. "Of course it is possible that you might get off with five—but even five years is a slice, a distinct slice out of a young man's life."

Lindsay made use of Mr Drayton's impressive pauses to adjust himself to the shock. One may dislike a cousin very much without being prepared to hear that he has committed forgery. No one cares about having even a second cousin in the dock. Family pride kicked. He felt an elementary desire to hit Drayton good and hard—the blackmailing swine! Froth, unfortunately, was not in a position to hit Drayton. Lindsay, as Froth, made a nervous movement and muttered,

"For heaven's sake—"

"What about taking my orders?"

"Yes—yes—of course. But I say—"

"Yes?"

"Suppose he just tells me to go to blazes?"

Drayton slowly withdrew the still upright pen.

"I hardly think he will do that—but he may, of course, put up a bluff."

"That's what I mean."

"In that case you will inform him that a copy taken from the register of St Mary's, Coldingham, under date of May 8th 1903 will be forwarded, with all other pertinent evidence, to the office of the Public Prosecutor."

"What is it?" said Lindsay. "Bigamy?"

"You can leave that to Sir John," said Drayton gently. He leaned back in his stiff chair. "You can add that, in case of his—shall we say— sudden decease, the same information will be sent to Lady Gladisloe and to the Press."

"*Swine!*" said Lindsay to himself. Aloud he achieved a nervous "Yes."

"And for yourself, you will remember that you are on probation. If you make a fool of yourself—there's the cheque. If I have any cause to distrust you—there's what you've had a taste of already, and more to come. You are on probation—and when I use a man on probation I keep a pretty tight check on him. Do you get that? You had better. If you say more, or less, to John Gladisloe than I've told you to say, I shall know it. Don't you forget that!"

Lindsay pushed back his chair with a jerk.

"I say, don't talk like that! I—I'll do my best."

"Nine-forty-five—7 Portesbery Square. You will give your name as Smith," said Drayton curtly.

Lindsay supposed that the audience was terminated. He got up. As he did so, something caught his eye. When he pushed his chair back, one leg had caught the hearth-rug and rucked it up. Against the fold something glinted. The sheet of paper that Lindsay had in his hand dropped. He exclaimed, and, bending to pick it up, retrieved the tiny glittering thing. He wrapped the paper round it and slipped it into his pocket.

Drayton had no more to say.

Lindsay went out by the second door, which led direct into the passage. His heart was thumping. His hands were cold. It seemed about a mile to his room.

When he had shut and bolted the door, he took the folded paper from his pocket and opened it. A small diamond flower like a miniature daisy slipped into the palm of his hand. It was just a fortnight since he had touched it last. It was the middle flower of a spray. He had stood with his hand on Marian's shoulder and moved it with the tip of his finger. He could hear their voices now, like the voices of two people in a play:

"It's loose—you'll lose it."

That was Lindsay Trevor.

"I must remember to have it mended."

That was Marian Rayne.

The flower had been warm then because it lay against Marian's bare warm shoulder. It was cold now. She had not remembered to have it mended. She had lost it in Drayton's room.

Chapter Twenty

LINDSAY LEFT the house just after nine o'clock. He carried with him a report of his conversation with Drayton. Before posting it he had to make sure that he was not followed. He did not think that he would be followed on this occasion. Drayton would be tolerably sure of his keeping his appointment with Sir John Gladisloe. He knew—perhaps he alone knew—just to what extent he had the whip hand of Trevor Fothering. Lindsay, in Froth's shoes, could only guess at the raw places the whip had flicked. That Drayton was prepared to bring it down with smashing brutality, he had no doubt. Froth wasn't the man to face penal servitude for the sake of what remnants of conscience he had left. No, he thought that Drayton would feel quite easy about his instructions being carried out. On the other hand, you never could tell, and he wasn't taking risks.

When he was quite satisfied that he was not being followed, he posted his report and went on his way to Portesbery Square. He wasn't at all sure what he was going to do. He would have liked to give the man a hint, but he had a conviction that Drayton had not been bluffing when he declared that he would know whether his instructions had been exactly carried out. Lindsay hadn't, of course, any idea of how Drayton would know. He had the solid conviction that he would know.

As he rang the bell of 7 Portesbery Square, it occurred to him that of all the jobs he had ever undertaken he liked this one the least.

He was shown into a study and left alone there. A man's room gives the key to his character. This was the room of a wealthy man; but the wealth was subordinated to comfort, and as Lindsay judged, to sentiment. The mantelpiece and the top of a book-stand were covered with photographs, most of them old and faded. The chairs were in their comfortable middle age. On a clear space of wall immediately opposite the writing-table hung the portrait of a woman with big sad eyes and an air of fragile dignity. The hair above the dark sad eyes was silver white. The long pale fingers held a scarlet carnation.

Lindsay was still looking at the portrait, when the door opened and Sir John Gladisloe came in, tall and spare, with a grey face and grey hair, and the look of a man who is sleeping badly. He came to a halt with the shut door behind him, fixed a bleak look upon his visitor, and said,

"Mr Smith?"

"Er—yes," said Lindsay. He had decided to play the part as Trevor Fothering would have played it. Froth would undoubtedly have been nervous. The last accounts of him did not present the portrait of one who would do his blackmailing with an air.

Lindsay registered conscious guilt and admitted to the name of Smith in a nervous whisper. All the time his mind was working on the question of how Drayton was going to check up this interview. He had already deduced a spy in the garrison. Someone in the Gladisloe household was in Drayton's pay. Listening at doors would be rather crude. He had made sure that the window curtains did not conceal a listener. But it would be easy enough to contrive a tube leading from the cornice to one of the upper rooms; those heavy mouldings with their alternate acanthus leaves and pomegranates would shelter a much larger hole than the one required.

"You made an appointment," said Sir John curtly. He had the air of a man who wishes to avoid as far as possible an undesired proximity.

"Yes," said Lindsay again.

Sir John crossed the room, keeping well away from him. He reached the other side of the writing-table and spoke from there:

"Will you kindly state your business?" Lindsay advanced a step.

"I am here," he said nervously—"er—in continuation of the correspondence under dates of December 15th and 21st, and January 2nd and 7th."

Sir John looked at him beneath straight grey brows. Lindsay could admire his bearing.

"Well?"

Lindsay moistened his lips.

"I am to say that there is to be no further correspondence."

"Indeed?" said Sir John. "Is that all?"

"Er—no—there's a message."

"Give it to me."

"You are to begin to make cuts in the wages of all grades of your employees within the next fortnight."

The grey face was a little greyer.

"Indeed? Is that all?"

"Er—no. You are to be prepared to go on making cuts until there is a strike. There must be a strike not later than the first week in February. Er—it is to be understood that it is the Government's disarmament policy which is responsible for the cuts."

Not a muscle of Sir John's face moved. His eyes looked past Lindsay. Lindsay had a feeling that he was something too foul to be looked at. He would have liked to call out, "Well played!"

Still without moving, Sir John spoke:

"Do you happen to know that blackmail is punishable with penal servitude for life?"

Lindsay did not feel called upon to answer this. He remained silent. He thought that if he had really been a blackmailer, he would not have chosen Sir John Gladisloe as a subject. After a moment Sir John spoke again:

"Is that all that you have to say to me?"

"Er—it all depends on you."

"You had better explain yourself."

"It depends on your answer."

"And if I have no answer?"

"Er—I suppose that would amount to a refusal of the—er—terms."

"It is open to you to put your own construction upon it."

"If you refuse," said Lindsay, "I was to tell you what the next step would be."

Sir John, standing beside his table, had one hand upon it. He leaned upon this hand very slightly now. "Deliver your message," he said in the same controlled voice that he had used throughout.

Lindsay reminded himself that this was a matter of more than one man's peace of mind, and that there was almost certainly a hole in the cornice or some equivalent accommodation for Drayton's spy.

"If you refuse, I was to tell you that a copy taken from the register of St Mary's, Coldingham, of the date of May 8th 1903 will be forwarded, with—er—other evidence, to the office of the Public Prosecutor."

That grey control held. After a moment Sir John took his hand from the table and straightened himself. He was, perhaps, afraid to lean on anything just then. When the walls and the roof of the house are falling in, it is better not to lean on anything."

"Is that all?" he asked.

Lindsay forced himself on.

"Not quite."

"Finish what you have to say."

"I was to say that, in case of your death, the same information would appear in the Press."

He could not, after all, bring in the sad-eyed woman who looked down on them with the red carnation in those thin, frail hands. If Drayton knew of the omission, the eavesdropping would be fairly proved. He could play a nervous lapse of memory. These were his thoughts afterwards. At the time he merely baulked at Lady Gladisloe's name.

For an instant Sir John looked at him. A flush rose painfully to the roots of the thick grey hair.

After that one instant Sir John had looked away. At last he said, "I will give an answer—later. You had better go."

Lindsay went.

After the door had shut behind him Sir John Gladisloe remained standing just where he was for perhaps five minutes. Then he straightened himself with a jerk and went out of the room and up the broad, easy stair.

In a small room on the half-landing the original of the portrait was waiting for him. She sat in the corner of a sofa, her head with its thick silver hair very erect, her fine pale hands clasped together on her knee. The room was brightly lighted, and the light picked out the jewel colours of the embroidered Chinese shawl which draped her slight figure. She had been looking down at her own hands, but when the door opened she lifted her eyes and smiled. It was rather a heartbreaking smile.

"Come and tell me," she said.

He came and stood beside her.

"It is what we thought."

"What are they going to do, John?"

He said, "I wonder," and looked down, frowning heavily.

"What do they threaten to do?"

"Send the entry from the register with other evidence to the Public Prosecutor."

Her hands pressed each other and she became, if possible, a little paler.

"Do you think they will do it?"

His frown deepened.

"I don't know."

She looked up at him then. Her eyes had more blue in them than the portrait showed.

"What do they want you to do?"

"I'm to force a strike by cutting wages."

She exclaimed faintly at that.

"How wicked!" Then, after a pause, "What are you going to do?"

"I don't know," said John Gladisloe. He went down on his knees and put his arms round her. "I can't face it for you," he said.

"John—don't! Don't, darling! It—it isn't as if you'd done anything wrong. You thought she was dead."

"I hoped she was. I thought—oh yes, God knows I thought she was dead. Evans wrote and told me, but I didn't keep the letter." He controlled his voice with an effort. "I don't suppose the Public Prosecutor would move in the matter. If he did, nothing would come of it." He laughed bitterly. "Nothing except the washing of all our dirty linen in public."

"If it comes to that, you must bear it, John."

"It will kill you," he said.

She shook her head.

"No—I won't let it."

He got up and walked away from her to the other side of the room. From the mantelpiece a pretty fairhaired girl in a fluffy dance frock smiled on them both. She had a gay, confident air and bright unshadowed eyes.

"And Cynthia?" said John Gladisloe.

A look of agony passed across Mary Gladisloe's face. With John's back to her, she could for a moment relax the self-control which had kept a smile on her lips. When she spoke, her voice was steady and sweet.

"Cynthia isn't—brittle."

Still with his back to her, John Gladisloe said,

"In the eyes of the law she will be—illegitimate."

Mary Gladisloe got up and went to him. Her shawl slipped, and she caught it up with her usual gentle composure. She leaned against him and spoke softly:

"John, we are just one family. If there are these wage cuts and—a strike, there will be—suffering—for hundreds—children—and old people. I don't want to push our sufferings on to them. I don't want to be saved, and I don't want Cynthia to be saved—at their expense."

He dropped his head on her shoulder, and they stood without speaking for a long time. When he lifted his head again he looked like a man who has set himself to a hard day's work.

"You're sure, Mary?"

"Yes, I'm quite sure." She lifted her chin. "We'll fight them. Perhaps we'll win—but if we don't, we'll keep our self respect. Why, if we gave way this time, what would the next demand be, and where would it end? If it hadn't been for me, you would never have dreamt of giving way."

John Gladisloe walked to the telephone table and picked up the instrument.

"What are you going to do, John?"

"I'm going to make a clean breast of the whole thing to old Benbow Smith."

Chapter Twenty-One

Lindsay reported to Drayton. The interview was of the shortest. Drayton, sitting at his desk, his shoulders stooped, his head thrust forward, listened to what he had to say in a silence that remained unbroken on his side. He did not even look at Lindsay. The heavy pouched lids were almost closed. Some imp pushed into Lindsay's mind the lines: "Heard melodies are sweet, but those unheard are sweeter." A little zigzag flash of amusement went off like a squib. Drayton's eyes were beastly enough when you could see them—lizard's eyes, snake's eyes; but when you couldn't, when the bulging eyelids hid them, they were a good deal worse.

He was dismissed with a curt, indifferent nod, and departed with relief. Half way up the main stair, with its gilded pillars and its caryatides, he encountered Restow—this also with relief. Villain for villain, he preferred Restow every time. Restow was bull to Drayton's serpent. If he had to fall foul of one of them, he would rather take on brute force than poison. Not that Restow hadn't plenty of brain—he wouldn't have been Restow without it. He had starved in every capital in Europe, and he would still have been starving if he had not had the brain that can coin itself into gold. Ruin Restow to-morrow, and he would be a millionaire again whilst another man would still be casting about for a job that would keep him out of the workhouse.

Restow came charging down the stairs.

"Aha, Fothering! You have come! Where have you been? What does it matter where you have been?" He flung a huge arm about Lindsay's shoulders. "You are here—you are the watched pot that has boiled—and I do not care a halfpenny damn where you have been."

"Did you want me?"

Restow clapped him on the back.

"Would I look for you if I did not want you? Would I go running up and down these stairs like a squirrel in a cage if I did not want you?"

Restow as a squirrel was very nearly too much for Lindsay. He laughed.

But Restow himself was laughing too.

"I am a fine well-grown squirrel, *hein*?" His enormous cheeks crinkled, the little pig eyes almost disappeared, on either side of the big open mouth the crooked canine teeth came into view. Lindsay was again smitten on the back. "You will go to your room, and you will pack your bag."

For a frightful moment Lindsay thought that he was being dismissed.

Restow roared with laughter.

"Did you think I was giving you the chuck? By Jing, I believe you did! Have you a conscience that makes you a coward—what?" He took Lindsay by the arm and began to mount the stairs two steps at a time. "Hurry! Hurry! Hurry! Pack the bag! Take everything for a week—ten days—a month! Perhaps we shall only be there twenty-four hours—perhaps we shall never come back. 'To-morrow and to-morrow and to-morrow.' That is Shakespeare—*hein?* But I do not know where from. It all goes round in my mind like a whirlwind, and when I fish in it something comes up, and how shall I know what it is and where it comes from? It is the wise reader who knows his own quotation—*nicht?*"

They arrived at the top, and Lindsay was suddenly released.

"Where are we going?"

"To Paris," said Restow. He blew out his cheeks and made a schoolboy grimace. "Paris—*why?* Aha! I will tell you. Because we are not expected there. Or do you think that she will expect me—that she has done it on purpose? How is it possible to tell with a woman who always goes a different way like an Irish pig in a poke? What do you say, Fothering?"

"You haven't told me what you're talking about yet, sir."

Restow ran his hand through his thick black hair.

"I haven't told you? Have I stopped telling you? Your head is wood all through from one side to the other! I suppose you have clockwork somewhere that makes you go. If you had either a brain or a heart, you would know that I am going to Paris because Gloria is there. Do you hear that? Does your clockwork miss a stroke when I tell you that you are to see Gloria Paravicini—to meet her—to meet her—to be an ambassador, a go-between, a plenipotentiary—a whole peace conference? By Jing, I am sorry for you, my Fothering, because I do not think that Gloria is feeling peaceful. She makes a splendid gesture of war, and I send her my Fothering—and a formula. That blessed word formula! We right like cat and dog—no, these are too small animals—it is like tiger and elephant that we fight—but—let us find a formula, and let me see my Gloria's magnificent face when you bring it to her! Aha! She shall learn that I too can make gestures! Did I tell you what she has done?"

"No, you didn't," said Lindsay, as drily as he dared. Restow caught him by the shoulders and shook him to and fro.

"She has gone back to the circus—she has herself billed to appear in Paris in three days' time. Gloria Paravicini—*Première Dompteuse* of the habitable globe—the Python Queen—the Serpent Sorceress—Tiger Tamer—Lion Witch—Panther Pet. Bah! What do I know how many dam foolish names she calls herself? But I know this"—he stopped shaking Lindsay and held him solemnly at arm's length—"this I know for sure, because my head is not wood, it contains brains, so I know when Gloria placards herself all over Paris that she does it to cock a snook at me." He took his right hand from Lindsay's shoulder, pressed his own nose with the thumb, and twiddled the four fingers derisively. "She cocks a snook—she says 'be dam!' I too can cock a snook—but I do not swear at a lady, not even when she is my wife. Aha! She and her Gloria Paravicini! I am divorced, am I? There is no Gloria Restow any more? By Jing, then, we shall see!" He pushed Lindsay away. "Go and pack your bag, my Fothering!"

Chapter Twenty-Two

LINDSAY WENT to Paris in something of an unreasoning holiday spirit. To leave Drayton behind and to go off into the blue with Restow felt absurdly like coming out of prison. They had a smooth crossing, and an encounter which, to Lindsay at any rate, was unexpected.

He was standing by the side looking down at the oily, even flow of lead-coloured water, when he felt a touch on the arm and, turning his head, found himself very close indeed to a lady whose fine eyes looked smilingly into his. A single line of plucked eyebrow surmounted the eyes, which shone like dark jewels in a sallow mobile face.

"What a happy encounter!" said a voice with a marked French accent.

Lindsay produced a smile of pleased recognition, at the same time stepping back a pace. As he had never set eyes on the lady before, he imagined that she must be a friend of Froth's. As he smiled, he snatched off his hat and displayed the red hair. A pleasant consciousness of having given it a fresh wash of henna overnight sustained him; even in this bad light it would put any carrot to shame.

"Fortunate for me," he said, and remembered to pitch his voice high.

The lady was a thin vivacious forty. She had exquisite ankles, and expensive shoes. Her dress was the smart, inconspicuous black of the travelling Frenchwoman. She asked him if he was going to Paris, and where he was staying, and for how long. He told her that he was staying with Restow at the Paris Luxe, but that he had no idea how long they were to be there. He began to wonder if he was talking to Madame Ferrans. After a few minutes she left him. The incident was over. He wondered whether Froth knew many people in Paris. And then suddenly, as he stood looking out towards the grey horizon, there was Madame Ferrans brushing past him. She did not stop. Just beyond him she hesitated, spoke a few words in a low voice, and then walked away. He had no time to say anything to her; the whole thing was over in a moment, leaving him puzzled and interested.

What she had said was just this:

"Take care, *mon ami*—he suspects you."

Lindsay left the boat with relief. On the gangway Restow stood aside to let Madame Ferrans pass. She thanked him with a murmured *"Merci, monsieur"* but with no trace of recognition. Lindsay put that away to remember.

It was just after six o'clock that he knocked at the door of Madame Paravicini's sitting-room. She was registered as Madame Gloria Paravicini. Restow had been oddly divided between the sense of the honour done to the hotel by the world-famous name and the insult offered to himself by the repudiation of his own name, equally world famous. He had dispatched Lindsay to this interview with plenipotentiary powers and a number of extremely conflicting instructions.

A voice said, "Come right in!" and Lindsay came.

He was a good deal intrigued, and a good deal afraid that it would not be possible for Madame Gloria to be as exotic as Restow's account of her. Even as he turned the handle of the door, he told himself that he must be prepared to meet a merely civilized woman. At the first glance his spirits rose. Gloria Paravicini wasn't going to be merely anything. To use her own vocabulary, she was two hundred per cent, and then some. In the midst of an untidy room littered with clothes, flowers, parcels, cocktail shakers, and a variety of other articles, she drew the eye and held it.

She had grown stouter since the offending artist had painted her with a panther because the tiger she desired would take up too much room. It would have required a colossal canvas to accommodate Gloria Paravicini and a tiger now, but she was still magnificently handsome. She wore a loose wrapper of cloth of gold lined with the vivid emerald green of the portrait. Her hair hung in two enormous braids. They appeared to Lindsay to be some yards in length, and though afterwards he had moments of doubt, yet, at the time, he received the impression that they were at least six inches across. They were certainly looped and threaded with emeralds. A ruby and an emerald of about the size and appearance of the side and rear lights of a bicycle lamp blazed upon the curves of Madame Gloria's bosom. It was of a surprising whiteness. Lindsay found everything about her surprising, and the most surprising thing of all was the deep contralto voice with its purely American accent. Gloria Paravicini might be her name, but God's own country had had the raising of her.

"Come right in!" she said.

Lindsay came in, shut the door, and shook hands. He received a grip which he felt would have inspired his respect had he been a refractory lion; after which he was waved to a chair and wondered what he was going to say first. He confessed to feeling just a trifle dazed. He repressed a desire to stretch his fingers gingerly and discover whether any of them were broken. He achieved a pleasant deprecating smile, and said,

"It's very good of you to see me, Madame Paravicini."

"Cut it out!" said the lady with a frown. Then, on a rising note, "You're Algy's secretary, aren't you?"

"I'm Mr Restow's secretary—yes."

"Isn't that what I'm saying? Cut out all that politeness stunt! I'm not seeing you—I'm seeing Algy's secretary. And I'm seeing Algy's secretary because I'd a darned sight rather see Algy's secretary than Algy—and you can tell him I said so."

Lindsay found this rather a difficult gambit. It seemed to him that tact was going to be wasted. With ingenuous frankness as the order of the day, he might perhaps be able to hold his own.

Gloria Paravicini flung back one of her massive plaits and fixed him with a compelling gaze.

"And you get this straight right here and now!" she said in forceful tones. "If Algy guesses he's going to get across with any he-man stuff, well, he's guessing the wrong side of the multiplication table, and he'd better go right out and buy himself a calculating machine, because I reckon that brain he thinks such a sight of has got the blue mould sprouting all over it."

"I don't think that's Mr Restow's idea at all," said Lindsay firmly.

"And what is his idea? No—hold on! What he wants is to get it right into his head that his ideas don't cut any ice with me. What you want to hand him is my ideas."

"Well, I shall be delighted—if you will tell me what they are."

She was sitting on a small gilt sofa piled up with cushions. So little of the sofa was visible that, except for the fact that the lady and the cushions must have had some means of support, it would have been rash to assert its existence. Madame Paravicini now seized a scarlet cushion, tucked it behind her head, and said,

"You listen to me!"

Lindsay listened. The lady's ringing voice would indeed have made it difficult to do anything else.

"The first thing you've got to hand to Algy," said Madame Paravicini, "is that he isn't my husband any more. We're divorced, and he'd better not forget it. There isn't anyone on this planet that's got any reason to talk scandal about me, and there isn't going to be anyone. I've always been mighty careful of my reputation, and I'm not going to have Algy compromising me by coming to Paris and butting in on my hotel."

"It's a very large hotel," said Lindsay mildly.

"It's *my* hotel," announced the lady. She put a good deal of vigour into the pronoun. "It's my hotel, and I consider it very bad taste for Algy to come butting in—very bad taste and very compromising—and that's the first thing you can tell him. And the next thing you can tell him is this—I'm billed all over Paris to appear before the public with four lions and a tiger that have never been tamed, and if he wants a box to see the show, he can have one with my compliments—with Gloria Paravicini's compliments." She threw back her head against the scarlet cushion and looked at Lindsay through the longest and blackest lashes he had ever seen. Behind them her eyes were bright, lazy, and intent. She reminded him of one of those great cats she had been speaking of—the drowsy pose; the full, graceful curves; the unsleeping wariness.

"I'll tell him," he said.

A curious flickering smile just stirred her rather heavily cut lips.

"He'll be *mad*," she said with considerable satisfaction. Then she sat up with a suddenness that sent the scarlet cushion toppling. "He'll be real mad. And when he's real mad you can tell him that just as soon as I get through with this engagement I'm going to be married."

Lindsay was rather taken aback.

"Don't you think you'd better tell him that yourself?" he said.

"Nope!" said Madame Paravicini. "I've got my reputation to think about, and the gentleman I'm going to marry has got a very jealous disposition."

Lindsay smiled affably. It had obviously become necessary to return the lady's fire. "But in the circumstances," he submitted, "the gentleman surely wouldn't be jealous—er—not in the circumstances?"

"I don't know anything about circumstances. He's jealous—do you get that? He's got Othello beat to a frazzle."

I But if Mr Restow is also expecting to be married, there would surely be no occasion for jealousy?"

Madame Paravicini sprang to her feet. Some seven or eight yards of cloth of gold swished sharply to the floor. She stood like a towering golden pyramid and glared at Lindsay.

"Say that again, young man!"

Lindsay got to his feet, and felt safer.

"Since Mr Restow is also thinking of getting married—" he began, and was at once interrupted.

"He can't do it!"

"Well, he's thinking about it."

Her voice sank to an ominous purring note.

"Let him think about it! He can't do it."

"Well, I don't see—"

Her voice seemed to spring at him, it rose so suddenly.

"Cut it out! He can't do it. I've got him where he can't move. I've got him where he's tied up and I'm free. I've got him where I'm divorced and he's married. It's great—isn't it?" She began to laugh. "Isn't it just great?"

"Well, I don't think I've quite got there."

She went on laughing.

"I'm an American citizen, and my divorce is good in American law; but Algy's a British subject, and they won't take any stock in an American divorce. I've been to the best people, and what they say goes. I'm not married, but Algy is. I can marry to-morrow—Algy's got to wait till my tombstone's ordered. Isn't that just the slickest thing you've ever struck? Now you get going with that little packet of samples and put Algy wise. The only thing I mind is not seeing his face when he tumbles to how I've got him fixed."

The folds of her gold wrap lay all about her feet. She kicked them out of her way, swept to the door, and flung it open.

"Quit!" she said.

Lindsay quitted.

He had gone perhaps a dozen yards down the corridor, when it occurred to him that he had not heard Madame's door close. He glanced over his shoulder and saw her standing on the threshold. He received a curious fleeting impression of a mood in the very process of change. She looked triumphant, a laugh still moulded her lips; but her eyes had clouded, her brows sketched a frown.

As he looked back, she made a gesture that recalled him.

"You're in a mighty hurry," she said.

He came back into the room, and wondered what would come next. At first it seemed as if nothing would come at all. Madame Paravicini walked away to the window, where she stood parting the curtains a little, her long gold draperies gleaming against their rosy colour. She stood like that for quite a time. Then, with one of those sudden graceful movements, she swung round and came towards him again.

"You haven't told me how Algy is," she said in something nearer an ordinary conversational tone than he had yet heard from her.

"Oh, I think he is very well."

She lifted her chin. One might almost have said that she tossed her head.

"He hasn't worried himself sick then?"

"Oh, I don't think so."

"Hasn't got thin!" She laughed rather angrily. "He was right down fleshy when I left him. He hasn't gone away into a decline fretting about me?"

"Oh no—I think he's very well."

This time she certainly tossed her head.

"I'm sure I'm very pleased to hear it. Has that Drayton got himself fired yet?"

"Mr Drayton is still librarian."

She made a sound which could only be described as a snort. It disposed of Drayton as far as she was concerned.

"I didn't have you back to waste time on him. I'd like to have you tell me about my snakes."

"Your snakes?"

"Didn't I say it loud enough? How is Typhoon?"

Lindsay looked blank.

"Young man, aren't there any works in your brain-box?" Then, her voice breaking angrily, "You're not going to tell me he's dead!"

Lindsay remembered suddenly that Typhoon was the python of the portrait.

"I'm sorry, but I don't know anything—"

"That's a mouthful anyway!" said the lady. "I'd be tickled to death if you'd start in and tell me something you do know. Typhoon's dead for all you can say—and mind you, if he is, then Algy's going to be sorry he didn't hand in his checks at the same time. What about Romeo and Juliet?"

Lindsay smiled affably.

"I'm doing my best," he said, "but—"

"But it don't amount to much! They're my cobras, and Romeo is a real smart snake and one I wouldn't lose for the world. Juliet's kind of bad-tempered-bites first and asks who you are afterwards; but Romeo is real smart—fond of me too, and I'd got him so that he'd travel in my pocket and never move an inch. I wish I'd taken him away when I quit, but I was afraid Juliet would fret. She'd a real tender heart, but a mighty uncertain temper."

"I don't know anything about the snakes, I'm afraid," said Lindsay.

A look of passionate anger crossed Madame Paravicini's face.

"Then you can git!" she said. She strode after him to the door. Her voice echoed down the corridor. "You can tell Algy he'd better be dead if those snakes have come to any harm!"

Chapter Twenty-Three

LINDSAY WONDERED how Restow was going to take his account of the interview. He might be quiet, or he might blow up, or he might be devastated. He began by being quiet, and passed rapidly through various stages of angry emotion. Upon the legal point, he reverted to an ominous calm. He had been striding up and down the room, but stopped now in the middle, his arms folded across his enormous chest, his jaw jutting out, his little pig eyes brightly aware.

"Aha! We have it! What a woman! By Jing, what a woman! She is to be free, and I am not to be free! I am a good, quiet, tame, faithful husband, and she is not to be a wife at all—she is to be a blushing demoiselle—she is to marry whom she chooses—some whipper-snapper, some riff-raff, some...Bah! I spit at him! Aha! She is to be divorced, and I am not to be divorced! She is to marry, and I am not to marry!" He flung out his arms like the sails of a windmill. "We shall see—we shall see!"

He swung round on Lindsay.

"And there is a thing she has not thought of. She and her legal advisers! I spit at them! She has not thought that just as soon as she marries another man—Why do I talk of marriage? She is my wife—just so soon as she goes to another man I can file my divorce petition, and there is no one who can stop me. Aha!" He burst into a roar of schoolboy laughter, caught Lindsay a buffet on the shoulder and, still laughing, made for the telephone.

"Shall I go?" asked Lindsay.

Restow shook his head.

"Why should you go? Listen, and you will see—Ah!" He broke off and began to talk into the mouthpiece. "Ah, Gustave, *mon vieux*! Is that you? Aha! Yes! Algerius." He slipped into French as easy and slipshod as his English.

Lindsay reminded himself that Froth would have understood no more than a word here and there, and kept a wooden face.

"Now, *mon vieux,* there is something you can do for me...On the instant—yes. It is at this moment—" He glanced at his wrist-watch. "Yes, it is a quarter to seven. I dine in this hotel...Yes, yes, the Luxe! I dine at the Luxe at a quarter past eight, and I require urgently two ladies to dine with me...Mock then, imbecile! I require two ladies, and if you do not wish me to hire an assassin to put an end to your atrociously ill-spent life, you will now give me your attention...*Juste Dieu!* Serious? Have I not said that I am serious? And when my assassin has his knife in your heart it will also be serious for you—yes, an apache of the most ferocious. Attention now! As I said, I require two ladies—one middle-aged, respectable, *comme il faut*, a little impoverished and *démodée*—that would not hurt. She must appear to be the mother who has made all possible sacrifices for a single much loved child. The other—the other is to be a young girl—*blonde, bien élevée,* modestly conscious of my respectful adoration...Yes, yes—they will dine with me—and afterwards I have a box for the Opera. For the fee, I give you *carte blanche*, and since you have wasted the little time there is, you had better hurry yourself."

He rang off and turned a grinning face on Lindsay.

"*Pas si bête? Hein?* No, by Jing!"

"I'm afraid I couldn't follow—er—er—"

Restow raised his hands above his head.

"The English public school!" he jeered. "It teaches you to win the battle of Waterloo, but not to talk ten words of Napoleon's language! Aha! I have my thoughts of that! The battle of Waterloo is won on the playing-fields of Eton? What a magnificent camouflage! We are a school, but we do not educate, we do not teach anything at all—but when anything happens in the world we can say superbly, 'Alone we did it. This we learned upon our cricket field!' Eton! Harrow! Bah! All your schools are the same!"

He snatched up the receiver again and became immersed in an effort to get on to Madame Paravicini's suite. After saying to three people running, "No—*Madame Paravicini!* No, I will not give a message!" his voice suddenly altered and became so smooth and agreeable that Lindsay would hardly have known it. He dropped at the same time into English.

"That Gloria?...Why, this is great! My secretary tells me I'm to congratulate you... What's that?...Oh, no, no, no, *no*! I am not the dog in the manger. Why, I have hopes myself...Ah yes, I hope. She is dining with me to-night...Yes, she and her mother...Ah, yes, yes, yes—a young girl-quite young—the violet on the mossy stone...No, that is not Shakespeare—that is Wordsworth...Yes—very blonde, very timid—a violet—yes, a white violet...Ah, yes, yes—another time. I know I have all your sympathy and good wishes."

He hung up the receiver and shouted with laughter. "Aha! She boils with rage! A woman scorned has hell beat to a frazzle! Isn't that Shakespeare all right? Why don't I have a secretary who can put my quotations right?"

"'Hell—er—has no fury like a woman scorned,'" said Lindsay with modest pride.

"Aha! Good! Good! Good! Pearl of a Fothering! When you have learnt French I will quote Racine too."

They descended to the lounge at precisely ten minutes past eight. Restow took up a commanding position with his back to a pillar inlaid with gold and blue mosaic. Lindsay thought to himself that his appearance certainly gave the expected damsel a good deal of excuse for timidity. He himself was looking about with amused interest and wondering at what stage of the proceedings Madame Gloria would put in an appearance, and what would happen when she did. The lounge was full of people. Lindsay watched them idly, his glance passing from an immense Jewess hung with pearls to a group of English people who had just come in. In a moment his heart was thumping. In the next he was telling himself savagely that if he was going to see Marian Rayne in every black-haired girl, he had better book a room in the nearest lunatic asylum and have done with it.

The girl had her back to him. She wore a black dress. She had Marian's height and Marian's carriage of the head—the little air that marked her out from other girls, the something that drew his heart. His heart beat harder. She turned and met his eyes. And it was Marian—as pale as when he had seen her last—a sad, pale ghost of the Marian who had worn his ring. The shadows under her eyes were like bruises. She took a single forward step and stood still, looking at Lindsay.

He looked back at her in shocked consternation. The girl was Marian, and there was no doubt of the recognition in her eyes. For perhaps half a minute the look of recognition persisted. Then with a piteous groping gesture she put out her hand and slipped down on to the floor.

Lindsay was half way across the space between them before he remembered that, whoever went to Marian's help, it must not be he. He forced himself to stand still. A stout elderly man of obviously British nationality had her head propped up against his knee. A bun-faced woman with pale blue eyes and sandy hair was fanning her. Her head drooped. Her eyes were closed. The black lashes lay upon cheeks as colourless as milk. Her hands were open palm upwards as if they had let go of everything.

And then she stirred—stirred and opened her eyes. A long, deep look went past him.

With a very great effort he turned and went back to Restow. Nothing felt quite real. Restow, the blue and gold pillar behind him, the two women who had joined him, were pictures with hard clear edges. They had no relation to each other, or to him, or to reality. He did not feel real himself. But Marian—there behind him, struggling out of her faint—Marian was real.

He approached the picture of Restow. His pulses were still thudding. He heard Restow say:

"Mr Fothering—Madame Grandier—Mademoiselle Ursule Grandier."

He was being presented to the perfect picture of a depressed French gentlewoman, and to that young girl *bien élevée* whom he had heard Restow demanding of his friend Gustave.

Madame Grandier was dressed in an out-of-date black silk. She wore a scarf of carefully mended lace about her drooping shoulders, and a piece of black velvet round her neck. She had the anxious, beady eyes of a hen. Mademoiselle Ursule was in white. Her frock was neither new nor well cut, but she wore it with a certain modest grace. As they crossed the lounge and made their way to the restaurant, Lindsay found himself noticing these things mechanically.

Madame Grandier addressed him, and he had sufficient composure to produce a stumbling excuse for having no French.

"But you speak very well," said Madame as they took their seats.

"Tray poo," said Lindsay firmly. He was coming back to himself.

Madame Grandier, with a valour which he admired, addressed him in a series of painstakingly simple remarks, to which he replied at intervals with *"Wee" "Nong,"* or *"Je ne comprong."*

Mademoiselle Ursule, on his other side, sat silent and discreet, her pale blonde hair demurely neat, her pale blue eyes occasionally lifted in grateful admiration to Restow's face. She ate very little. A small pleased smile came and went upon her pale rose-coloured lips.

Restow was in great form. He toasted Mademoiselle Ursule. He toasted Madame Grandier. He demanded special wines, special dishes. The head waiter himself was called into consultation. If it was Restow's desire to focus public attention upon his party, he achieved it. His orders given, he began to tell tales of vivid adventure, illustrating them with a good deal of expressive gesture.

Mademoiselle Ursule hung modestly upon his words. Madame Grandier ceased her efforts at conversation, and listened spell-bound.

Lindsay constrained himself to look round the big dazzling room in search of Marian Rayne. She would not be there. He told himself that. She certainly would not be there. A girl does not faint at one moment, and the next come in to dinner as if nothing has happened. She certainly would not be there.

And then he saw her. She was with a party of six. There was the stout elderly man, the bun-faced woman, another middle-aged couple, an indeterminate young man—and Marian. They had a table by one of the windows at the end of the room. He saw her profile relieved against the deep bright blue of the curtains. It was as colourless as if she were fainting still. She sat back in her chair with her head high. The young man was talking, but he could not see any movement of Marian's still, pale lips.

Lindsay brought himself back with a jerk. Restow was speaking.

"My good Fothering, if you stare like that, you will be in a duel before I know what is arriving. Ladies do not like being looked at—*hein, Mademoiselle Ursule?*" He repeated his remark in French. "They shrink from the bold admiring eye—is it not so? It is their study to be unobserved, to pass in the crowd, to live in a modest seclusion, in a kind of cloister of all the virtues. *C'est vrai—hein?*"

"Ah, monsieur, I do not know," said Mademoiselle Ursule.

"Like that beautiful lady just coming in, *par exemple.* Would she wish to be looked at, to be noticed, so that everyone might say, 'There is the most beautiful woman in the world?' Never! *Jamais de la vie!* She blushes unseen. And the reason for that is that it is not possible to see a blush when there is no blush to see—no, by Jing!" His voice had dropped; its soft huskiness became almost harsh.

Lindsay looked over his shoulder and saw Madame Gloria Paravicini come slowly up the room. He thought at first that she was alone, but presently discerned behind her a small, fair gentleman with a neat imperial and an air of considerable self-importance. It appeared unlikely that Madame's aim was to avoid attention. She wore a sheathlike garment glittering with emerald and sapphire sequins and billowing out below the knee into a foam of peacock-coloured frills. The frills swept into a train. Her shoulders and arms were magnificently bare. Her two enormous plaits were caught behind her with a jewelled clasp. She frowned upon the crowded room and advanced with a measured, hesitant grace. "Like a cat on a strange roof," was Lindsay's impertinent comment.

Restow leaned sideways in his chair and watched her, his wide mouth smiling, his eyes narrowed. When she was quite near, he sprang up and bowed.

"But what a pleasure!" he said in French.

From his great height he looked down over her shoulder at her escort. What he saw appeared to amuse him. He made the sort of face that he might have made at a Pom or a Pekinese, transferred his attention to Madame Gloria's lowering face, and dropped back into crude English:

"Say, Gloria, couldn't you do better than that?"

The furious blood ran up into her cheeks. For a moment Lindsay thought that she was going to strike him. Then she looked past him at

Mademoiselle Ursule, who was leaning back in her chair in wide-eyed alarm. Gloria Paravicini did not speak. She lifted her eyebrows and passed on. The little man with the imperial followed her. It was obvious that he had understood Restow's remark; he controlled a pale fury. Lindsay rather admired the way he took the encounter. He breathed more freely as the two passed to a distant table.

Restow sat down.

"That is the most beautiful woman in the world," he said complacently.

"And who is she?" asked Madame Grandier.

"She is my wife," said Restow, and threw a magnificent chest.

Chapter Twenty-Four

LINDSAY COULD never have said what opera they heard that night. He sat in a box with Algerius Restow and the Grandiers. Algerius talked the whole way through the opera. It must have been obvious to any onlooker that he was paying his respectful attentions to Mademoiselle Ursule. At intervals Madame Grandier remarked, *"Ah, que c'est beau!"* Whereupon Lindsay said, *"Wee."*

It was a nightmare of an evening. He saw, not the stage or the opera singers, but Marian's profile as he had seen it across the crowded dining-room of the Luxe. He heard, not the prima donna's high C, but the clamour of his questioning thoughts. What was Marian doing in Paris? Who were these people she was with? Was it a coincidence that she should be here, and at the Luxe, just when Restow was here? Why had she fainted?

The answer to this was, unfortunately, easy enough. She had fainted because she recognized him. She had seen Lindsay Trevor, and not Trevor Fothering. She had seen Lindsay Trevor, and Lindsay Trevor was dead. It was bound to be a shock. That's what it was a shock. It didn't mean anything in the way of affection; it was just a shock; because of course she had been thinking of him as dead. He felt sorry that she should have had such a shock as to make her faint.

He went back to that pale profile against the deep blue of the curtain. Its pallor touched some hidden spring of compunction. He had not been able to keep his eyes from it for long. He had looked, and then immediately looked away, not once but many times. And once, looking, he had caught, not her profile, but a fleeting startled glance that showed him how thin she had grown. After that he did not dare to look at her again.

All things come to an end. The ladies were put into a taxi. Restow, in great spirits, insisted on walking back to the Luxe. He narrated apocryphal stories of famous opera singers. Did his dear Fothering know that Maria Celeste sang entirely on winkles and sliced cucumber?

"But I give you my word for it." This with much gesture. "I myself have sliced the cucumber. But you shall not get any wrong ideas into your head about my relations with this lady. They were of an absolutely outstanding propriety—yes, by Jing! I sliced cucumber for her at midnight, and no one can cast an aspersion—for at that time, my Fothering, I was a waiter. I called myself Jules Dubois. Aha! I tell you I saw some life! And in six months I made three hundred pounds in tips. I do not say that every waiter can do this. Every waiter is not an Algerius Restow under a *nom-de-guerre* any more than every woman who opens her mouth and squalls is a Maria Celeste.

"Once—" he grasped Lindsay by the arm, hurrying him along and talking all the while in his soft husky voice—"Once I was at the opera in Majorca...Was it Majorca? I do not know. Yes, I think-but if not, it does not matter. I was selling programmes, and there was a girl singing Marguerite—a pretty girl—fair hair, fine eyes, fine figure—just a little fat for Marguerite, but no matter, she is well enough, and her voice is well enough—plenty of it, and high to lift the roof. And all goes on well enough until she comes to the 'King in Thule', and there she sings just a quarter of a hair's-breadth flat. In Paris in London, no one would take any notice. No, by Jing! in London I have heard the great Antonella sing flat—oh, flat enough to turn the milk sour—from one end of *Bohème* to the other. Aha! Yes! She kissed flat, she coughed flat, she died as flat as a piece of blotting-paper—and I went deaf on both sides with the applause. But in Majorca—no. There one is a purist— one has an ear. If anyone sings flat, they come to bury that person, not to praise him. That girl was very nearly buried. The first flat note she sings, a gentleman in a' box takes out a revolver, and when she does it a second time he fires three shots and she falls to the ground with a bullet in her shoulder. Fortunately, he is too excited to be a good shot. I have heard many singers whom I would gladly send to Majorca. Either you sing in tune there, or you are soon dead."

He stopped suddenly, still holding Lindsay by the arm.

"Aha! I talk—I jest—I laugh! Like Shakespeare says, I jest at a scar, but I have a wound in my heart. No, that is not how it goes, but it does not matter. Courage! Courage! Courage! You do not understand French, but there was a great Frenchman who said, *'de l'audace—de l'audace—et toujour de l'audace!'* Do you know what that means?"

Lindsay had the sensation of being looked through for a moment. Then Restow burst out laughing and began to tell him that Giulio Carozza smoked cigars made out of seaweed.

They reached the hotel with Restow still talking, but arrived at the door of his suite, he fell silent. A sitting-room divided his room from Lindsay's. Restow passed to his own door, opened it, clicked on the bedroom light, crossed the threshold, and shut the door, all without a word.

Lindsay had his hand on his own switch, when the door across the room opened abruptly. He turned, and saw Restow looking round it grinning.

"To-morrow I decline a duel," he said. "Pff!" He blew out his cheeks, grimaced, and vanished, slamming the door.

Lindsay undressed and went to bed, but when an hour had passed he had not slept. He went into the sitting-room for a book, and felt envious of Restow's snores, which were plainly audible. When he had been reading for half an hour he began to drift towards sleep. The print became first very black, and then so hazy—hazy. He realized that he had actually dropped off for a moment, and stretched out his hand to turn the light off. The action woke him, but by degrees the dark began to wash in amongst his thoughts and drown them. He could hear the lapping of the tide—soft on the sand, and hard with a dash of spray against the rock—hard with a grating of stone upon stone—water-rounded pebbles moving one on another—grinding.

He opened his eyes and looked out into the darkness. He was quietly and clearly awake, but the sound that had been in his dream went on. It came from a couple of yards to the left of his head. Someone was knocking at the door. No—knocking was too loud a word; the sound was the softest and most hesitating of sounds.

Lindsay slipped silently out of bed. He wanted badly to know who was tapping at his door at two in the morning. He thought that he would prefer to see without being seen. If he felt his way to the sitting room door and opened it softly, he might with luck manage this. He was very good at moving in the dark. He made no noise and knocked nothing over, and, turning the handle of the sitting-room door, he eased it ajar and looked through the opening.

At the moment that the door opened a sigh struck on his heart and warned him of what he would see. Marian Rayne stood in front of his door in an attitude of the most utter weariness. She wore a black evening wrap over her dinner dress. Her right hand held the jamb; with her left she leaned against the door. Her head rested against the middle panel. It was as if she had been flung there by wind or water, or by some overwhelming impulse, and had caught at the door and so stayed. He was shocked beyond all power of speech. If anyone should come—should see her...

Before his shocked thoughts had ordered themselves, she sighed again heavily, lifted her head, and saw him. The same recognition which he had seen in her eyes just before she fainted came flooding into them now. A half caught glimpse of his face looking at her from a dark room, and she was filled with an utter certainty. The weariness went out of her. The certainty rushed through her like a flood. Before Lindsay could move she was pushing the door, and him with it. And then the door was shut upon them and she was holding him in the dark.

"Lin—Lin—*Lin!*"

He felt her whole body tremble. And what was he to say? It was dark; but, darkness or daylight, there was no hope that Marian could be brought to believe that he was anyone but Lindsay Trevor. He stretched out a hand and put on the light. She had been leaning on him, holding him; but when the light came her hands dropped and she stepped back, leaning against the wall and looking at him with shining eyes. The pale ghost was gone. Before his eyes life and colour bloomed in her lips and cheeks.

"Oh, *Lin!*" she said.

Lindsay reminded himself of many things. He said, in a dead, cold voice,

"You are making a mistake. My name is Trevor Fothering."

And Marian laughed. It was just the faintest ripple of sound, the whisper of a laugh, but her eyes laughed too.

He said, "Lindsay Trevor was my cousin. I know we are alike."

Marian's eyes went on laughing.

She said, "Oh, *Lin!*" And then, with the laughter suddenly gone, "Lin—why? I thought I had driven you—oh, I thought—*Lin!*"

"I'm Trevor Fothering."

Marian threw up her head.

"Very well. Then it doesn't matter if I tell everybody about the likeness. I can tell Mr Drayton, and you won't mind?"

Lindsay would mind very much indeed.

With a quick, darting movement Marian caught him by the arm.

"Oh, Lin—Lin—*Lin*—don't be stupid! Do you suppose you can keep me from knowing you by dyeing your hair? It's *you* I know, not the outside of you. If you dyed yourself pea-green all over, it wouldn't stop me knowing you. And I'm safe—I'm really safe. Lin—can't you trust me?"

Lindsay said what he had no intention of saying.

He said,

"Why did you break off our engagement?"

The glow died.

"I can't tell you."

"I think you'd better tell me."

"No, I can't."

He put a hand on her shoulder and tilted her chin.

"Look at me, Marian!"

She looked at him for a moment. Her eyes were no longer full of joy.

"Why did you come here, Marian?"

"To see you." Her voice broke a little. "I had to see you."

"Why?"

"To be sure."

"To be sure that I wasn't dead?"

He was still holding her. She turned her head aside.

"Yes."

"But you didn't care for me. Why did it matter to you? You told me you didn't care."

She looked up at him with eyes suddenly bright, cheeks suddenly flushed.

"Why did you want to marry me if you thought I was the sort of girl who is ready to marry a man one minute and quite pleased to hear he's been drowned the next?"

"But you weren't ready to marry me, Marian."

"And you thought I'd be pleased, and glad, and happy to think you'd committed suicide because of me! It's the sort of thing that makes one happy—isn't it?" Her cheeks burned, her breath came quickly. I "Is that what you thought?" said Lindsay.

"What else could I think? Everyone—everyone thought so. Why did you do it?"

"I never dreamt—" said Lindsay. "I—Marian, I never meant you to think—I—it was to be an accident."

She went on looking at him for a moment, and then, pulling her wrap round her, turned to the door.

"I must go."

"No—not yet."

She said quietly, "I won't give you away," and put out her hand to the door.

"Marian—what do you know of Drayton?"

She turned the handle, but he put his weight against the door and kept it shut.

"Marian, I know you went to see him. Tell me why."

She shook her head very slightly. She was trembling again.

"Oh, Lin, let me go!"

"Marian—trust me!"

She threw him a curious tremulous glance.

"Don't I trust you?"

And then his nearness—the joy, the utter joy of knowing that he was alive—rushed in on her and carried her away.

"Oh, Lin!" she said, and was in his arms.

At the first touch of her trembling lips Lindsay knew that she loved him. He had no idea why she had broken off their engagement, but he knew now that it was not for want of love. He would not have believed her upon her oath if she had said she did not love him. He held her close and kissed her tears, and felt her strain towards him.

"Marian!" he said. "Why did you do it?" And then, "You love me—you do love me!"

She put up her face and kissed him solemnly and sadly.

"I mustn't—"

"Mustn't love me?"

"No—Lin."

"Why? Is it anything to do with Drayton?"

He felt her shudder.

"Marian—tell me the whole thing. Don't you see that you must tell me?"

She began to draw away from him.

"Perhaps. I don't know. I must think."

Lindsay came back to time and place. She mustn't stay here now; it was too frightfully risky. With his arm still round her, he said,

"No—you mustn't stay. But you'll meet me tomorrow? You will? *Promise!*"

She nodded.

"Honest, Marian? No hanky-panky?"

"No. Where?"

Lindsay stood frowning. Anywhere in the hotel was out of the question. It would have to be Madame Marnier. Not a very nice part of the town, but Marie Marnier was safe. It was half a dozen years since he had seen her, but he wrote to her always for the New Year, and got a few scrawled lines in reply.

He released Marian, went over to the writing-table, and printed the address carefully.

"Will you come to this address to-morrow—no, it's to-day—at—what time could you come? Who are these people you are with?"

"She is a cousin of Aunt Louie's—her name is Merson. She always rests after tea."

He frowned again. He couldn't have Marian coming there alone after dark.

"Could you leave the hotel at five?"

"Yes, I think so."

"All right, that will do. Turn to the left and walk as far as the first corner. I'll be waiting for you there. Now you must go. Wait till I make sure that the coast is clear." Then, with his hand on the door, he turned and flung his other arm about her. "Are you glad I'm not dead?"

When she was gone, he switched the light out and went back to his room in the dark. He had reached his own door before he noticed the silence in the room behind him. Restow was no longer snoring. The room was full of a listening silence.

Chapter Twenty-Five

THERE WAS A certain solemnity about Restow's demeanour next morning. He drank his coffee and broke his rolls with an air. Lindsay was reminded of an actor holding the stage. Presently it would be, "Enter—someone." He awaited this entrance with interest.

Restow finished his coffee, leaned back in his chair, and remarked grandly, "I am a conscientious disbeliever of the duel."

Lindsay hadn't anything to say at all. From his experience of Restow he felt that it was quite unnecessary for him to say anything. Algerius could sustain a monologue as well as any man living.

"I am about to be challenged," said Restow abruptly. "And when I am challenged I shall say, 'No thank you—run away and play.' Yes, by Jing! And that will be very amusing—much more amusing than if I am a laughing-stock in all the papers for shooting pistols in the air with Gloria's little yellow puppy-dog. Bah! The duel! Everyone laughs at it! On the other hand, why should I kill this yellow puppy-dog? He would not be a loss to the world. I might even consider that I was a public benefactor. But on the other hand, if I had wished to become an executioner, I have had my chances—yes, when I had not one single bean to my name and I was offered to be executioner to the republic of Santalena. And I refused. And if I refuse the job when I have no money and I am a young man very hungry and with nothing to give my hunger—if I refuse it then, why should I now take the bread out of the mouth of the no doubt excellent M. de Paris? Can you tell me that?"

As he spoke, there was a knock on the door and there came in two gentlemen very punctiliously dressed; the one small, dark, and youngish; and the other elderly, stout, and with something of the air of a military man.

Restow had risen to receive them. He appeared larger than usual as he returned their formal bows. The elder man introduced himself as M. Denoyer, and his companion as M. Georges Martel. He spoke in French, but Restow's reply was couched in the English of the United States.

"Very pleased to meet you," he said, and beamed upon them.

"Perhaps you can guess our errand," pursued M. Denoyer.

"Any errand that makes me acquainted with you two gentlemen—" said Restow, and bowed again.

"We are here, monsieur, as the friends of M. Charles Arêsne."

Restow smiled affably.

"The yellow puppy-dog," he said in English; and then in French, "But I don't know him—this M. Arêsne."

"Yet you insulted him last night in the restaurant of this hotel."

"Is it possible?"

"We are here to demand an apology or, failing that, to arrange a meeting."

Restow spread out his hands.

"But I have met your friend once, and I assure you that is enough for me. I have not the very slightest desire to meet him again."

Both gentlemen stiffened noticeably.

"But you cannot refuse a challenge!" said M. Denoyer.

"And why not?" said Restow.

The friends of M. Arêsne looked at one another. The younger man burst into speech.

"Then, monsieur, you are a coward!"

Restow shook his head negligently.

"No, it is not that. I do not like your friend, but I do not wish to kill him."

"Or to be killed by him!" said the elder man with a sneer.

Restow smiled.

"I would not mourn if he were dead, but I do not wish to kill him. It would annoy my wife, and besides, if I were to kill every little man who reminds me of a puppy-dog, I should have no time to amuse myself. It is fortunate for M. Arêsne that I am too lazy to enjoy killing people, otherwise there would remain only the arrangements for his funeral."

"I repeat, monsieur, that you are a coward!" said the dark young man with considerable heat.

"You are wrong," said Restow placidly.

He turned to Lindsay.

"My Fothering, these gentlemen are asking me to fight a duel, and as you do not know any French you have not just had your feelings harrowed by hearing them call me a coward. The word is *lache,* so you can look out and be ready to sit up and take notice next time you come across it. And now I'm going to show them what would happen to their friend if I wasn't a very good-tempered man. What sort of nerves have you got this morning—*hein?*"

"The usual sort," said Lindsay gravely.

Restow went back into French.

"Messieurs, I invite you to witness an improvisation after the manner of the celebrated William Tell, deceased. It is, perhaps, a little hackneyed, but the human interest—that is always fresh. You will be on tenterhooks to see whether my esteemed secretary is to lose a finger or two, or whether you are to go back to your M. Charles and tell him what a lucky escape he has had." He darted a quick malicious glance at Lindsay, then clapped his hands and smiled expansively. *"Allons! Allons! Allons!"*

He stepped briskly up to the table and plucked from the dish of fruit which stood there a banana.

"Now, my Fothering!" He handed it with a flourish to Lindsay. "We play William Tell with a difference. Ha! That is Shakespeare! And I have forgotten where it comes. 'Rue with a difference,' isn't it? But this shall be a banana with a difference, and you shall hold it over there against the wall—yes, at arm's length. And if your hand shakes, perhaps you will spoil my aim and get a bullet in your knuckle—*Hein?* Hurry, my Fothering—hurry! These gentlemen are naturally impatient—they are on hot cockles to return to their friend and to assure him of my humanitarian objection to the slaughter of this yellow puppydog."

He turned a little and repeated his remarks in French with an apology.

"My secretary, messieurs, is a barbarian—he speaks only his own British tongue. Come now, my Fothering—we begin!"

Lindsay walked across the room with the banana in his hand. He was wondering what Restow was driving at. He was wondering whether there was going to be an unfortunate accident—perhaps even a fatal accident. He recalled Madame Ferrans' warning. He recalled Froth's motor smash. It was, of course, open to him to refuse to hold up a banana as a target for Restow.

Restow's mocking eyes were daring him as he turned.

"If you are afraid, I will hang my banana from a string," said Restow's mocking tongue. "Aha, my Fothering, you are afraid—nervous? Your feet turn cold? A cold perspiration bespangles your brow, like the tit willow bird out of Gilbert and Sullivan—*nicht?*"

Lindsay was perfectly well aware that, as Froth, he would do better to turn sulky under Restow's chaff and leave him to his trick shooting. What he actually did was to hold out the banana at arm's length and laugh.

M. Arêsne's two friends looked towards him involuntarily. Neither they nor Lindsay saw Restow draw, the movement was so quick. There was a sharp report, and the green tip of the banana vanished.

"One," said Restow pleasantly. He had fired from his hip. He raised his automatic and counted:

"Two."

The second shot pierced a neat hole about half an inch from the stubbed end of the banana.

"Three," said Restow, and drilled another hole, very neatly spaced half an inch nearer to Lindsay's fingers. Four, five, and six followed rapidly.

Restow's hand went back into his pocket again.

"Bravo, my Fothering! After all, your nursing home made a good job. I shall write them a testimonial—'Good nerves for bad ones'!"

Lindsay came back to the table and laid the banana down upon it. Restow had chosen a firm unripe fruit. His first shot had carried away the green tip. The other five accounted for five neat holes at intervals of half an inch.

Restow turned to the sofa, where an open cardboard box displayed a froth of tissue paper. He came back with a couple of sheets in his hand.

"My Fothering, I make bad parcels. Wrap up this little souvenir and give it to these gentlemen. Their M. Alphonse—M. Charles—I have forgotten his name—it is of no consequence—he had better see for himself what kind of an escape he has had." He bowed with much politeness, and continued in French: "Messieurs, I present you the banana and I make you my farewells. My Fothering, these gentlemen tear themselves away. Perhaps you will be so good as to show them out."

M. Martel ground his teeth. He began to speak, and was checked by M. Denoyer, who straightened himself and addressed Restow with dignity and self-control.

"You refuse definitely to meet M. Arêsne?"

"I am a humane person," said Restow.

"Then there is no more to be said." M. Denoyer bowed stiffly and went out.

M. Martel did not bow. He glared at Restow, hesitated on the threshold, shook his fist, and banged the door with violence.

Lindsay came back to find Restow regarding him. He had a moment's uneasiness, but it passed when Restow said,

"I have a letter here from my good Drayton. He is excited because there is a first edition of a very dull book which I hope never to read, and he says it is to come into the market, and if I buy by private treaty first, I will save it from going out of the country. What a curious mind! He thinks of nothing but his books, and not even of what is inside them—which I can understand. Ah! Bah! That bores me! By and by Drayton will turn into one of those long, flat, grey, unpleasant insects which live in the bindings of old books. I have warned him of it. I tell him he becomes rapidly sub-human. Pfst! Enough of Drayton!"

He picked up the banana and tossed it with excellent aim into a waste-paper basket on the other side of the room. He turned back to Lindsay with a grin.

"There are six holes in the wall-paper. You have a very steady hand, my Fothering—almost as steady as mine."

He came quite close, dropped both hands on Lindsay's shoulders, and held him at arm's length. He said nothing. Lindsay said nothing. Restow's brows were drawn together, his eyes half closed. The silence lasted.

Suddenly Restow released him, and as suddenly asked,

"Have you seen Drayton?"

Lindsay was really taken aback. What did this mean? He said, "No."

"You have not?"

"No." He spoke seriously, his eyes on Restow's face.

Restow turned and went out of the room.

Chapter Twenty-Six

At a quarter to five Lindsay walked out of the hotel and, having turned the corner, strolled to the end of the street. From there he proceeded quickly about half a mile, and then made his way back by a series of twists and turns. Arrived at the street down which he had strolled, he resumed that pleasant pace. As he walked, his thoughts returned to the morning. What did Restow mean by asking him if he had seen Drayton? Right on top of telling him he had just heard from Drayton too. He would have given a good deal to know just what was in Restow's mind. Madame Ferrans' words came back: "Take care—he suspects you." What did Restow suspect him of? And hadn't he been the world's worst fool to play up to his absurd William Tell act? He ought to have stopped, funked, played the nerve-shattered invalid—in fact done anything he chose except join in and play up to Restow's gasconade.

He tried to think why he had played up. He had acted on impulse, when quite possibly his life was depending upon his never acting on impulse. And at the back of the impulse he discovered a reluctance to let Restow down. He had been as keen on Restow bringing off his bluff as if his own safety had hung on it. He had been backing Restow. He *liked* Restow. This was an odd point to arrive at. He was frowning over it as he reached the corner again.

He stood for a moment lighting a cigarette. That allowed him to waste several matches and some time. He did not wish to appear to be waiting for anyone. He had just got the cigarette to light, when Marian turned the corner. She wore the fur coat and the little black cap which she had worn when he had come on her in the train after she had broken off their engagement. There was almost as much difference between that pale Marian and this glowing one as between life and death.

She came up to him with a smile in her eyes, and they walked down the street together. When they had turned a second corner, Lindsay hailed a taxi and told the man to drive them to the Arc de Triomphe.

"Why the Arc de Triomphe?" said Marian.

The taxi darted into the traffic.

"I've got to talk to you," said Lindsay—"and I've got to make sure that neither of us has been followed."

She pressed up against him in the dark.

"That sounds—horrid."

"Yes—it might be horrid." He looked back once or twice.

Marian did not speak again. She felt a little chilled. She had thought that he would put his arm round her, and perhaps kiss her. It was the most wonderful thing in the world that he was alive. She couldn't look past that yet.

When the taxi stopped, Lindsay paid the man quickly and walked her away at a brisk pace. Ten minutes later they took another taxi.

"I think that's all right," said Lindsay.

"Where are we going?"

"To see an old friend of mine. I can't risk eavesdroppers. She'll let us talk in her room."

"Who is she?"

Lindsay hesitated.

"She's mixed up with the time I was doing Secret Service work. There's a son—an awful young rip, but they're both under the impression that I saved his life, so I'm *persona grata*." He laughed. "I don't know that I should be with the police if they knew. Gogo's a pretty bad hat, I fancy."

They were set down in a dreary, ill-lighted locality. Another ten minutes' walk brought them to a dark street where tall rickety houses leaned together.

Madame Marnier lived on the top floor of the third house on the left. They mounted a close, slippery stair, and at the top Lindsay knocked and next moment was being kissed on both cheeks by one of the fattest women in Paris.

Madame Marnier was immense. Her still coal-black hair was strained tightly back from a face like a large white cheese, in which two very shrewd dark eyes twinkled. She wore a blue checked apron over her dress. The room behind her had a sloping roof which on one side nearly touched the floor. It was scrupulously clean, but full of an overpowering smell in which garlic and cabbage struggled for the upper hand.

Madame Marnier, having embraced Lindsay, stood back from the door and beckoned them in, talking all the time.

"And you are married? Ah yes, you told me that in your letter. And what a happiness to meet madame your wife! Ah, madame, not till you have a son of your own will you know how I regard this husband of yours. Has he told you? But no—he would always say that it is nothing, and that he has done nothing. But I—I will tell you. Figure to yourself my Gogo, my only son, and the best son in France—"

Lindsay put an arm through hers and marched her over to the other side of the room.

"Now, now, *la mère*—no reminiscences! Amongst other things there's no time for them."

Madame Marnier's hands went up over her head.

"*Mon dieu!* What has arrived to your hair?"

"A little dye," said Lindsay, laughing.

"You're in it again?"

"Up to my neck. And I want the loan of your room for half an hour whilst I talk to mademoiselle."

"What? She's not your wife!"

"Not yet. I'm playing a part, as you guess, and I can't see her safely. It is of the first importance that I should be able to talk to her undisturbed."

"Well, well—who is going to disturb you here?"

"No one, I hope." He put a hand on her shoulder. "It is a very serious affair this time. For one thing, I am dead."

"Aha! You are dead! And then?" Her little eyes twinkled at him.

"Well, if some people were to find out that I was alive, it wouldn't be very long before I was dead enough to stay dead."

Madame Marnier said "Aha!" again and laid her forefinger along her nose.

"I'm putting my life in your hands by coming to you. It's not the first time—is it?"

She spread out her thick work-roughened hands palm upwards.

"It's safe enough," she said; and then, "So you did not come to see *me* at all! But of course not!"

Lindsay laughed again.

"I should have come to see you anyhow. I don't forget my friends."

"And they don't forget you. Gogo is out on a job. If he misses you, he will be ready to throw himself into the Seine."

"Perhaps he won't miss me."

Lindsay came back to where Marian waited in bewilderment. The rapid French was quite beyond her. She saw Madame Marnier shrug her great shoulders and go out through a door on the other side of the room. She saw her shut the door. Marian gave a sigh of relief. Now Lindsay would come.

He came and put his arm round her.

"Now!" he said, and took her to a bench by the attic window. "Now! We haven't got very long, and I want you to tell me everything."

Marian turned her startled eyes on him. She hadn't been thinking of what she was going to say; she had only thought of how lovely it was to be with him again. But now she had to think of what she was going to say.

Lindsay took both her hands in his.

"My dear, this is all so very much more important than you've any idea of."

She did not look at him. She looked down at her hands and said, "Is it?" in rather a shaky voice.

Lindsay watched her colour come and go. His hands closed hard on hers.

"You are going to tell me first why you broke off our engagement. And then you are going to tell me why you came to see Drayton the other night."

He heard her draw in her breath, and felt her hands quiver. And then all at once her resistance was gone. He could feel her reaching out to him, leaning on him, wanting him to help her. She said, almost in a whisper,

"Yes, I'll tell you—I must tell you—I've been so frightened."

"Don't be frightened. Just tell me everything. Begin with why you broke our engagement."

"Lin—it—it nearly killed me."

"Why did you do it?" Then, sharply, "You told me it was because you were in love with someone else."

The grey-green eyes looked up at him. They were full of tears, but under the tears there was a sparkle.

"No, I didn't, Lin! I said it was because I loved—someone. I didn't say—someone else."

"So you broke our engagement because you loved—me?"

She nodded. The brimming tears fell in two bright drops. The sparkle remained.

Lindsay didn't kiss her. He held her hands.

"You'd better tell me all about it."

She tried to draw her hands away, and when he still held them she said, "*Please*, Lin."

He let go then. She turned her head aside and said in a troubled whisper,

"It's not easy. I'll try. You mustn't look at me."

"You'll feel a lot better when you've told me."

Marian looked away across the room. There was a dark stain on the wall there rather like a star. She kept her eyes on the dark stain and spoke with pauses between the sentences as if each was an effort.

"It began that Sunday night. You know. We all said good-night. I went upstairs. I didn't go to bed at once. I was feeling hot. Aunt Louie always has her room so hot. I put out the light and opened the window. I sat there looking out. It wasn't cold a bit. There was a smell of leaves and wood smoke. And the moon made everything look like a dream. I didn't know what sort of a dream it was going to be." Her voice stopped.

Lindsay put an arm about her.

"Nothing to worry about. Just go on, darling."

For a moment she leaned against him. Then she said,

"You mustn't touch me or I shall cry. I'll try and tell you."

He took his arm away again. What could have happened in the few hours of that moonlight night to change their lives? He began to be afraid without quite knowing why.

"I sat there for a long time. You know I can see a bit of the rose-garden from my window. I was thinking I would like to be walking there—with you—"

"Yes?" said Lindsay.

"I'm going on."

She seemed to find it hard to go on. Her hands came together in her lap and gripped one another hard. She began to speak with a rush of fluttering words.

"I saw someone—go down the garden. I thought it was you. I thought we hadn't had any time together. I put on a coat and went down. I thought I could get out of the study window—" She paused. "The study window was open. I thought you had gone out that way. When I had gone half way down the path I nearly went back." Her voice broke piteously. "Oh, Lin, why didn't I go back?"

"Tell me what happened."

"I went on—" She drew a long sighing breath "I went on. When I came to the yew hedge I stopped and listened. I couldn't hear anyone moving. I went through the archway and stood by the big peacock that is cut out of the hedge, and then I could see something move by the pergola. I didn't call you, because I wasn't sure it was you. There was deep shadow by the hedge. I kept in the shadow and went over to the pergola. Just as I got there, I saw two men in a little patch of moonlight. One of them was Uncle Robert. The other—" Her voice shuddered and was still.

Lindsay's sharpest fear left him. He laid his hand over hers.

"You're just frightened," he said. "Go on and tell me what happened. Who was the other man?"

"I didn't know—then. He frightened me. There was something frightening about him—" She was almost inaudible. "So tall—like a shadow all lengthened out. I couldn't see his face."

"Go on, darling."

"I wanted to run away, but I was afraid they'd see me. I stood quite still where it was very dark. They came towards me. I heard Uncle Robert say, 'She thinks she's my brother's daughter.'"

Lindsay's hand closed hard on hers.

"What?" he said.

Marian looked up at him with a funny little twisted smile.

"That's what he said. It's like a tract—isn't it? If I hadn't listened, I shouldn't have heard—things. I should have gone happily to bed and we'd have been married on Saturday." She caught at his hand and held it. "I *did* listen."

"What did you hear?"

"Uncle Robert said—*that*. Then the other man said, 'Why didn't you tell her?' Uncle Robert said, 'Her mother didn't wish it—no, no—of course—I don't mean her mother—my sister-in-law, Mary. Why, Louie and I didn't know until Mary was dying, and she wouldn't have told us then, only she said something when she was out of her head.' Lin—when he said that, I knew they were talking about me, but it didn't seem really to get into my head. It was like something horrid *trying* to get in. I just stood there, and the man who frightened me said, 'What a pleasant surprise for her to meet her father!'"

Lindsay was holding her now, and she leaned against him.

"Uncle Robert said, 'You won't tell her. She's just going to be married.' They began to walk away. *He* said, 'Have I no paternal feelings?' And when he said that everything began to go round. I thought I was going to faint, but I didn't. They walked to the end of the pergola and came back. When they came back he was saying, 'We can get a pull on him through the girl—he's crazy about her.' Uncle Robert said—Lin, you won't hurt Uncle Robert—will you, if I tell you what he said?"

"My dear, I think you must just tell me everything." He felt her tremble.

"He said—Uncle Robert said, 'I suppose you know what you're risking. A man got a life sentence the other day for blackmail.' *He* said, 'I shan't get a life sentence, my good Rayne!' *He*—laughed. He said, 'Trevor might be a useful tool. If not, he could be easily—eliminated.'" She turned with a sob and flung herself against him, burying her face on his shoulder. "Lin—Lin—don't let him! *Lin!*"

She seemed in a paroxysm of terror, and for a time he could only hold her and say all the comforting things he could think of. Presently she drew away.

"I'm sorry—I didn't mean to—I told you you mustn't touch me."

Lindsay had been thinking.

"When he said Trevor, did you think he meant me?"

"Didn't he mean you?"

"I don't think so. He was talking about my cousin Trevor Fothering—the man whose shoes I'm in."

She passed her hand across her eyes.

"I thought he meant you—I thought he was going to do something horrible to you—through me."

"And that was why you broke our engagement?"

She nodded.

"If he didn't mean you, who was the girl?"

"No one you know—someone Trevor was fond of. Trevor was Trevor Fothering. They thought that they could put the screw on him by threatening her."

"You're *sure* he wasn't talking about you?"

"I'm not sure about anything. I don't think he was."

She looked at him in a puzzled, doubting way.

"I don't understand—but I'd better tell you the rest."

"Yes—go on."

"They walked away again. I was at one end of the pergola, and they were walking up and down. When they came back again, they were talking about strikes."

"What were they saying?"

"I couldn't understand it. Why should *he* want there to be a strike in Uncle Robert's works?"

Lindsay imagined that he knew.

"What did Mr Rayne say?"

"He said it was ruinous. And he said, 'It's all very well for you— *you've* made enough on the side to weather it.' They went on a long time. Uncle Robert was angry."

"Did he give in?"

"I think he did. They walked away again. This time they didn't come back. They stood at the far end of the pergola talking. I was afraid to stay any longer. I went back to the house. I didn't go to bed at all. I sat by the window and thought it all out. I didn't see how I could marry you. I wasn't Marian Rayne at all—I didn't know who I was. I was afraid of knowing. If he was—my father—" Her voice faltered away.

"Why didn't you tell me?" said Lindsay.

"I didn't think I could because of Uncle Robert."

"You ought to have told me."

She shook her head.

"I couldn't. I thought he was talking about you and me when he said he could get at Trevor through the girl. I—I can't explain why I was so frightened, but there was something frightening—dangerous…It's no use, I can't explain."

"All right," said Lindsay—"that's why you broke our engagement. Now why did you go and see Drayton?"

He saw her take a pull on herself.

"After I'd seen you in the train I went to the Mersons for a few days. When I came back I told Aunt Louie that someone had told me I wasn't really Uncle Robert's niece. She wanted to know who told me. And then she cried a little and said they hadn't ever meant me to know. And then I got it all out of her. I knew she'd be easier than Uncle Robert. She told me the whole thing."

"Yes?"

"Uncle Robert's brother John went out to Australia with his wife. They had a little girl who was born out there, and when she was about two and a half John Rayne died. I've always thought he was my father, but he wasn't. His wife came home. The little girl died on the voyage. Aunt Louie said they'd never written much. She—my mother—no, she wasn't my mother—I don't know what to call her—Mary Rayne—it sounds so strange—she was nearly off her head. She landed, and went into rooms in London. She didn't write to anyone. She hadn't any relations of her own. The woman where she was lodging was in great trouble—her husband had gone away and left her. She had two children—a little girl of three, and another a year younger. She was trying to make enough to keep them by letting rooms. Mary Rayne took the elder child. She told Aunt Louie the child was the only thing that held her back from going mad. It had the same name as her child. She said the mother was willing for her to take it. She thought the husband was a bad man, and that the woman wanted to get the child away from him."

"You said he had left her."

"She was afraid he would come back. She was dreadfully afraid. Mary Rayne told Aunt Louie she'd never seen anyone so afraid. It made her afraid too. She got my mother—my real mother—to promise she would never tell anyone where the child was. Then she left the rooms, and a week afterwards she went down to stay with Uncle Robert and Aunt Louie, and no one had any idea that the child she brought with her wasn't her own. She died when I was ten, and when she was ill she told Aunt Louie the whole story. She and Uncle Robert hadn't any children.

They took me. It was very kind of them." She fell silent for a minute. Then, "They've been good to me," she said. I "I ought to be fonder of them. I've never—been able to feel—they belong—"

It was difficult to imagine Robert and Louisa Rayne inspiring strong attachment. No—Marian hadn't ever—belonged to them, or they to her. Did she "belong" to Drayton? It was a chilling thought.

"Why did you go to see Drayton?" he said.

"He sent for me. I think Uncle Robert told him I knew. He—sent for me."

"Yes?"

"I can't tell you," she said.

"Oh yes, you can, Marian."

She shook her head.

"My dear," said Lindsay, "this is going to be a very dangerous affair for both of us if you're going to keep me in the dark."

She looked up then, her face colourless, her eyes dark and frightened.

"Dangerous—for you?"

"Undoubtedly."

She put her hand on his. It was very cold, and if it did not tremble, it was because she was holding it steady with a deliberate effort.

"There isn't much—to tell. It's just—I—hated him so—and he is—my father." There was no colour even in her lips. Her eyes were despairingly frightened. "Lin—it's like a—nightmare—only—I don't wake up."

Lindsay put an arm round her and shook her.

"Wake up now! People aren't tied up to one another like that. The prophet Ezekiel has some good stout words to say on the subject of the fathers having eaten sour grapes and the children's teeth being set on edge. The people of his day believed it almost as firmly as some people seem to to-day, and he said it was wicked nonsense—and so it is. You're not any different from what you were before you knew all this. You're Marian—you're not just someone's daughter. Now tell me what happened when you went to see Drayton."

"He said I was his daughter."

"If he said so, it's probably not true."

"He said my mother was American. Her name was Manning. He said he had changed his name for reasons of his own. He said she had died years ago. He said my sister was dead too."

"Well, that's a lie anyhow," said Lindsay, and saw the colour rush into her face.

"Oh—Lin!"

Lindsay laughed. He was tingling with excitement.

"Lin, what do you mean? Isn't she dead?"

He laughed again.

"When I watched you go in at the back door of No 1 Blenheim Square I'd just been having a very interesting talk with your sister Elsie," he said.

Chapter Twenty-Seven

Marian sprang to her feet.

"My sister! Is her name Elsie? How do you *know*? Oh, Lin, tell me quickly!"

"I know by putting two and two together. Perhaps I don't know at all—I just guess."

"Oh, Lin, tell me!"

"She's the girl Trevor Fothering—my cousin Froth—is fond of. I found that out right at the start. Her name is Elsie Manning. Then I met her. Of course she knew at once that I wasn't Froth."

"Are you so awfully alike?"

"Elsie said I was good enough to pass—and as a matter of fact I have passed—or at least I hope so. Well, I don't know what terms Elsie was on with Froth. I don't think there's much on her side, because she seems to have a perfectly good young man called Jimmy Thurloe—a nice lad. I know him a little, and when I walked into him in a fog he recognized me. Elsie seemed so sure she could keep him quiet that I imagine it's a case."

"Lin, you're not telling me why you think she's my sister."

"Well—she's Elsie Manning. She described a man who was either Drayton or Restow. I wasn't sure then, but now I think it was Drayton. She's a very plucky girl, but she fairly stiffened with fright when she talked about him. She told me two very interesting facts about him. He is a blackmailer, and—his name used to be Manning."

"Oh—" said Marian faintly. She dropped back upon the bench beside him.

"So you see I put two and two together. Mrs Rayne told you you had a sister. Drayton corroborates that but says that your sister is dead. Drayton says he is your father. Drayton's name used to be Manning. Elsie's name is Manning. Well, I guess that Drayton wasn't telling the truth when he said your sister was dead. I think that's a pretty safe guess. He wouldn't risk your meeting Elsie. Now go on and tell me what happened when you went to see him."

There was not much more to tell. It was odd how much terror Drayton seemed to produce without anything very much to account for it. Marian, it is true, had gone to him shaken and unnerved from the shock of Lindsay's death; but Elsie had been just as much afraid.

"Did he ask any questions about me?" said Lindsay.

"He asked why I had broken off my engagement."

"What did you say?"

"I wouldn't tell him."

"Did he ask any more?"

"He went on asking. I wouldn't say."

"And then?"

He felt her wince away from the recollection.

"He—I hate it. Must I—Lin?"

"I'm afraid you must. You'll feel better really when you've got it off your chest. What did he say?"

"He said—" Her voice went away to a whisper.

"He said, 'The damfool has just got himself killed, hasn't he?'"

In a flash Lindsay could see Drayton, designedly brutal, thrusting his question at a sore place. Perhaps he wanted to see if the place was really sore.

He put a comforting arm about her and asked,

"What did you do?"

Marian leaned against him, shaking a little.

"Lin, I made a fool of myself."

"What did you do?"

"I fainted."

"You poor child!"

"He made me feel—absolutely defenceless—as if I couldn't do anything—against him. I felt as if he was battering at me. And when he said that—about you—something seemed to give way."

"Poor darling! What happened next?"

"I came round again. It seemed like a long time afterwards. He was looking at me. He said, 'You really fainted. Do you often do that?' I said 'No.' I wasn't so frightened, but I was crying—I couldn't stop myself. He gave me some water to drink and told me to go home." Her voice stopped.

Lindsay held her. He was thinking. He didn't like his thoughts very much.

"My dear," he said, "has it occurred to you that our meeting last night in the lounge strains the laws of probability rather heavily?"

"What do you mean?" Her colour came and went.

"How do you come to be in Paris with the Mersons? How do the Mersons come to be at the Luxe?"

"I don't know. Uncle Robert arranged for me to come with them."

"Exactly—Uncle Robert arranged with them. And I wonder whether Drayton arranged with Uncle Robert."

"But why?"

"I think someone was interested to see what would happen when we met." He wondered whether Restow had been an interested spectator.

"Oh, Lin—and I fainted!"

"You mustn't make a habit of it, darling—it's rather compromising. Now look here—this is what you've got to do. You must have a nice confidential heart-to-heart talk with Mrs Merson. Recur to the faint. Say you're so sorry, but the likeness upset you. Say you've been making inquiries. Better really make some first—never neglect your local colour—and then say you find that there's a Mr Trevor Fothering in the hotel, and that he's a cousin of poor Lindsay's."

"I *wouldn't* say 'poor Lindsay'!"

"Say anything you like, darling. But this is the important part—say you've seen Mr Fothering again and convey to Mrs Merson that the likeness isn't nearly so strong as you thought it was at first—it struck you painfully at first, but when you saw him again it sort of evaporated.

It's a way likenesses have, so you'll be on good firm ground. Do you think you can do that?"

"I'll try."

He kissed her. Then:

"We ought to be going."

He went to the inner door and knocked. Madame Marnier opened it, and as she did so, Lindsay was aware of something—

There was no outward change. She smiled all over her broad face, twinkled at him, and rolled into the room with a genial air of banter.

"Aha! You have amused yourselves? One is only young once!" she said, and twinkled again.

That was on the surface, and on the surface Lindsay gave back her banter with a laugh. But under the surface there was something—a change—a withdrawal a watchfulness. He became aware that she desired them to *go*; and yet her welcome had been perfectly spontaneous. Something had happened whilst she was in the other room. He remembered that it had its own door on to the landing. He wondered if it was Gogo who had happened. He thought so. He sprang his guess at Marie Marnier. "Isn't Gogo going to come out and speak to me?"

The shot hit some mark. The twinkling eyes blinked at the shock of it.

"Gogo?" Shoulders and eyebrows went up together.

Lindsay flung open the door with a laugh and called,

"Gogo, you ruffian, come out and let's have a look at you!"

There was a moment's silence, a moment's tension, perhaps a moment's indecision; and then, with a crowing laugh and a quite amazing swagger, Gogo Marnier stood on the threshold.

Madame Marnier joined in the laughter.

"A good surprise—*hein?* He wouldn't let me tell you. He must have his joke, my little Gogo. Always such a one for a joke, my Gogo."

Lindsay admired her presence of mind, but he didn't believe in Gogo's joke. It suggested to him so many thoughts that he found it impossible to deal with them all. In the foreground was the fact that Madame Marnier had been overjoyed to see him until Gogo turned up, after which she was passionately anxious to see him go. It had been in his mind to fish in the muddy waters of Gogo's experience. Well—he could still do that.

He began to talk of their last meeting, of a foolish comical adventure in which a gendarme, a goat and a too zealous journalist had all played spritely parts. As he talked, he was aware of Gogo relaxing. Lindsay possessed a very useful faculty of being able to talk of one thing whilst thinking of another.

Gogo hadn't changed for the better in the last few years. He looked the gutter rat. He had been rather a good-looking boy of the sharp-featured, dark-eyed type. The sharpness had become accentuated; the black eyes had a restless ferocity; and the effects of army drill had worn off, leaving him a crouched, wizened creature with a swagger that sat ill enough on his almost misshapen figure.

Lindsay went on talking. It had been in his mind when he came here that if Drayton was in touch with the criminal underworld, Gogo might be useful. In that underworld news circulated with astonishing rapidity. A successful coup is commented on and discussed. Star performers have their admirers, their imitators, their jackals, their receivers, and their places of refuge, in more than one great city. They are known by hearsay to almost as large a public as a popular movie star. Gogo might know quite a lot of useful gossip.

From the back of Lindsay's mind emerged his recollections of the Vulture. He had never seen the Vulture. No one had ever seen the Vulture—no one, that is to say, in the Secret Services of the five countries whose concentrated efforts to lay hold of him during and after the war had been frustrated. Perhaps one should not say that no one had seen him. It is believed that Hugo Leroy met him face to face. Hans Gottfried Müller certainly did. It is possible that Hiram J. Lee did so too. But they did not, unfortunately, survive to describe him. A profiteer of the underworld, he sold both sides in the war with impartial cupidity. Garrett had hunted him in vain. Lindsay, Garrett, and Gogo had shared a very dangerous adventure in the course of this hunt. It had been in Lindsay's mind that if the Vulture still lived, it might be expected that he would have a finger in any international movement against law and order.

As he talked, he was aware of a sort of quivering sensitiveness towards the impressions coming to him from Gogo and from Madame

Marnier. His consciousness resembled a photographic plate deliberately exposed. He finished his story, and whilst Madame Marnier still shook with laughter, he said,

"And the Vulture? Going strong?"

He was watching Gogo's eyes as he spoke. Nothing in Gogo's face changed—nothing except the pupils of his eyes. Lindsay saw them wince as if a flash of light had passed before them. It was the slightest, most uncontrollable of movements. If it had been less slight, it would have been less damaging. He might have sworn at the Vulture—his face might have become convulsed with rage or with fear—he might have grimaced a reluctant appreciation—or he might frankly have admired. Instead, that slight uncontrollable wince, where everything else was under rigid control. It told Lindsay more than he had bargained for. The sensitive plate recorded what it told him. It recorded also the sudden nervous movement of Madame Marnier's hand. It hung down upon her blue checked apron. At the Vulture's name it closed upon a fold of the stuff and stayed there, rigid.

Gogo laughed—oh, quite naturally and with not more than a breath of delay.

"That one?" He made an unpleasant sound indicative of contempt. "Pah! He is dead."

"And you take orders from a dead man?"

Gogo's hand flew to his right side and checked there. Lindsay guessed at a knife in his belt. The hand remained clenched above an unseen hilt. It occurred to Lindsay that if he had been anyone else, the blade might have been in his heart.

Marian Rayne had been watching the scene. She had risen. She could not understand a word of what was passing, but she understood Gogo's gesture well enough. A faint scream rose to her lips.

Gogo threw her a glance of mingled ferocity and suspicion. Lindsay's right hand fell on his shoulder. His left was ready for any movement of Gogo's right. His mind dealt with a new and startling thought. How did Gogo happen to make so opportune an entrance? Coincidence? There were too many coincidences in this affair. The thought and the fall of his hand on Gogo's shoulder were simultaneous; and immediately upon thought and movement he laughed.

"*Tiens, mon vieux!* You're a wonder! Nobody else could have done it without my spotting him! A good piece of work!" He clapped the shoulder again.

If it had not come straight on the story that had brought up the old adventurous companionship, if Lindsay's laugh had been less certain, Gogo would have maintained his defence; but the look, the touch, the tale brought back the time when Lindsay had had for him the glamour which the older boy has for the younger—the time when they both served and worshipped Garrett. He was shaken, afraid, unnerved by Lindsay's assumption of knowledge. His hand moved on the hilt of the hidden knife, his eyes wavered before Lindsay's. Then with a jerk of the shoulder he freed himself and stood back a pace.

"What's all this?" he growled.

Lindsay was now sure of what before he had only been guessing at. He was laughing with his eyes as he said,

"Why, you followed us—didn't you?" Gogo went back another pace. The movement had the effect of a recoil.

"Why should I follow you?" he said.

"Because the Vulture told you to," said Lindsay.

Madame Marnier threw up her hands with a sharp exclamation. Gogo did not exclaim. He remained looking at Lindsay with a curious expression in his narrowed eyes. He was plainly startled, plainly afraid, and plainly unable to hide his fear. But over and above all this there was a spark of the old admiration.

Marian looked from him to Lindsay and back again. She was horribly afraid of the knife and of his twitching fingers. If she had not held on to herself with all her might, she would have screamed again.

"Where did you pick us up?" said Lindsay, still laughing. "I really would like to know. Was it at the hotel?"

"*M'sieu! M'sieu!* What are you talking about?" cried Madame Marnier.

"Ask Gogo," said Lindsay. "Come, Gogo, be a sport and tell me how you did it."

Gogo relaxed suddenly.

"Since you know everything, you know how I did it. You say I follow you? Well, well—you know how it is done. And I who say, 'Why should

I follow?' what have I got to answer when you say, 'Tell me how you did it'?"

"Professional secrecy, in fact! All right, I won't ask you to give anything away—we've all got our trade secrets. What's the Vulture like to work for?"

Gogo's hand went to the knife again. His brows drew together with a jerk.

"What are you talking about?"

"The Vulture," said Lindsay with a long, steady look.

Gogo came closer. He came so close that Marian felt the scream rise in her throat. He came closer still.

"Why do you talk about him?" said Gogo, whispering.

Lindsay made a gesture with his hand. He kept his smiling eyes on Gogo's eyes.

"It's dangerous," said Gogo.

"For him?"

"Nothing's dangerous for him—you ought to know that. The other people die—and he lives. The other people are pinched and put in jug— he goes free. He's a bad one to cross—you ought to know that." There was an extraordinary ferocity about the whispered words. "Why are you crossing him?" he said at Lindsay's ear. His hand shook on the knife. "Why are you crossing him?" he said again.

"Am I crossing him?" said Lindsay.

Gogo came out with a violent oath.

"Are you crossing him? You ask me that!"

"Certainly. In what way do I inconvenience Monsieur the Vulture?"

"*M'sieu! M'sieu!*" said Madame Marnier. "Not that name—for the love of Heaven!"

Her enormous face was as white as a milk cheese. She shook. Her fingers plucked at her apron.

"Well?" said Lindsay. "In what way do I inconvenience him?"

"How should I know?" said Gogo.

"You might."

"I know nothing."

"Yet you followed me?"

There was a pause of perhaps five seconds. Then,

"Not you," said Gogo.

Lindsay's pulse gave a jump.

"You were not following me?"

Gogo jerked a shoulder at Marian Rayne.

"Ma'mselle," he said in a sullen voice.

The pulse jumped again.

"You were told to follow ma'mselle and see whether she met me?"

Again the fleeting spark of admiration.

"Eh bien, Gogo? And what will you have to report? Did ma'mselle meet me, or did she—merely do a little shopping?"

There was a pause. This time it was a long one.

Marian had sunk down again on the bench. She leaned forward on one hand watching them. She watched Lin. It was so odd to see him with red hair. She didn't like it. But she loved the little smiling crinkles at the corners of his eyes; he looked as if he was enjoying himself. She wondered if he was—really. She watched Madame Marnier, and could make nothing of her; she wore her fat like a mask. She watched Gogo, and all at once Gogo looked straight at her, a spiteful, savage look that brought the angry blood to her cheeks. Then in a moment the look changed to a grimace. He snapped his fingers almost in Lindsay's face.

"Bah!" he said. "A little shopping! A little this—a little that! And for me"—he made a horribly expressive gesture—" a little throat cutting, and a drop into the Seine on a black night! There are too many people in this. Someone talks—I am dead. *Voila!"*

"Ma'mselle will hold her tongue," said Lindsay. "Your mother hasn't got one, has she?"

Gogo scowled at him.

"And no one followed you, *par exemple*? Do you think I don't know his way? Do you think he hasn't got a check on everyone he uses? If I was following her"—he jerked a sharp elbow in Marian's direction—"then he'd have someone else following you. Isn't that his way?"

"Certainly. But you needn't worry—I shook him."

"You thought you'd shaken me—didn't you?"

"My dear Gogo, I never knew you were there at all," said Lindsay laughing.

"Eh bien?"

"Well, I did know about the other one—and if I know about a man, I can shake him all right. You know that."

Gogo made an impudent grimace.

"So you say!"

Lindsay repeated the words with gravity.

"So I say. And I say also that ma'mselle has been shopping."

Gogo grimaced again.

"Do you take me for a fool?"

"Certainly not. A fool would make his report and say that ma'mselle met m'sieu, who is an old friend—a very old friend and good companion of Gogo Marnier and of the excellent Madame Marnier, *mère*—and after they had met they all went together to M. Gogo's ancestral home, where they had a famous talk about old times. That would make a very interesting report for the Vulture—don't you think so, *mon vieux*?"

Gogo swore.

"It sounds well—doesn't it?" said Lindsay. "You know, Gogo, I shouldn't wonder if the Vulture were to think it sounded a little too much of a good thing. If everything were to come out, he mightn't care very much about your old association with Garrett and myself. I'm afraid you might be rather badly compromised—and he's got rather a short way with people who have compromised themselves—hasn't he?"

Gogo's skin had been slowly turning the colour of cheap tallow. He saw himself pinched between two dangers. If one deceived the Vulture, death was the very least that happened to one. On the other hand, to offer—positively to offer him the proof of one's past association with a notorious member of the British Secret Service...He recoiled in a fervour of self-preservation. The tallow melted in the heat of it. He mopped a streaming brow.

"*M'sieu*—what am I to do?"

This was surrender.

"It's quite simple," said Lindsay. "You followed ma'mselle, and she went shopping. She met no one—she spoke to no one. She returned to the hotel at"—he glanced at his wrist-watch—"half past six, and—she'll have to hurry to do it! Marian!" He called to her. "We've got to hurry."

His hand fell on Gogo's shoulder.

"Well, *mon vieux,* you understand. It may upset my plans a bit if the Vulture recognizes me, but as far as you are concerned, my dear Gogo, it's just sudden death—that is unless he has contracted softening of the conscience lately."

He embraced Madame Marnier, clapped Gogo on the back with a "Be wise, my child," and ran Marian out of the room and down the stairs.

Chapter Twenty-Eight

"WHAT WAS IT all about?" said Marian ten minutes later.

Lindsay had hurried her round corners and along dark streets, finally hailing a taxi.

He put his arm round her.

"I'd like you to get out of Paris."

"Why, Lin?"

"It's too dangerous."

"For you?"

"For both of us. You were followed when you came to meet me."

"Oh—I didn't see anyone."

"One doesn't see Gogo. He'd follow a needle through a bundle of hay and the hay would never know he was there. We mustn't meet again, I'm afraid."

"Oh, Lin—mustn't we?"

She clung to him, and they kissed. After a moment he took his arm away and straightened himself.

"As soon as I get through with this job we'll be married. Meanwhile I think you'd better droop and be depressed. Write and tell the Raynes you're homesick, but don't overdo it. The safest thing is for them to think you're just bored and moping."

"What a horrid word! It sounds like a hen."

"You're thinking of 'moulting'."

"It's all the same thing."

"Darling, be serious. I've got to go. The next traffic block we get into I shall slip out. I've told him to drive you to Amedee's. Dash in and collect some parcels—anything. You mustn't be more than ten minutes. You're supposed to have been shopping, and you'd better have something to show for it. When you've done, take a taxi to the Luxe."

He had the door open as he finished speaking. His left hand reached back and closed hard on hers. Then he was gone.

Marian shut her lids on two burning tears.

Lindsay slipped through the traffic and made his way to the Rue Jean Jacques, where he called for letters, which were not addressed to Trevor Fothering. The first letter contained some very interesting information. Under a heading, 'The Vulture,' Lindsay read:

"Nothing had been heard of this man for some years. His last coup was the Jarnac affair in '22. Was believed to be dead until very recently, when the arrest of Ferdinand Schreck in Vienna on a charge of heroin smuggling resulted in the reintroduction of his name. Schreck resisted arrest was severely injured, and in the prison infirmary became delirious and talked repeatedly about 'the Vulture.' On his return to consciousness he was confronted with the notes which had been taken of his ravings. He at first denied any knowledge but later admitted that 'the Vulture' was alive, and that he had been acting under his orders. He stated further that half the proceeds of his smuggling went to him—he made use of the expression 'He wrings us all dry.' Pressed further he denied knowledge of 'the Vulture's' identity. He sent the money in notes addressed *poste restante,* using a different name and sending to a different place each time. He was notified of name and place by the receipt of a sheet of paper with the words printed on it in block capitals. One of these sheets was found when he was arrested. It bore the words, *'Achtung'*; and below, plainly printed, 'Johann Gessner, *poste restante, Salzburg.'* Inquiries at Salzburg showed that the packet containing the notes had not been claimed. Pressed on the subject of how he received his instructions, Schreck became excited and declared that all the hard work and initiative were his; 'the Vulture' merely raked in the money. Interrogated as to why he paid this levy, he refused to answer. He was remanded for a week whilst inquiries were made. When he was being brought from the prison at the end of this time, he was shot dead by an unknown person who escaped in the crowd. 'The Vulture' having operated in most European countries before 1922, the Vienna police informed us in detail and requested us to follow up any indications on this side."

Lindsay read all this through a second time. Then he struck a match and burnt the sheets.

He opened the second letter. It contained an answer to his request for particulars of Drayton's antecedents. He read it with a puzzled frown:

> "Edward John Drayton. Born 1870. Third son of the Reverend John Drayton, Vicar of Vincton Parva, Glos. Educated at Burgate Grammar School. Scholarship at Caius College, Cambridge. Honours—history, literature. Became assistant librarian at the Carrington Foundation library, 1893; in 1906 became librarian. In 1910 offered appointment of librarian to Mr Henry Lewindorf of 400 Park Lane. On Mr Lewindorf's death in 1922 passed in the same capacity to the service of Algerius Restow."

A blameless chronicle—"beautifully regular, icily dull," as Algerius might have put it. Lindsay twisted his lip over it in an odd smile. At what period in this beautifully regular life did the third son of the Reverend John Drayton of Vincton Parva adopt blackmail as a recreation?

He walked back to the hotel thinking deeply. It seemed to him, quite plainly and soberly, that his life was in the Marniers' hands. To the Marniers he was Lindsay Trevor. What was he to the Vulture? Lindsay Trevor, or Trevor Fothering? An adversary, or a tool? If he was Trevor Fothering, what coincidence had sent Marian Rayne to Paris, to come face to face with him in the lounge at the Luxe, and why had Gogo orders to shadow her and to see whether she met Trevor Fothering? On the other hand, if it was known that he was Lindsay Trevor, why hadn't he already met the fate of his predecessor and of Ferdinand Schreck?

Restow—

Was Restow the Vulture?

His mind dealt with the possibility in detail. His instinct rejected it.

He returned to Vincton Parva and Burgate Grammar School. Was the Vulture by any chance a product of these blameless surroundings? He went over the dates in his mind. Assistant librarian in '93—librarian to Henry Lewindorf 1910—passed into Restow's service in 1922.

1922—

The Vulture disappeared in 1922.

Lindsay stopped a hundred yards short of the hotel and put a match to the record of Drayton's blameless past.

Chapter Twenty-Nine

GLORIA PARAVICINI stood in the middle of her apartment and contemplated the square wooden box which a waiter had just set down upon the table.

"Open it!" she said.

"Madame desires that I should open it?"

Madame Gloria presented him with a dazzling smile which displayed her wonderful teeth in all their strength and even whiteness.

"Step to it!" she said, and waved her hand very much as she was wont to wave it before the eyes of a refractory tiger.

"But it requires tools, madame."

Gloria clapped her hands. They made a sound just like the crack of a whip.

"Rosalie!" she called. "Rosa!" Then as the bedroom door began to open, "Bring a chisel—a hammer—a penknife—a pair of scissors—a nail file—or any old thing that'll open a packing case!"

A stolid, grey-haired maid appeared at the half open door, looked without emotion at the box, and presently appeared with one of those large clasp knives whose handles conceal an astonishing variety of implements. She handed it to the waiter, and the waiter addressed himself to the box.

It was not a very terrible proposition. Four light strips of wood crossed one another in such a manner as to form a skeleton crate. On these being removed, the box was seen to possess a simple fastening consisting of an iron staple and hook. It also had a number of small holes drilled in the lid.

"It's a snake!" said Madame Paravicini in a tone full of enthusiasm.

The waiter, who had only recently been transferred from the London branch, dropped the knife upon his foot and leapt back acrobatically. Rosalie remained unmoved.

Madame Paravicini, who was dressed for dinner in an exotic mediæval robe of ruby velvet and cloth of gold, with a gilded net across the back of her head and strings of rubies wound into her plaits, picked up the box, exclaimed at its weight, held it fondly to her bosom, and reiterated,

"It's a snake! Someone has sent me a snake!"

The waiter reached the door, bounded through it backwards, and was about to shut it, when he saw Madame Paravicini replace the box upon the table and raise the lid. He remained, his hand upon the door, at gaze. The box apparently contained a quantity of coarse greenish-white flannel. And then, just as he had allowed himself to become conscious of relief, there shot up out of the flannel a yard or two of snake topped by a flat seeking head. He shut the door so vigorously that the act remained on his professional conscience as a bang.

But Madame Paravicini did not even hear it.

"My! Isn't he cute?" she said. "Rosa—isn't he just a real honey boy? Say—do you think Algy sent him to me? Because if I thought that, after the way he behaved last night, I'd come pretty near sending him back again."

"Perhaps it wasn't him," said Rosa. "Perhaps it was the other one."

"Charles?" said Madame Paravicini. She took the snake behind the head with a firm grip and drew it out of the box. It was about five feet long and beautifully marked. She began to talk to it in a low voice, and presently had it coiling about her arm, darting its head this way and that at her golden net and the jewels in her hair.

"It might be Algy," she said.

"Well, it might—but I should say he was mad with you, and if he was mad with you, why should he be sending you a snake?"

Gloria Paravicini flung across to the telephone and demanded Restow's number. The snake, passing behind the plaits of her hair, looked down beside her cheek and watched the mouthpiece as she spoke into it.

"That Algy?"

"It's Trevor Fothering," said Lindsay at the other end—"Mr Restow's secretary."

"I don't want any secretaries—I want Algy, and I want him right away."

Lindsay retired. He had no need to ask who was speaking.

"It's Madame Paravicini," he said, and saw Restow get up smiling from a chair beside the stove.

He took the telephone, winked solemnly at Lindsay, and spoke into it.

"That you, Gloria?...What's that?...You speak too close to the telephone—I have told you a hundred times! 'Bzz—bzz—bzz'—that is all that comes through, instead of your beautiful voice...Oh, go on speaking! I love to hear your voice, as the song says—but how can I hear it when nothing but a 'Bzz' comes through? If you say 'Adored one' to me, my heart cannot beat with rapture when I hear only 'Bzz.' It is those fine mezzo notes of yours—there is no room for them inside one poor little wire—they fight with one another and are strangled... What do you say?" He paused, and for a moment the mezzo alluded to could be heard doing its best. Restow showed all his teeth in a grin. "Six inches farther away, and you will roar as gently as a sucking-pig— as Shakespeare says in his *Midsummer Night's Dream*. Say Gloria, it isn't often I know where they come from and when I do, I find I'm looking round for a bouquet...All right, all right—you shall speak. I am listening—I am all attention."

Lindsay, bidden by a gesture to remain, now caught the ghost of Madame Paravicini's voice. It appeared to be a very angry ghost.

"Algy Restow—will you quit fooling and tell me whether you've just sent me a snake!"

"What would I do that for?" said Restow after a brief stupefied pause. Then, recovering himself, "By Jing! A snake! Someone has sent you a snake? That would not be sweets to the sweet—would it? No, by Jing!

"Again that ghost of a full, angry voice:

"Did you send it—or didn't you?"

"Does one send snakes to the woman one is in love with? A bouquet of cobras—a shower of vipers—a python—for a *gage d'amour?* And scorpions for *billets doux?*"

"Cut all that out! Did you send it?"

"I would rather die!"

A determined click announced the close of the interview.

Restow struck himself on the side of the head, swore volubly in Turkish, and demanded to be reconnected with Madame Paravicini's suite.

It was not Madame Paravicini but Rosalie who answered him.

"Is that you, Mr Restow?...Yes, it's Rosa speaking...No, she won't come, Mr Restow. She says you've been insulting her. She says if you want to insult someone, it's just got to be someone else...No, it's no use my telling her that, Mr Restow. She won't come—she's real mad...Yes, someone did send her a snake...Oh yes, she'd have been real pleased if you had sent it...Oh yes, Mr Restow, she's real mad with you now."

Restow, who had been making a series of horrible faces at the telephone, here brought down his fist upon the table with a resounding bang.

"And why haven't I murdered that woman when I have had the chance?" he declaimed rhetorically. Then, in a slow, malignant voice, "Woman—be silent! You have a tongue like a Persian wheel! Are you there? Are you silent? Are you listening? Here is a message for my wife. I have been challenged to a duel by that precious M. Arêsne of hers, and if to-morrow she has no husband and no little yellow puppy-dog, it is not I who am going to be sorry for her—no, by Jing!"

He flung the receiver back upon the hook and came striding across the room laughing, with his head back and his long teeth showing.

"And now we dine! Mademoiselle Ursule honours us. Is she not the perfect type that I described to you? Is it possible to be more blonde, more *fade*, more amiable—more damnably amiable? Aha! We shall see! *Qui vivra verra!* We will wait upon the hind leg of opportunity. Perhaps it will kick us—perhaps not. Also I present Mademoiselle Ursule with an offering of flowers. Now I give you three guesses what they are, these flowers that I present to this blonde young girl!" He waved a hand towards a florist's carton which reposed on the sofa. The half open lid showed nothing but a crinkle of tissue-paper.

"Forget-me-nots," suggested Lindsay.

Restow made an indescribable grimace.

"*Jamais de la vie!* To live in hearts we leave behind is not to die—*hein?* What a fate! What an immortality! The pale, cold, insipid thoughts of an Ursule Grandier for all eternity—*Dieu!*" He blew out his lips on the word and let it go with a loud plop.

"Lilies," said Lindsay with a spice of malice.

Restow shook his head vigorously.

"My good Fothering—" he began, and then stopped short with his head cocked on one side listening.

Lindsay listened too.

There was undoubtedly a row going on in the corridor. Somebody banged against the wall. There was a reverberation of voices, a scuffling of feet. Somebody banged hard against the door. The door burst open. Gloria Paravicini appeared upon the threshold. She looked extremely handsome and she was in a towering passion. She held M. Charles Arêsne by the shoulders, and she had opened the door by the simple process of banging him violently against it. His collar had burst from its stud, his hair fell dishevelled over one eye, and a long scratch which ran down his nose and cheek testified to the well-known cutting powers of a diamond ring.

"My angel!" said Restow.

Madame Gloria propelled her puppy-dog into the room, banged the door behind her, and turned a furiously commanding gaze upon Lindsay.

"Send for the police!" she said in a deep booming voice.

"What has it done?" said Restow.

"But I have done nothing!" said the unfortunate Charles. "Messieurs—I call you to witness—she has attacked me—she has torn my collar—she has scratched my face—she has lacerated my nerves— she has outraged my feelings!"

As he spoke, he placed Restow between himself and the indignant lady.

Madame Paravicini put her back against the door and glared at him.

"You little murderous thug!" she said. Then, with a sudden change to unbelievably bad French, "Will you deny that you had the atrocious intention of assassinating my husband? Will you deny that? Will you say that you didn't challenge him to a duel? Little apache! Do you think that you will be safe from the vengeance of Gloria Paravicini? Do you imagine that my Algerius has no one to protect him? Do you think that you can murder him with impunity?" She dropped back into American. "If that's what you think, you gotter think on the other side of your head!"

"*Gloria*—" said the unhappy Charles.

"Don't you call me Gloria! I'm Madame Paravicini to murderers, and don't you forget it! Algy Restow, do you call yourself a man—standing there and letting me be insulted by an assassinating apache?"

Restow made her a deep bow and stepped aside.

"It's seconds out of the ring, I guess."

The wretched Charles exhibited a good deal of terror.

"Madame, I do not insult Monsieur Restow. I wish to leave this apartment."

Gloria Paravicini stamped her foot.

"If Algy was a man, he'd beat you!" she said in a voice choked with fury. She whirled round upon Restow. "Do you know who sent me that snake? Well then, it was *him!*" She pointed at the uncomfortable Charles. "And didn't you say yourself that a man that sent snakes to a woman would be all out to insult her? And what are you going to do about it? That's what I want to know."

Charles Arêsne burst into a propitiatory stammer.

"But—you say you like a snake—you adore a snake—you are lonely without your snakes—you weep for them. I wish to please you—I buy a fine, large, expensive snake—I send him to you. *Gloria!*"

"Algy Restow," said Madame Paravicini in a voice like the lower notes of an angry harmonium, "are you going to stand there and let another man make love to me under your very eyes?"

Restow produced a bland smile.

"And why not—if it amuses you?" he said.

Madame Gloria sprang away from the door, wrenching it open as she did so. She banged it back against the wall with all her might, and the next instant she had taken the unfortunate Charles by the shoulders and hurled him into the corridor.

"Git!" she said succinctly.

Charles now asked nothing better of fate. His goddess was no longer a woman, she was a cataclysm of nature. He would as soon have aspired to a volcano in eruption.

She slammed the door upon him and stood panting before Restow.

"Are you going to fight him?" she said.

"No," said Restow.

"And why not? Don't you want to kill him?"

Restow threw back his head and laughed.

"He made love to me!"

Restow shrugged his shoulders.

"He kissed me!" cried Gloria. Her bosom heaved tumultuously.

"What has it to do with me?"

She said "Oh!" her voice all fallen away to a whisper. Her whole big magnificence winced.

Lindsay saw Restow's large hairy hand clench upon itself so hard that the knuckles went white. He spoke, however, with an effect of pleasant ease,

"By Jing!" he said. "He has a curious idea in presents, that puppy-dog of yours! Now, for me, when I wish to offer my respectful homage to a lady, I do not send her reptiles—*pfui!*—no! I offer—yes, by Jing, I offer her the flowers of love."

He turned magnificently to the florist's box, ripped off the lid, and plunging into the silver paper, drew out a long sheaf of velvety crimson roses. The scent came out into the room and filled it.

"That is better, is it not?" said Restow.

Madame Gloria looked at the roses, then she looked at Restow. Then she said, "For me, Algy?"

Restow smiled diabolically. He held the roses up and rolled his little eyes at them.

"By Jing—no!" he said. "They are for a very beautiful young girl who dines with me. You have seen her—*hein?* Is she not blonde? Is she not beautiful? Is she not a rose? Oh, no, no, no—a rosebud—she is too young to be a rose. And youth's the sort of stuff that don't endure, as Shakespeare says—*hein*, Madame Paravicini?"

She threw back her head and laughed quite softly.

"Skim milk!" she said. "If you think you're going to get me all worked up over skim milk, you'd better think again."

She looked at him, the amazingly long dark lashes just veiling the amazingly large dark eyes.

"Algy, I guess those roses are for me."

Restow brought his nose to them and sniffed.

"They smell good—*nicht?* You would like to dine with me and wear my roses, which suit your dress *à merveille*—and go to the Folies Bergères and have a good time—*hein?*"

"I guess I would, Algy."

He sniffed the roses again. His face took on a malicious grin.

"Then what a pity I should have a previous engagement! *Schmerzliches Zeug—hein?*"

Lindsay began to feel very much *de trop*. On the other hand, something violent seemed due to occur at any moment. Due? It was overdue. And as the thought went through his mind, Gloria Paravicini snatched at the roses.

Restow sprang back, but not in time. Her hand grasped at the stems—grasped and slipped. Restow wrenched free, and Madame Gloria with a piercing scream collapsed upon the floor, wringing a wounded hand. The rose had had its thorn, and the thorn had ripped a long scratch across the lady's wrist and palm. Large drops of blood welled up upon it, the very colour of the roses. Gloria Paravicini gazed at them in horror. Then she began to cry exactly as if she were five years old. She screwed up her eyes, contorted her face, and sobbed passionately, while a really remarkable flow of tears poured down her cheeks.

In a moment Restow had cast the roses upon the carpet and was on his knees beside her.

"My angel! My little one! My Gloria! *Herzens-allerliebste!* I love but thee! *Querida! Carissima!*"

"You love that whey-faced doll!" sobbed Madame Gloria.

Restow, with his arms round her, struggled for prudence, but as the weeping lady's head declined upon his shirt-front and a large white arm encircled his neck, he abandoned the contest.

Lindsay slipped out of the room. He closed the door upon a love duet in half a dozen languages.

Chapter Thirty

As LINDSAY undressed that night, he considered that he had earned his salary. He had dined alone with Madame Grandier and Mademoiselle Ursule, conversing with them carefully in a style modelled upon the simplest French exercises. When you know a language perfectly it is not at all easy to talk it as if you do not know it at all.

Madame Grandier, who in ordinary circumstances possessed an unfailing flow of conversation, was disappointed at Restow's absence and devoted herself sulkily to her dinner.

If Mademoiselle Ursule was disappointed, she dissembled very well. She toyed prettily with the prettier courses and cast glances of an almost aggressive modesty at Restow's deputy. Her foot touched Lindsay's foot beneath the table. Her hand lingered against his—purely by accident. She succeeded, in fact in putting him very much on his guard. Altogether an arduous evening.

He put out the light and lay watching the darkness until the oblong of the open window snowed against the black outer wall. A dark night, a cold night—cold without frost, and dark without rain. He lay on his back, his hands clasped behind his head, divesting his thoughts of all the speculations and theories of the day. He made it a rule to put such things away and plunge into sleep with a consciousness ready for new impressions. He let go of Restow, of Gloria Paravicini, of Madame Grandier, and Mademoiselle Ursule. He let go of Marie Marnier and Gogo, of the Vulture, and of Drayton. He would not let go of Marian, but only of his anxieties for her. Marian might come with him into the even fields of sleep. He began to, drift towards them pleasantly.

The window hung like a picture on the black wall—a secret picture hung with veil upon veil of dusk. Then the first veil rose, and he saw— He could never remember what he saw, because all at once he was vividly awake. Something had waked him. He had not the slightest idea what the something was. He had not been here. He had taken the first step over the borderland of sleep, and something had put out a touch and brought him back. He frowned intently in the dark. That was it—a touch. Something had touched him. Something had moved.

He stiffened, every muscle rigid; not with the fixed rigidity of fear, but with the strung rigidity that waits for action. He waited. There was nothing. A most interminable minute passed.

He had begun very slightly to relax, when something moved under his hand, under his head. His head rested upon his hands, and his hands upon the pillow. Under the pillow something moved like a muscle moving under the skin.

Lindsay shot out of bed. There was apparently no interval between that sensation of movement and his finding himself barefooted on the floor feeling for the switch of the electric light. The light in the ceiling came on. Lindsay, a yard away from the bed, stared at the rumpled pillow and the hastily cast off bedclothes. He saw a pillow-case, white sheets, the corner of a blanket bound with blue. There was nothing else.

And then, with the faintest rippling motion, the broad hem-stitched edge of the pillow-case lifted and something thin and dark showed like the loop of a leather lead—one of those round leads which old ladies attach by one end to a wrist and by the other to some plump, surfeited lap-dog. This lead moved along the edge of the pillow-case, and all at once it had a little flat head which came darting out and hung in the air, questing, on the self-same spot where Lindsay's head had been not half a minute before.

By the time he had snatched up a stick, the creature had left the shelter of the pillow. It was a small, active snake of a dull brownish colour. Lindsay broke its back with one blow and finished it with a couple more. Then he picked up the pillow gingerly. There appeared to be no more snakes.

He sat down on the stiff hotel chair and contemplated the corpse. He thought it was a *Krait*. He had seen *Kraits* in the reptile house of the Zoo. He recalled that they had a fancy for getting into houses and that the majority of deaths from snake-bite in India were laid to their account. If this had happened in India, it would be so easy. But *Kraits* don't wander about Paris looking for an hotel under whose hospitable pillows they may find shelter.

His thoughts slid to Gloria Paravicini. Someone had sent her a snake. There had been a snake under his pillow. But Gloria Paravicini's snake was certainly not a *Krait*. He did not see Charles Arêsne selecting that little mud-coloured death as a *gage d'amour*. Gloria had displayed the creature after dinner, detaining him from his duties as escort to Madame Grandier and Mademoiselle Ursule. Her snake was a large, handsome, and perfectly harmless rock snake. Now that M. Arêsne had been demolished, she was taking a good deal of pride in his gift. She wished to display both her snake and her husband. Lindsay had been put to it to get away.

What was the connection between Gloria Paravicini's rock snake and the dead *Krait*?

Lindsay considered. As a coincidence, he simply wasn't having any; another coincidence was more than he could induce his mind to receive. He was of the opinion that he had to thank the Vulture for a very characteristic attention. The Vulture? Drayton? Someone had put the *Krait* under his pillow. This someone had known of M. Arêsne's offering of a rock snake to Gloria Paravicini. Lindsay felt sure that he had known. He had known, and he had at once acted upon his knowledge. One snake was to explain the other. Charles Arêsne had probably procured his rock snake from some regular dealer. If the *Krait* came to light, it would be said that it had got into the same box by accident and, escaping, had made its way along the corridor to Lindsay's room. Lindsay would be found dead. The *Krait* might never be found at all; and if it were found, a regrettable accident would have occurred and the dealer would be blamed. It was a diabolically clever plan. Of course Charles Arêsne might be in it. Madame herself might be in it for the matter of that—or Restow.

Lindsay left that point. Someone had attempted his life—probably Drayton, either personally or through an agent. The question was—why? Was it simply because Trevor Fothering had outlived his usefulness and, as an ex-tool, had become a potential danger? Or had he played his part with less skill than he had thought, and was it Lindsay Trevor who was to be eliminated—finally this time? He found himself quite unable to say.

The point that now arose was—what was he going to do about it? What, in a word, would Trevor Fothering do if he found a snake under his pillow? Lindsay rather thought Froth would gibber. He recalled a cryptic word of Drayton's and wondered whether Froth's nerves had given under some such pressure as this.

He felt distinct disinclination to gibber. After some thought it seemed to him that there was a perfectly good alternative. He picked up the *Krait* on the end of the stick with which he had killed it, and tossed it as far as he could out into the middle of the road. A little traffic, and there would not be much left of the corpse. Even if it were noticed, there would be no harm done. Drayton, if it was Drayton, or the Vulture, if it was the Vulture, would not be sure of what had happened. The snake might have wriggled out of the bed, fallen down the lift shaft—been killed accidentally in a dozen ways. No one could possibly know that Lindsay had killed it.

He pulled the bed to pieces, shook each piece of bedding carefully before he put it back, and finally fell asleep and dreamed that he was catching snakes with a butterfly net in a trench which he was defending single-handed. If he could catch all the snakes, he would have won the battle; but Marian kept calling him to come and buy her an engagement ring, and that took his attention off the snakes. He wanted her to take a net and help him, but she wouldn't. And then all at once Garrett put a hand on his shoulder and said, "He's done it again!"

It was at this point that the man who was listening at the door crept noiselessly away.

Chapter Thirty-One

Next morning Restow swept his entire party back to London. He burst into Lindsay's bedroom at six in the morning like a jovial whirlwind.

"We pack—we depart! Life is not made for sorrow, my Fothering. Pack clouds away and welcome day, and all the rest of it. We go back to London just as quick as it can be done in a train and a boat. I would like to fly. What is the good of living in the twentieth century if one does not make use of its beneficent inventions? But Gloria will not fly. She will face a hundred wild beasts, she will handle a serpent that turns me as cold as pickled pork, but she will not set her foot in an aeroplane."

"Madame goes with us?" said Lindsay.

"By Jing, yes! We are reconciled. We are two hearts that beat as one. But whilst we are in France I do not know where we are. In America we are divorced. In England we are married. In France—I do not know. I prefer to go to England where I can say,' My wife—the most beautiful woman in the world is my wife.' *Ach! Yes!* Also there shall be no more of this damfool nonsense of an exhibition with untamed tigers. I will not have it—my foot is down—I keep it there. And I take Gloria to London and let myself be sued for breach of contract—if that is the law—I do not know. In one hour we start—I—you—Gloria—that wooden Rosa whom I detest—and the new reptile whom Gloria has named Fidelio. If you will lose it in the Customs, you shall have my blessing. It is a pity we do not fly. I would like to drop, this moment, plop upon the doorstep of my house. By Jing, yes—the whole lot of us!" He clapped Lindsay on the shoulder. "I have a strong wish—oh, the very strongest wish to know whether my good Drayton is at home."

The hand that had clapped his shoulder rested there. Lindsay wasn't quite sure whether he had jumped or not at Drayton's name. It had taken him so completely by surprise.

"Don't you expect him to be there?" he said.

Restow stepped back from him, laughing.

"Oh yes, he will be there—he will be there. He is not like Gloria—he has a high esteem for inventions. Yes, by Jing he has—my Drayton! He will be there. And he will have been busy whilst we are away—he will not have gone to sleep. I think he will have bought that first edition he wrote to me about. I think he will be able to show me how busy he has been whilst we are idle in Paris. I think he is always busy, that good Drayton of mine—*hein,* Fothering?"

At Dover Madame Gloria required refreshment. She would not take the boat train. She did not care whether there was another train or not. She did not care whether she ever reached London. She hated, loathed and detested England, a country that was only to be reached by tossing on the sea or endangering one's life in an aeroplane. She couldn't imagine why she hadn't stayed in America. She seemed to think that it was Restow's fault, and *anyhow* she required food—an omelette, a beefsteak, a *pêche* Melba, and several cups of black coffee.

Lindsay wandered away. He found a public call office and ultimately achieved the person he wanted. He gave, not his name, but a code number:

"I have just crossed...Yes, back in town tonight...Yes, I had the letters. Look here, will you try and get hold of someone who knew Drayton between 1910 and 1922—that is, whilst he was with Lewindorf? Beat up Lewindorf's butler or someone like that. I want the closest description you can get—a photograph if it's possible. Height is very important. I do not believe that my man was born at Vincton Parva, Glos...Have you got that?...All right. Then I want to know anything that is to be known about a man called Manning. I think he probably disappeared as Manning in 1922...No, I'm sorry—that's the best I can do. Then will you get hold of a young fellow called Jimmy Thurloe?

He's a junior reporter on the *Daily Round*. I want to get a message to him...Thanks. Will you tell him I must see Miss Manning? I'll try and come to the same place as before between nine and ten. Will he let her know? It's too dangerous for me to try to communicate with her direct. Oh, by the way, he knows who I am, so you needn't beat about the bush. He recognized me. I think he's quite safe. Tell him it's very important that I should see Miss Manning. He can be there if he likes...Yes. Oh yes, if you think so...All right I'll come on then...Yes, one must take some risks...Yes, that's all for the moment."

An hour later Madame Gloria was ready to proceed upon her journey.

Restow was right—Drayton had been busy during their absence. He had not bought the first edition, but everything was in train for Restow to buy it.

Restow temporized, chaffed Drayton affably, congratulated himself on having so zealous a librarian, and was dragged away by Madame Gloria to assist at a joyous reunion with her python, Typhoon, the cobras, Romeo and Juliet, and her other adored snakes. Lindsay discovered that they lived in a superheated snakehouse on the far side of the swimming-bath under the charge of an Egyptian youth called Ibrahim.

There had, fortunately, been no casualties. Typhoon was comatose after a heavy meal, his great head laid flat upon his massive coils, his eyes dead and lustreless; but Romeo and Juliet rose swaying at Gloria's call.

"I suppose their fangs have been removed?" said Lindsay as she opened the glass front of the cage and picked up first one and then the other, stroking them and talking to them in a deep crooning voice.

Restow shook his head.

"She says she is immune. I used to have my feet so cold that blocks of ice would be warmer. Even now something touches my spine with a cold finger. But they do not harm her, and they do not harm Ibrahim. He comes of a snake-charmer's family—for fifty generations they have handled snakes—perhaps ever since Pharaoh—I do not know. Ibrahim! This snake business—how long has it been in your family?"

Ibrahim grinned a cheerful grin. He wore a bright brown tweed suit and a jaunty red fez. His teeth were as white as the kernels of nuts.

"Always, master," he said, and grinned again.

Lindsay was looking at the last cage on the left. On the freshly sanded floor two small snakes of a dull brownish colour lay motionless. They had probably just been fed.

"What are those?" he said quickly.

Ibrahim grinned again.

"*Krait*, master—Indian snake. Very bad tempered snake, *Krait*."

Lindsay looked a moment longer. His mind showed him something moving, just moving, under the edge of a hem-stitched pillow-case. He looked steadily, and turned away.

Chapter Thirty-Two

LINDSAY DINED OUT. He did not think that he was followed, but he redoubled his usual precautions. After dinner he turned in to a big cinema, put the stub of his ticket in a convenient pocket, and after ten minutes or so slipped out unobtrusively.

By the time he reached Santa's he was quite sure that it was safe to do so. The shop window was dark, but the moment he knocked on the door it was opened—by Jimmy. They passed into the inner room where Elsie sat on the corner of the table, her feet swinging, her eyes round and bright.

"Well?" she said when the door was shut. She cocked her head just a trifle impudently, and for an instant the turn of the neck, the moulding of the chin, gave him that startling something that was like Marian. They had not a feature in common—eyes, hair, and skin were as unalike as they could be—and yet there was that something which tugged at his heart.

"It is very good of you both to come." He was aware of Jimmy on the defensive. "Thurloe, I don't know how much you know. If you know anything at all, you know that Elsie is not in a particularly safe position."

"Well," said Jimmy, "that's just it. Who put her there?"

"Not I," said Lindsay. "She will tell you that herself. She's in it because she knows things. I want her to tell me just what she does know, and then she needn't be mixed up in it any more."

"What do you want to know?" said Elsie.

"I want to know about Drayton."

"I told you."

"I'm sorry, but I've got to ask—is he your father?"

"What!" said Jimmy.

Elsie nodded. The colour stood high in her cheeks, her eyes were bright and hard.

"Will you tell me all about him?" said Lindsay.

She did not look at Jimmy at all. She looked first at Lindsay, and then down into her lap.

"He's a devil," she said. "Look here, this will show you—I haven't lived with him for eight years, and I'm still so afraid of him that if I were to meet him in the street, I believe I'd drop." She paused, jerked up her head, and said, "He killed my mother."

Jimmy exclaimed. He came nearer, flung an arm about her, and looked defiantly at Lindsay.

Elsie took no notice of him.

"As far back as I can remember we were frightened of him. She—wasn't strong. She—couldn't stand things. She died eight years ago."

"In 1922?" said Lindsay. The date kept cropping up.

Elsie nodded.

"You asked me about Trevor Fothering. He lodged with us—that's how I knew him. I was thirteen. When my mother died, he—that man—Drayton—came back. He used to come and go. Sometimes we didn't see him for months, and then he'd come down on us." She lifted hurt, angry eyes to Lindsay's. "You're making me think about things that I don't let myself think about."

Lindsay was conscious that he had received a shock. His mind had not travelled beyond her statement that Trevor Fothering—Froth—had lodged with the Mannings. If he had lodged there, he was known to Manning. Manning was Drayton. Drayton had known Froth eight years ago. He could not move his thoughts from this. It might mean that eight years ago Froth was implicated in Drayton's undertakings. It certainly meant that when he, Lindsay, set out to pass as Froth he had taken on a far more difficult job than he had any idea of. Had he ever deceived Drayton? He thought so. Yes, looking back, he was sure that he had. If Drayton had suspected him, he would not have been used in the Gladisloe affair. But something had roused his suspicions then.

Marian's appearance in Paris had not been accidental. Someone had confronted them there. Drayton?

And what did Drayton think now?

He was suddenly afraid for Marian. He moved, frowning. Elsie was staring at him.

"I'm sorry," he said. "I must ask you these things. About Fothering now—Drayton knew him?" He had to make sure.

"Yes—of course—I told you. He lodged with us. I don't believe you were listening."

"Do you think Froth was—well—*in* with him?"

Elsie flushed scarlet.

"I don't know—I thought sometimes—oh, I don't know."

So even eight years ago Froth had been running with the hare and hunting with the hounds. A racking game. No wonder his nerve had gone.

Lindsay frowned. Then he said,

"Will you go on?"

"I don't know what you want to know. My mother died, and Trevor helped me to get away. He sent me to school."

"Trevor did?"

"Yes. He—he was fond of me. He sent me to school till I was eighteen. Then he wanted to marry me. It doesn't matter my telling you that, because he used to tell everyone himself. He used to say he'd brought me up to marry him."

Jimmy's arm dropped from her shoulders. She had been leaning against it. When it dropped away she looked round and said in a small, quivering voice,

"Don't be a mutt, Jimmy!"

"Are you going to marry him?" said Jimmy Thurloe. He had turned rather white. Neither of them seemed to remember that Lindsay was there.

Elsie did not speak. She lifted her eyes and looked at him—hard. Then she turned away. Lindsay gave her a moment before he said,

"He called himself Manning. What Christian name did he use?"

"Robert."

"Do you think Manning was his real name?"

"I don't know."

"Did your mother ever tell you how she met him—or anything about him? Had he a profession?"

"She never told me anything. She was afraid all the time. We didn't talk about him. When he was there I kept out of his way, and when he was away I used to try not to think about him."

"He was away a good deal?"

"Most of the time. He used to come and go. Sometimes we didn't see him for months, and then he would come back for a night—two nights—a week—and go off again."

"But you never saw him after 1922?"

"No—not until the other day." She leaned back again, relaxing a little. Jimmy's arm was there for her to lean against. His hand rested for a moment upon her shoulder.

"Did your mother ever tell you you had a sister?" said Lindsay after a pause.

He saw her flush brightly.

She said "Oh!" in a startled voice; and then, "A sister?

"Did she?"

"I think—she did—"

"You *think*?"

"Yes—when she was ill—she talked. I couldn't make out what she was saying most of the time. There was a lot about someone called Lee, but sometimes she kept on saying 'Marian—Marian,' like that—over and over. Once she said 'Marian's safe'; and then, 'My little baby—she's out of it.' And then she caught my wrist and said, 'I've never regretted it, though it has broken my heart.' I said, 'Don't trouble'; and she said, 'I've had the trouble. But she's safe—Marian's safe—she couldn't have stood it as well as you—you're stronger—she couldn't have borne it.'"

"What do you think she meant?" said Lindsay.

Elsie looked at him questioningly.

"I thought she meant I'd had a sister who had died. Please tell me what she meant—*please.*"

"She meant that you had a sister who is alive," he said gently.

She jumped off the table and came to him.

"You're sure?"

"Yes, my dear."

She turned half round.

"Oh, Jimmy!"

"Shall you mind me for a brother-in-law?" said Lindsay laughing.

Elsie turned back, clutching Jimmy by the arm.

"A brother-in-law?"

Lindsay thought that Jimmy Thurloe brightened.

"Marian and I are engaged."

He told Marian's story in as few words as possible. Telling it over made it seem more real—and more dangerous. Marian's danger came more vividly before him with each short sentence.

"Does *he* know she is alive?" Elsie's voice was quick and frightened.

"Yes, he does. You mustn't try and see her, or write to her. It would be very dangerous for both of you."

"Where is she?"

"In Paris at the moment, but I don't expect she'll be there for long. I think she was taken over there in order to try and trap her into recognizing me."

"Then they know who you are?"

"They are not sure—at least that is what I think."

"Then it's dangerous for you—very dangerous?"

Lindsay gave a dry laugh.

"Middling," he said. Then abruptly, "Who is Lee?"

"Lee?"

"You said your mother talked about Lee when she was ill. Do you know what she meant?"

Elsie hesitated.

"She never talked about any friends or relations. I think it was someone she cared for. She had a picture he had painted—a water colour. She kept it hidden. I never saw it till she was ill. It is signed L.A. She said, 'Lee painted it.' She had it on her bed and kept looking at it. She told me to hide it from *him*. I'm trying to tell you everything. The last thing she did before she got too ill was to mend the back, which had got torn."

"A paper back?"

"Yes. She told me to make some paste and get her some strong brown paper, and she pasted it over. She did it herself."

"You've got the picture?"

"Yes—of course I have."

"May I see it? Will you let Jimmy have it? I'll try and get to his rooms to-morrow or next day about this time. And now I must go."

He had turned to the door, when they came up close on either side of him. Elsie slid a hand inside his arm.

"You'll be careful, won't you?" she said. "He-he's *cunning*—you don't know him."

"I say, can't I take a hand?" said Jimmy. "I'd like to most awfully."

Elsie looked at him with round anxious eyes and a tilt of the head that reminded him of a friendly bird. She was prettily flushed. The brown eyes were a little moist.

Jimmy, on the other side, was at once embarrassed and as friendly as Elsie. The blessed word brother-in-law had had its effect.

Lindsay went on his way feeling warmed and cheered.

Chapter Thirty-Three

"I THINK THAT is all," said Lindsay Trevor.

He stood with his back to the mantelpiece in Mr Smith's library. The fire behind him was low, a mound of glowing ash with the skeleton of a great log across it, but the long room was full of the warm comfort which the hearth had been giving out all day. In the window Ananias, Mr Smith's parrot, snored gently behind the green baize extinguisher which covered his cage at night.

Mr Benbow Collingwood Horatio Smith lay stretched at full length in a large leather-covered armchair, his long fine hands on either arm, his feet to the fire, his half closed eyes fixed dreamily upon the topmost of the many rows of books which covered the walls.

On the arm of a second chair there sat a little sandy man with a bottle-brush scalp and small grey eyes like points of polished steel. He wore the worst clothes in London and carried a brand of bright red cotton bandanna which could be seen at least a quarter of a mile away. Lindsay had once said, "When Garrett wants to disguise himself, all he has to do is to leave his bandanna at home and buy a neat gent's suiting." At this moment he wore a light tweed suit with a pink check. All the pockets bulged like a schoolboy's, and it had the air of having been made for an elder brother and cut down. A blue and white shirt, an exceedingly frayed green tie, and bright orange boots completed his attire. He made Mr Smith look almost incredibly distinguished.

Garrett snapped his fingers.

"*All!*" he said in a contemptuous tone. "If that's all, it's not a ha'porth of good! Nothing but a lot of dam theories, and not enough evidence to swat a fly!"

Lindsay laughed.

"Well," he said, "they've thought it worth while to try and wipe me off the map, so I suppose they have a better opinion of my evidence than you have, sir."

Garrett had one leg over the other; he crouched forward and hugged the uppermost knee.

"What's it all about? The Vulture disappears in 1922. Lewindorf dies in 1922. Drayton goes to Restow in 1922. Your young friend Miss Elsie Manning sees the last of a wicked parent in 1922. Therefore—Oh Lord—the Vulture is Drayton!"

"Not quite fair, sir," said Lindsay.

"Oh, put it yourself!" said Garrett.

"You've left out Gogo. Gogo admitted he was working for the Vulture in shadowing Miss Rayne. She was undoubtedly brought to Paris to see how she would react if she met me unexpectedly—"

"Conjecture!" snapped Garrett. "Arbitrary, unsupported conjecture!"

"Not quite unsupported. Gogo, admittedly working for the Vulture, is told to shadow Miss Rayne and to see whether she meets *me*. There's my support."

Garrett snapped his fingers within an inch of Mr Smith's left hand.

"How's that, umpire?"

"Oh—Trevor's point—undoubtedly Trevor's point," said Mr Smith, continuing to gaze at Gibbons' *Decline and Fall of the Roman Empire*.

"All right, you may have that," said Garrett. "But a fat lot of use it is to any of us. We should look nice running Drayton in and putting up evidence like, "He hired an apache to follow my fiancée in Paris, and I found a snake in my bed." He clutched his head and rocked on the arm of the chair. "Oh, Lordy *Lord*!"

"There's the blackmail," said Lindsay.

"My good Lin! Have you gone dotty? Do you propose to stand up in the witness box and swear to having blackmailed Sir John Gladisloe entirely *pour le bon motif*? You've only your own unsupported word for it that Drayton gave you your instructions. Drayton will have his pockets full of alibis. He's a learned, scholarly librarian, is Drayton—he don't meddle in strikes and suchlike. 'He is an intellectual chap and thinks of things that would astonish you." He hummed the snatch from *Iolanthe,* thumped on his knee, and ended, "*That's* no good."

"I didn't think it was."

Garrett thumped his knee again.

"What Gogo says isn't evidence, and what you might say 'ud be dam queer evidence. And the evidence we've got on the political side is all very entertaining and informative, but it's about as much good as a sick headache from the practical point of view. That Madame Ferrans you put us on to—she's an old hand. She used to call herself Marie Morel. Gouraud very nearly shot her twice, but she'd luck. Drayton's working up a ramp against the Naval Conference. We've identified the people she was sent to ginger up. F and J are prominent journalists. N is a party leader." He gave the names. "N will probably commit a blazing indiscretion to order some time in the next ten days. It's a new line in blackmail, but I'll go so far as to admit it's just the sort of thing one might expect from the Vulture. He collects scandals; then he turns some of 'em into money and buys more scandals—there are always plenty of scandals to buy, if you can afford the price. Well, he sells some of 'em for money, and he sells some of 'em for strikes and suchlike, or for anti-everyone articles in the Paris Press, or for calculated indiscretions in the Chamber, or the Reichstag, or any other old talking-shop. And I've got my guess—and a pretty good guess too—that he sells some of 'em for opposition to things like international agreements about drug traffic, the white slave trade, and oddments of that sort. Our friend Ferdinand Schreck got his in Vienna the other day. Why do you suppose he paid tax to the Vulture? *Tax!*" He laughed a short dry laugh like a terrier's bark. "You might call it sur-tax! Ferdinand was pretty sour about it, I gather. But why did he pay it? Did you ask yourself that? I did, and I decided that it was dam well worth his while. The Vulture blackmails the politicians who make the laws and the officials who administer 'em—and it's better to pay a sur-tax to the Vulture than to have your activities restrained by international agreements or to get jugged."

Lindsay stood on one foot and warmed the other.

"You began with Drayton, and you end with the Vulture," he said.

"Trevor's point again, I think," said Mr Benbow Collingwood Horatio Smith.

Garrett flung out an impatient hand.

"He can have it! It isn't worth a tinker's cuss. He may think Drayton's the Vulture, and I may think the Vulture's Drayton, and it's worth exactly nuppence to nobody unless we've got cold, cast-iron proof. That's about the size of it—isn't it, Lin?"

Lindsay nodded.

"We've got to get the proof," he said.

Garrett grinned.

"Carry on! You have my blessing. We'll hunt up Lewindorf's domestic staff and try and get a line on Drayton under the Manning alias—but eight years is a long time. And meanwhile if anyone attempts your life again, try and grab him in the act. Candidly, that's our best chance of evidence."

Without opening his eyes Mr Smith inquired,

"What was Mrs Manning's Christian name?"

"I don't know," said Lindsay.

"But Miss Rayne, her elder daughter—I have an impression that her name is Marian."

"Yes, sir."

"She might have been called after her mother."

"I don't know."

"It is possible. And Mrs Manning talked about Lee during her last illness—an artist, I think you said."

"Elsie Manning has a picture painted by him."

"One picture does not make an artist," said Mr Smith in a vague, abstracted tone. "No—no—certainly not. But I think you mentioned that the picture was signed L. A."

"Yes—Elsie said so."

Mr Smith rose slowly, strolled across the room, and came back with a portfolio in his hand. When he had seated himself, he took a pair of glasses out of his waistcoat pocket, placed them upon his nose, and began to turn over the leaves of the portfolio.

Garrett sat watching him intently.

"There are probably," said Mr Smith, "several thousands of persons who combine the initials L. A. with the ability to paint at least one picture. I knew one of them—oh, rather over twenty years ago. Yes—let me see..." He relapsed into calculation. "Yes, it would be twenty years ago, I think." He took a sketch and handed it to Lindsay. "You will see the initials in the corner."

Lindsay looked at the sketch. It showed running water, and trees blowing in the wind. The water ran, and the trees really blew.

"A young American," said Mr Smith. "Thaxter wrote to me about him and his wife. They were pleasant young people. They had no money, and they did not know anyone. There were two babies. His name was Lee Abinger. The wife's name was Marian. Thank you." He took the sketch and closed the portfolio upon it.

Lindsay felt the blood rush to his face.

"*Sir!*" he said.

Mr Smith nodded.

"Perhaps another coincidence—perhaps not. We shall know more when Garrett has discovered when Mrs Manning became Mrs Manning."

"What happened to the Abingers?" said Lindsay quickly.

Mr Smith laid the portfolio down upon the floor beside his chair.

"Now there I have no first-hand knowledge. I was—er—abroad—er—in Russia. When I returned I was told that Lee Abinger was dead and that his widow had married again. In the circumstances it seemed better not to write. I had in fact no address to write to."

Garrett whipped out a note-book.

"Where were they living when you knew them?"

"Earl's Court," said Mr Smith. "Rooms—" He closed his eyes. "The landlady had red hair that was always coming down—Irish—yes, her name was Carroll—Mrs Carroll—Frederick Street, Earl's Court." He opened his eyes again and gazed into the fire. "I am afraid I have forgotten the number."

The note-book went back into the pocket with the bandanna.

"Well, it's the first time in history if you have," said Garrett. "I didn't know you could forget anything. If you remember the number in the middle of the night, don't have me out of bed to tell me so, that's all. I can bear to wait." He swung round on the arm of the chair and fixed sharp grey eyes on Lindsay. "Now look here, my lad, so far we've been dallying. Let's get to business! Shed Drayton and the ladies and let's get to what about Restow!"

Mr Smith disposed himself in his chair as for slumber.

Lindsay met the steel of Garrett's eyes with his pleasantest smile.

"I don't know," he said.

Garrett snorted.

"You went to the dam place to watch Restow, and you come bobbing up with nothing to say but' I don't know.' Now listen to me and I'll put it to you. Someone gives Madame Ferrans her instructions. Your Manning girl—strong, persevering eavesdropper—overhears them. Now let's get quite clear—was that Drayton, or was it Restow?"

"Drayton."

"You're sure?"

"Yes. I wasn't at first, but I am now."

"And when the Ferrans woman warned you on the boat—was she warning you against Drayton or against Restow?"

"I thought Restow—now I'm not sure."

"And when you found the snake in your bed in Paris—whose room was next to yours?"

"Restow's," said Lindsay."

"Drayton wasn't in Paris?"

Lindsay smiled.

"I don't know. Restow gave me to understand that he was."

"Restow would, if he wanted to cover his tracks. Now let's hark back a bit. When Drayton sent you out blackmailing, he told you in so many words that Restow was his principal?"

"I shouldn't put implicit faith in a statement made by Drayton."

"Think with more than half your brain, Lin! Drayton would lie if it suited him—but he was risking your going behind him to Restow and saying, 'Look here, old top, what about this Gladisloe blackmail?' He was taking a bit of a risk, wasn't he, unless Restow really was his principal—unless Restow was the Vulture." He drawled out the last words, dwelling on them. "That's been my theory all along. Take the period of the Vulture's greatest activity, 1915 to 1922. Drayton was with Lewindorf."

"I don't admit that," said Lindsay quickly. "I don't believe that the Drayton who was with Lewindorf is the Drayton who is with Restow."

Garrett banged his knee.

"You needn't believe it if you don't like it! I'm putting my case. Drayton was with Lewindorf book-worming. Where was Restow?...I'll tell you. Restow was on the razzle-dazzle. He failed sensationally in the spring of '15, bobbed up again in '19, and failed again in '20—reappeared in a halo of millions in the spring of '22. In the intervals he was all over the shop—Madrid—Paris—Warsaw—Nizhny Novgorod—Sicily— and, for all I know, Timbuctoo as well. Sometimes he had money, and sometimes he hadn't. If Restow isn't the Vulture, I don't mind betting he'd find it difficult to produce a good rock-bottom alibi. D'you remember the night we thought we'd got the Vulture at Hazebrouck? Well, you try asking Restow with my compliments how he got away. I'd like to know—yes, by gum, I would!"

Chapter Thirty-Four

LINDSAY WALKED back to Blenheim Square. The night was cold and raw. There was no fog. The light from the lamp-posts fell clear upon the black wet streets. He was not sure whether it had been raining. The theatres were out and the streets beginning to be empty. He had taken a short cut through Leonard Street, when he first heard the footstep behind him.

The idea that he had been followed was a very unpleasant one. As he quickened his pace, the footsteps broke into a run and a man's voice hailed him as Fothering. He looked over his shoulder and saw a young man cross the circle of light about the last lamp. He was running. The light fell on a pale sharp face, on a tall hat tilted back, on a white muffler and a dark coat buttoned up. Lindsay had never seen the man before. He stood still for him to come up.

The street, which is only a couple of hundred yards long, was empty from end to end. Lights burned in the upper windows of the houses, but the ground floors had retired into darkness for the night. A street of respectability—a quiet, comfortable, family sort of street—not at all an appropriate street in which to be the object of nefarious attentions.

The young man came up with Lindsay rather short of breath.

"I—I saw you from my taxi. You—you walk the devil of a rate," he said accusingly.

"Well, it's getting late, and I'm supposed to be in," said Lindsay pleasantly.

"We'd better walk," said the young man. "You—you haven't been followed?"

"Why should I be followed?"

The answer came with a nervous laugh: "His way—his little way. Hang it all, you ought to know that!"

"Perhaps names are a mistake," suggested Lindsay, playing to his cue.

"Yes—yes. I say—my nerves are all in bits. You don't think—anyone's watching us?"

"No, I don't."

"My nerve's gone—that's a fact. Perhaps I've had one too many—I don't know. Would you say I had?"

He diffused an odour of varied drinks. As they walked, he showed a disposition to link arms.

"One too many," he repeated, leaning rather heavily on the arm he held. "Should always know when to stop. Dash it—I say—that's it!" He pronounced the words with a careful attention to consonants. "That's it! A fellow should—always know—when—he's had nuff." He stood still and leaned outwards, wagging an emphatic hand. *"Always."*

"You'd better get along home," said Lindsay.

"No," said the young man firmly. "Not home—can't sleep at home." He caught Lindsay's arm with both hands. "Is someone following us?"

"No. Why should anyone follow us?"

"His little way. I say—must pull myself together—what? Beastly thing to have nerves all go to bits."

"Beastly," said Lindsay. "Why have they gone?"

The young man sagged against him.

"You know, old sport. Not so long since you were in the same boat. Beastly kind of job to give a fellow—what? I mean—" He straightened himself and waved an explanatory hand. "What I mean is, you can't call it—kind of job—for a gentleman. What I mean to say is—can you?"

"Oh, I don't know," said Lindsay. He didn't know, but he began to want to know rather badly.

The young man slipped down on to the kerb in a sitting position, put his head in his hands, and burst into tears. They were not loud tears, but rather the sniffling weeping of a bullied schoolboy.

Lindsay looked up and down the road. It slept—most respectably it slept. He sat down on the kerb beside the weeping young man.

"After all—a fellow's a gentleman—what I mean to say is—isn't he, Froth?"

Lindsay patted the heaving shoulders.

"Of course," he agreed.

"An'—is it—the act-of-a—gentleman—taking a fellow's papers— what?"

"It would depend on the circumstances," said Lindsay cautiously.

The young man ceased to sob. He pushed back his hat and sat up.

"Circum—circum—" After two or three efforts he produced the word very slowly and solemnly—"Cir—cum—stan—ces. Hang it all, Froth, the poor fellow—poor old Ferdinand—poor old fellow—not friend of my childhood or any old rot of that kind—no. Ash a matter of fact—as a marrer-o-fact—yes marrer-o-fact—I never saw the poor old fellow. But all the same when a poor old fellow's been biffed by a bullet—biffed dead by a bullet—well—I put it to you, Froth, old bird—is it the act-of-a— gentleman to steal his papers? Well, I put it to you." He tapped Lindsay solemnly on the chest and wagged his head.

Lindsay tingled from head to foot.

"Poor old Ferdinand Schreck!" he said.

The young man shrank away from him.

"Mustn't mention names—mustn't ever mention names! Name of poor old Ferdinand Schreck never passed lips. Not act-of-a—gentleman to mention names."

"Only between friends," said Lindsay. "Did you get the papers all right?"

"Of course I got papers—English milord—tourist—lotsh and lotsh of money, no one sushpeck—sush—sush—peck—ted. But *not* act-of-a— gentleman. *No!*"

"He shouldn't have asked you to do it."

"Threatened me," said the young man with an access of misery. "Threatened me—*me*! And mind you, Froth, my governor'd have cut me off without a brass farthing, sure as my name's Dilling, he would. What was a fellow to do? Now I put it to you."

Dilling...There flashed into Lindsay's mind a picture of the large orange-coloured square which from every hoarding in the kingdom proclaimed the virtues of Dilling's Delightful Doughnuts. He wondered.

"Governor's so strict," moaned Mr Dilling. "Nonconformist consh—consh—conshentious objecshon. What's a fellow to do? I put it to you."

"Who gave you your orders?"

Lindsay kept his voice casual with an effort. This young fool couldn't know much; but if he knew something, that something might be pieced on to something else. Ferdinand Schreck had been shot dead in Vienna because he was on the point of giving the Vulture away. Dilling had been sent to collect Schreck's papers. What papers? Evidently papers that would incriminate the Vulture—papers that the police had missed. He repeated his question:

"Who gave you your orders?"

"Who gives you yours?"

"Drayton," said Lindsay.

"Who's he? Don't know Drayton—" He stared at Lindsay. "What've I been saying? Mustn't say things—mustn't talk—doesn't do to talk—must be getting—along." He scrambled to his feet and stood swaying a little. "What've I been saying, old fellow? Haven't been talking? Doesn't do to talk. No names—what? You're Froth, aren't you?" He came closer, peering. "Not Froth?"

He clapped his hat hard down upon his head and ran with surprising swiftness back along the way that he had come.

Lindsay let him go. Garrett could gather him in easily enough. Dilling's Delightful Doughnuts was what he sounded like—and once gathered he would talk.

Chapter Thirty-Five

Lindsay came into the hall of the house in Blenheim Square. The coloured lights in the peacock's tails shone down upon the green marble pillars and the green marble floor. It was after midnight and only one footman was on duty. He recognized the rosy faced Robert who had showed him the back way into the house and who usually waited on him. The boy looked owlish in his effort to keep awake. Lindsay gave him a friendly smile.

"Am I the last?" he said. "I'm afraid I've kept you up."

He went on towards the staircase, and then turned, aware of Robert at his elbow.

"I beg your pardon, sir—"

"What is it, Robert?"

"If I could speak to you for a moment, sir—"

"Yes—what is it?"

"Perhaps if I were to take your coat and be giving you a bit of a brush down—"

He took the coat and produced the brush. A resourceful lad.

"Well? What is it?" said Lindsay.

"It's that Abraham," said Robert gloomily.

"Abraham?"

"Him that looks after Madame's snakes."

"Oh—*Ibrahim*."

"Yes, sir—Abraham."

"What about him?"

"Well, sir, just before I come on duty here I went along to make up your fire, and as I come along the passage I see that Abraham come out of your room."

"Did he see you?"

"No, sir, he didn't." Robert hesitated. "I didn't want any unpleasantness, sir. He's got the name of being a bad one to get on the wrong side of, so I didn't want any unpleasantness, but seeing he hadn't any business where he was, I thought I'd mention it to you on the quiet."

"Thank you, Robert," said Lindsay.

He went up to his room and subjected it to an intensive search. Everything was there that should have been there, and nothing that should not. He pulled the bed to bits and remade it. And yet he did not fancy the idea of lying down in that bed and going to sleep. He had locked both his bedroom and his sitting-room doors every night since he had come to Blenheim Square. He locked them now, put on dressing-gown and slippers, and then passed into the sitting-room and, leaving the connecting door open, took a book and sat down to read.

The book might as well have been a Chaldean cylinder. There were characters in rows upon white paper. His eye looked at them, but his mind did not take them in. He shut the book, switched off the light, and sat in the firelight, thinking. Perhaps half an hour passed, perhaps longer. In the dark time loses its accustomed values.

At last he got up, stretched, and thought of bed with less repugnance. He went back into the bed-room. Through the open connecting door a warm glow of firelight followed him. A log had burned up so brightly that it had not occurred to him to switch on the electric light, but as he stepped out of the warm fire-lit patch, the darkness of the bedroom was unpleasant. He groped towards the switch by the door, and felt the hair on his scalp pringle as he did so. He had searched the room; he knew that there was nothing there. But as he groped for the switch, he could have sworn that something rustled—moved—rustled.

The switch was placed unusually low. Perhaps long ago the room had been a nursery. Feeling for it, he touched the handle of the door— and as he touched it, it moved.

It moved by no volition of his. It moved because someone was turning the handle from the other side. In a flash Lindsay knew that the rustlings had come from the other side of the door. The door was locked. The door was opening.

He could move as silently as a cat. He moved now in the only direction which offered a chance of concealment—behind the opening door.

It opened a bare inch and stayed. Lindsay stood with his right shoulder against the wall just clear of the jamb which carried the hinges. He felt an agreeable excitement. Here at last was someone who could be seen, touched, grappled with. He would let him get into the room and then spring on him from behind when he turned, as he surely would turn, towards the bed.

The door stayed just that bare inch open.

Lindsay went on thinking. If the man behind the door was Restow—could he count on overpowering him? He planned the grip which would turn Restow's bull strength against itself and bring him crashing down. But he did not believe that it was Restow who was there behind the inch-wide crack. He hoped that it was Drayton—his fingers tingled for Drayton—but he feared greatly that it was Ibrahim. What was the good of his throttling Ibrahim? It would be a most complete give-away. It would make it impossible for him to remain at Blenheim Square. It would bring this secret underground struggle with Drayton into the open. Was he ready to fight in the open yet? He said "No" so emphatically as to astonish his own thoughts. They scattered in confusion. He was left with a fixed resolve to wait upon the developing event, to see without being seen, and still remain if possible the unconscious tool.

The door moved slowly. The crack widened. When it was about a foot wide, the door stopped moving. Lindsay's eyes, accustomed to the darkness, could see the movement, but the door, swinging towards him, hid the opening. He could judge its width only by the angle in which he now stood. He had before him the length of the room, with the open door connecting with his sitting-room about two thirds of the way up it on the left. To the right was the bed with its head against the right-hand wall. Facing him, the curtained windows. The firelight was fainter now, but it still lighted the open doorway and made a warm diffused twilight at that end of the room.

Lindsay could see the window curtains dark against the lighter wall. He could distinguish the black shapes of wardrobe, chest of drawers, washstand, and chairs, and he could see quite plainly the white linen and blankets of his bed.

The door moved again.

It was now wide enough to let a man pass. The angle just left the bed visible. Lindsay took a half step away from the wall. If he stooped forward now, he could see round the door. He waited, listening intently, and heard a faint, a very faint, dragging would. It was not a footstep, or any sound that a man would naturally make in moving. It was slow, cautious, and only just audible; and it came fitfully, as if something was crawling forward, an inch at a time.

Lindsay's heart jumped. He had a sickening recollection of the great python, Typhoon, with his head propped upon coil on patterned coil. He thought that the slow rippling passage of the heavy, supple body would make just such a sound as this that he was straining his ears to catch.

He bent and leaned as far forward as he could. His heart jumped again. The thing that was coming slowly into the room was not Typhoon. He thought that he would have been able to see the python's sliding coils; but this thing he could not see at all. It was moving forward a yard from his eyes, but it was only his ears that told him of the movement. And then all at once between him and the white bed he saw the vague rounded outline of a man's head.

The head was about two feet above the floor. Behind it, Lindsay guessed at a crawling body supported by hands and knees. He remained bent forward and saw the shape of the head approach the foot of the bed by the slowest of degrees. Sometimes it remained quite still, and then again it moved inch by inch until not only the head but a humped outline of shoulder could be seen against the bedclothes.

Lindsay was on thorns. When would the man discover that the bed was empty? If it had been turned down in the orthodox way he must have discovered it by now, but Lindsay himself in remaking it had left the bedding in a comfortable huddle all ready to tuck about him. There was even a blackish blur against the pillow, which might have been the head of a sleeper. He puzzled over this, and then remembered throwing down a green silk handkerchief when he stripped off his coat.

The dark head was close against the side of the bed, low down towards the foot. Two dark hands rose and fumbled at the bedclothes. There was no sound. After a full minute the head dropped below the level of the bed.

Silence.

Darkness.

No movement that could be either heard or seen.

Lindsay waited, and after some most interminable minutes he saw between one black mound, which was the chest of drawers, and another, which was the dressing-table, a third and smaller blackness which moved.

He lost it—found it—lost it again—and, waiting there, was seized with an all but uncontrollable desire to yawn. By the dressing-table something was lifted and set down, and then the slow crawling began again, coming imperceptibly nearer.

Lindsay strained his eyes. The man would avoid the fire-lit patch. Would he? Why should he? It would not be visible to anyone lying in the bed. The shape of a man crawling emerged from the darkness, the lifted head turned for an instant towards the light, and Lindsay saw two little brilliant discs like red-hot sixpences in the middle of the head. Just for that instant the man's eyes caught the red firelight and reflected it, as an animal's eyes will catch light and reflect it, in orange, emerald, or red; and just for that instant the shape of the face showed plain.

"'That Abraham'," said Lindsay to himself, quoting Robert.

Ibrahim crawled on. He was less deliberate now. He made no noise, but he came without stopping to the door and passed out of Lindsay's sight. The door moved on noiseless hinges—closed and clicked to with the barest sound.

Lindsay moved back against the wall and stood there. He would give Ibrahim half an hour. The luminous dial of his watch told him that it was half past one. He would wait until two o'clock. Afterwards he thought that half hour one of the worst he had ever spent. It was of a most intolerable length, and it was enlivened by the conviction that somewhere in the room there were a couple of poisonous snakes.

Chapter Thirty-Six

THE HALF-HOUR passed. Lindsay opened the door noiselessly and stood looking up and down the corridor. In the ordinary way, a light burned in it all night long; yet when Ibrahim crawled into his room not the faintest glimmer of light had come with him. Now the light burned again and showed the passage empty from end to end.

Lindsay shut the door, switched on the light, and experimented with the key. It turned easily enough, but it no longer locked the door. He drew it out and looked at it. One of the wards had been filed away. He put the key back and gave his attention to the bed, which he approached stick in hand.

Ibrahim's operations having been directed to the foot of the bed, Lindsay came to the head and, taking hold of the bedclothes, peeled them back. When two thirds of the bed was exposed, he saw a small dark head, lifting, thrusting, as the movement disturbed it. He stripped the clothes right back with a jerk and brought his stick down upon the snake with a sharp cut.

It was one of the *Kraits* which Ibrahim, showing those white teeth of his, had described as "very bad-tempered snake, master."

Lindsay wondered where the other one was. For all he knew, there might be more than another *one*.

He went over to the dressing-table and looked about him. The shoes he had taken off were outside the door; the shoes he would put on in the morning stood beneath the table. He picked up the right shoe with his stick, held it dangling, shook it about, and set it down. As he hooked the stick into the other shoe, something moved against it. At the first shake a tiny snake fell out. If it was small, it was exceedingly active. It streaked across the carpet like the flick of a whip lash and disappeared under the wardrobe.

Lindsay had never seen a snake hustle before. He associated snakes with the slow, dallying movements which they exhibit in a cage. This exhibition of pace filled him with the liveliest dislike. He poked under the wardrobe, and nothing happened. He swept the whole space, and drew a blank. He had certainly got to find that *Krait*.

The wardrobe was too heavy to lift—a cumbrous mahogany affair with shelves on one side and a hanging space on the other. He got an electric torch, lay down, and peered underneath it, hoping that the snake would not suddenly decide upon a sortie. The space beneath the wardrobe was empty.

He got up rather quickly. There was a dozen inches of concentrated unpleasantness loose in the room, and he was bound to find it, if it took all night.

He shifted the chest of drawers. Nothing there. Then, standing on a chair, he shook the long dark curtains. There were four of them, and as he touched the third, the snake shot out. Lindsay flung the stick at it and ran in with the chair. He laid the corpse beside the other one, handling it gingerly.

The question now was whether Ibrahim had more than two strings to his bow. Lindsay thought not; but for nothing on earth would he have slept in the bedroom, which might or might not contain Ibrahim's third string.

He went back into the sitting-room, made up generous fire, and sat down to see the night out in a chair.

He read for a bit, and then became drowsy. After all, Ibrahim had shot his bolt. He put down his book and turned his attention to the clearance of the door from the bedroom. It fitted so closely to the carpet that it appeared gratifyingly improbable that the most persistent reptile could worm its way underneath it. He shut the door, put his feet up on a second chair, and turned out the reading-lamp at his elbow.

He had no idea how long afterwards it was that he was awakened by the sound of an opening door. He wakened, and was broad awake in a single flash of time, his mind sufficiently alert to keep his body still and his eyes so far closed that they would appear to be shut. They were not, however, so far closed as to make it impossible for him to, see. What he saw interested him very much. The door between his bedroom and the sitting-room stood wide open. The bedroom was brightly lit, and in the doorway, bulking dark and large against the lighted background, stood Algerius Restow.

Such a commingling of feelings surged up in Lindsay that no single one of them predominated sufficiently to decide his mood. A sharp disappointment—a keen surprise—a warm wave of relief—a sense of shock—of incongruity—

Restow stood still, looking into the fire-shot dusk of the sitting-room. Even with the lighted room behind him, he must surely be able to distinguish Lindsay's seated figure. Lindsay looked back at him between half closed lids. He remembered a picture of the Minotaur—a lowering beast-headed hulk leaning on the battlements of his rude Cretan tower. Restow, standing there, reminded him of this picture. Was Restow a modern Minotaur, taking toll of men, as the Cretan monster had taken his toll and tribute three thousand years before Christ? The thought ran like a blood-red thread through the long silent moments during which there was neither movement nor sound in the dark or in the lighted room. Then a log toppled and fell outwards upon the hearth. A flame sprang up from it, filling the room with a red light as clear, though not as bright, as day. Restow crossed the floor with two of his great strides and set a hand on Lindsay's shoulder. Had he come to see if his work had been done? Had he seen the *Kraits*? Had he—

Lindsay forced himself to the lax stillness of sleep. The hand on his shoulder rested lightly there, and went to his wrist and clasped it with a gentle pressure, the fingers feeling for the pulse. Lindsay experienced the strangest sensations. This contact, instead of alarming, reassured him. He was aware of concern—anxiety—and a great rush of friendliness coming from Restow. Was this the Vulture? Was it possible for any man so to act a part as to produce impressions so completely at variance with his real nature? He could not answer these questions. The groping fingers found and pressed the pulse in his wrist. It was time to awake. Lindsay flung out an arm and sat up with a choking cry of,

"What's up?"

"By Jing!" said Algerius Restow in a loud surprised voice. "By Jing!" he repeated and stepped back. Then without another word he strode across to the door and switched on the overhead light. He was revealed in crimson silk pyjamas and an emerald and blue shot dressing-gown. Lindsay blinked, yawned, and said sleepily,

"Is anything the matter? Do you want me?"

"By Jing!" said Restow again. "Do I want you? Aha! Do I *want* you, my Fothering? You ask me that!"

"Well—yes, sir—do you?" He had got out of his chair now and stood beside it.

"You do not sleep in your bed?" said Restow.

"Well, I must have fallen asleep in here."

"By Jing, yes! But why? I ask you that like a damfool idiot, because if I ask you, you will not tell me the truth. People who shove their noses in, asking damfool questions, get told lies, my Fothering—yes, by Jing— but sometimes the lies are damfool too. Have you thought of that?"

"I don't think I know what you mean, sir."

"My poor Fothering—are you then a half-wit? I have not thought so, though sometimes you would like it if I thought so—but no—I have had another thought—*Ach!* Yes!"

His brows drew together. His little pig eyes looked shrewdly out from under them.

Lindsay assumed a muddled stare and struggled not too successfully with a yawn. He had been wanting to yawn all night.

With a gesture of impatience that was purely Latin, Restow swung round.

"Come into your bedroom, my Fothering, and I will tell you why you sleep in a chair and make me think I may want my secretary and he will not come again whether I want him or not."

He went through the connecting door and Lindsay after him. The bed stood stripped, a pair of shoes lay widely separated upon the floor, and, stretched side by side on a sheet of newspaper between the windows, lay the corpses of two *kraits*.

Restow waved a magnificent arm.

"In the morning Gloria will want to know why you have killed her snakes," he observed.

"Er—I'm sorry—"

"*Nicht!*" said Restow emphatically. "What a liar you are, my poor Fothering, and what a fool you think me to imagine that I believe you are sorry that you have killed the snakes instead of the snakes killing you! Now I will tell you why I am here. I have seen Robert talking to you in the hall when you come in, very quietly. Robert has a red face, he blushes like nowadays the young girls do not blush any more. It is a pity. A blush is a very beautiful thing—*hein?* and sometimes it is also a very useful thing. I find Robert's blush not beautiful—no, but very useful. I send for him. He blushes again. I ask him what he has said to you. He blushes like ten virgins—all foolish. I go on asking. He tells me at last that he has seen Ibrahim, whom he calls Abraham out of the Bible, coming out of your room. Well, I go to bed. I do not think of it—*much*. I sleep. Gloria sleeps. Then I wake—I cannot sleep again. I stay awake, and something says to me, 'Go and see what is happening in your Fothering's room.' So I come. The door is not locked. I enter. I listen. I do not hear you breathe. Then the fire shoots, and I see the bed empty—stripped. I put on the light, and I see two of Gloria's snakes, quite dead, laid out very neat and tidy upon newspaper. Then I wonder whether you have killed them quick enough—*krait* is very quick, very slippy and nippy. I begin to be afraid and when I stand in the door and see you quite still-quite silent—quite as if you too were dead—then I am afraid. Yes, by Jing, I am afraid!" He paused, looked hard at Lindsay, and said in the same soft voice, "You do not believe me?"

The odd thing was that Lindsay did believe him. Against reason, against experience, he believed that Restow, standing in that doorway and looking in on a fire-lit room, had been very much afraid. He had felt Restow's fear. It had come throbbing towards him through the silence. He had felt Restow's fear, and he had felt Restow's relief; but at what lay behind them he could only guess.

Restow stooped and bundled the snakes into a rough parcel with the newspaper, then carried the parcel into the sitting-room and dropped it on the still blazing fire, holding it there with the poker until the room was full of an acrid smell and the floating black ash came quivering down upon the red embers beneath.

Then he spoke over his shoulder.

"Who are you, my friend?" he said.

Chapter Thirty-Seven

"Who are you, my friend?"

Restow asked the question with no more than a casual turn of the head, yet Lindsay was aware of something shrewd in the sudden glance. He had no time to consider, and no need, for Restow straightened himself, laughing.

"For how long do you think I took you for Fothering? *Fothering!*" He shook with his soft laughter. "Bah, my friend! When you went to steal Fothering's name, that was very poor trash indeed—such poor trash that I say to myself, 'Why—a thousand times why?' Yes, I ask myself why—and now I ask *you*."

Lindsay contrived a puzzled expression.

Restow laughed again.

"My dear friend," he said, "if someone shows you a line of French and tries to persuade you that it is Latin, he will lose his time—*hein?* That is because you learned Latin and French in your public school. My school, it was the streets of all the big cities in Europe, and I learned there to know men—therefore you cannot deceive me. You have Fothering's face, but you have not Fothering's mind. Just for five minutes, when you first arrive, you are Fothering; but after that—no—by Jing, no—you are not Fothering any more, and I ask myself who are you, and why are you here? And I think you are from Drayton, or you are from the police, but I am not sure. If you are from Drayton, then it is very serious. It may be that he no longer needs me. I have been useful—a screen, a camouflage, a shelter—but it may be that I am no longer necessary. I am perhaps an old glove. And the old gloves of Drayton—something happens to them very quick—by Jing, yes—dam quick! Yes, I begin to think that I am an old glove."

"And then?" said Lindsay in his natural voice.

Restow laid a hand on his shoulder.

"Then I see behind Fothering's face someone whom I like very much. Funny that—*hein?* I see behind Fothering's face a friend. I know very well that you are not from Drayton. I feel you are a friend—I talk to you—I tell you of Gloria. *Ach!* Do you think I would tell what is in my heart to someone whom I do not trust? No, by Jing! What I learnt in my school, that I know!" He paused and dropped his hand. "You have lied to me, and you have come into my house with a false name—and I trust you so much that now, at this moment, I am putting my life into your hands, and more than my life—but you do not trust me."

Lindsay felt oddly touched. Restow had spoken with a simplicity which he found touching. He said quietly and deliberately,

"You're wrong. I propose that we should both put our cards on the table."

Restow caught him by the arms and swung him to and fro, laughing like a great boy.

"Aha! *Aha!* By Jing, yes! And what are your cards, my Fothering? No, you are not Fothering—by Jing, no! And what do I call you—*hein?*"

"I think you had better go on calling me Fothering."

Restow nodded, tossing his head back and jerking it forward.

"Yes, *yes*—Fothering. By Jing, what a likeness!"

Lindsay felt himself flushing. Even now he resented the fact that he was like Froth—*Froth.*

"Aha! You do not like that—you do not love Fothering! Is he your brother?"

"No—only a cousin. And I am not really so very like him when my hair is not red and my eyebrows are their proper shape."

"He has them plucked! *Ach!* Like a young lady!" Restow laughed again. "Now come—come—*come!* Show me these cards of yours—spill out this what Shakespeare calls 'perilous stuff'—*hein?* Get it off the chest—he says bosom—but it is all the same meaning as when Gloria says 'spill it.'"

Lindsay spilled it. He did not mention Garrett or Mr Benbow Collingwood Horatio Smith; he did not in fact mention any names but those already known to Restow.

The big man listened intently, frowning here, laughing there, gesticulating angrily, his expression changing from one moment to another. He stood by the hearth, a towering figure in crimson emerald and blue. Like something out of the Arabian Nights, was Lindsay's thought—a djinn who might at any moment expand and carry off the house and all its occupants on smoky sable wings.

Lindsay leaned on the mantelshelf, one foot raised to the bright brass kerb, his eyes on Restow's changing face. When he had finished, there was an unexpected silence.

Into it Restow shot a question:

"And the girl who faints when she sees you at the Luxe—what about her?"

"She thought that I was dead."

"And you let her think that? You sacrifice the woman you love like that?"

"She had broken off our engagement." Lindsay found himself stammering a little. "She—I—"

"And you let her think she had driven you to your death? By Jing, you are hard and cold, you English! Yes, by Jing! You put that burden on those delicate lady shoulders, and when it is lifted suddenly she faints and tells Drayton what he is wanting to know. I think till then you have deceived him enough to make him not sure—and he wants to be sure. Then when your Marian Rayne—Aha, yes, I have informed myself about her name—when she faints—pft!—Drayton knows that you are not Fothering, and he sets the first snake on you. If you are bitten, it will be Gloria's fault, because she loves snakes and everyone will say that if she have one snake in an hotel, she probably have a dozen and they walk about at night, or hop like fleas from room to room and from floor to floor, and what a shame it is these artists—with their temperament, and their snakes who bite people in a large, fine hotel like the Luxe. No one at all will think of Drayton—who is not even in Paris. Why should he?"

"Was he in Paris?"

Restow threw a sombre look upon him.

"Yes—by Jing he was, but I cannot prove it. I cannot prove anything except the one thing that I will die to hide. Can you prove anything?"

"Not yet."

"Not yet? Not *ever*! He is too cunning. He has defended himself with too many secrets. Once—twice—perhaps half a dozen times someone whom he has tormented too much has had the thought of giving proof against him to the police—and they have died very suddenly. Did you hear ever the name of Ferdinand Schreck? Aha, you did? He was the last, and he was shot with a policeman on this side of him and on that, and a policeman in front and another behind, and no one knows who fired the shot." He paused, swung half round, bent forward, facing Lindsay. "Perhaps he listens now. Perhaps he aims now at me. Perhaps he shoots now before I can tell you what I know."

Lindsay looked involuntarily over his shoulder. Then he followed his glance, stood for an instant in the doorway between the two rooms, and came back to the hearth again.

"Well, he is not in there," he said with a laugh.

Restow nodded.

"No—not this time. Well, I will tell you—but it is not much—and you will have guessed some of it. He blackmails me, this devil—this Vulture who feeds on carrion."

"Drayton is the Vulture?" The words jumped to Lindsay's lips.

Restow flung up his hands.

"If I could prove that! But no one can prove it. He is a devil. Let me go on—perhaps there is not very much time. Eight years ago Lewindorf dies, and this Drayton comes to me with papers to say he is the best librarian in the world, and I take him. I know now that he has stolen these papers, and that he comes to me because he has need of a place to hide and stay quiet whilst Europe is raked out for him. Well, I take him. He stays quiet—oh, very quiet indeed. I think he does a little quiet blackmail, but no big coup—no—every place is too hot for him. He leads the simple life. How touching! Then one day I find something out—a quite little thing, and I take notice. The more notice I take, the more I do not like my good Drayton. I send for him. I tell him so. I say, 'You are dismissed.' And he says—*Ach, was!*" The blood ran thick and dark to the roots of Restow's hair. He turned away. His voice choked.

Lindsay waited. He was not prepared for the fury with which Restow flung round again.

"He blackmails me—*me*! He has found something—something that breaks my heart—something! Oh, my friend, it is Gloria that he threatens to torture, to drag before the public—to—to—*Ach!* Why do I tell you this? Can you understand that there may be a thing in her life? *Ach ja!* Think that she is left without parents, or friends, or home! Think of this! This Vulture battens on what he has found. He blackmails me. If it were me that he threatened, I would let him go to blazes—I do not care. But it is my Gloria, and I suffer anything rather than let him spit his poison in her face. I tell you, my friend, I have been in a pit of torment. This man makes my home his place of refuge—he hatches his plots here—he does his vile business here—and because of Gloria I cannot take him by the throat and choke him. He taunts me with that. On the next day after he dies he says all this that he knows will be in the hands of others who will deal with it more hardly than he has dealt. My hands are tied. By Jing, you think I am a fool! And I say, yes, I am a damfool—for Gloria—and a coward—for Gloria—and weak like a woman—for Gloria. And you are the first to whom I can speak and get it off my chest—yes, by Jing!"

"What hold has he over Madame Gloria? Do you mind telling me?"

"I will tell you anything," said Restow. "It is a letter that he has—a letter that she has written when she was a young girl, very proud, very friendless. It is a letter to break the heart. If she ever knows that I have seen it—I who love her—it will be something that she cannot forget."

"She does not know?" Lindsay spoke in amazement.

"No, she does not know. For that price I give this Drayton a den to hide in. If he were to tell her, I would care no longer—I would drive him out—and this he knows. For the rest—for this letter—I offer him to the half of what I have. But it is not for sale like that—he will not take money for it—it is to keep him a refuge—he will not part with it. What can I do?"

Lindsay was silent.

"What is there to do?" repeated Restow. "I ask myself that. Sometimes I think, like Hamlet, that it is better to take a whole sea of troubles into my arms and make an end of it. *Hein?* He said that, didn't he?"

Lindsay grinned.

"Something like it," he said.

"What did he say?"

"'Whether 'tis nobler in the mind to suffer
The slings and arrows of outrageous fortune
Or to take arms against a sea of troubles
And by opposing end them.'"

"By Jing—yes! He says that well, Hamlet! I find him very sympathetic—but not cheerful—no. Let us come back to your Marian Rayne. I have seen her. She is a young girl, well brought up, good, beautiful. What else is she?"

"I think—Drayton's stepdaughter. She broke off our engagement because she thought that she was his daughter."

"And the other girl, Elise—no, Elsie Manning, to whom Fothering used to write love-letters—or perhaps not love-letters—I do not know?"

"She is Marian's sister, and Drayton's stepdaughter too. I do not know why he has pretended to be their father—a matter of bolstering up another identity, I imagine—but there it is. I believe Marian and Elsie are the daughters of a young American artist called Lee Abinger. Drayton married their mother when they were too young to remember anything about it. He was Manning then."

"By Jing he did!" He paused and laid a hand on Lindsay's arm. "And do you think that they are safe, these two girls, who know that Drayton was once Manning? Do you think that they are safe?"

Chapter Thirty-Eight

At ten next morning Lindsay was called to the telephone. An apologetic lady enquired if she were speaking to Mr Restow's secretary.

"Oh—I am the secretary—the—er—honorary secretary of this branch of the S.P.C.A. and I want to know whether you think it would be possible to interest Mr Restow to the extent of obtaining a permanent subscription."

Lindsay's heart beat a shade faster. Garrett had arranged to send him necessary information under cover of this code. He wondered what could have happened so soon after their parting last night. He said,

"Well—he is very much interested in animals—but he sees no one without an appointment."

"Then—oh—I wonder—would it be possible for me to see you? Could you make it possible?"

Lindsay said, "Yes." Something must have happened. He felt an acute anxiety.

"Could you come round presently, do you think?"

"Oh, at once," said the voice.

The matter then was urgent.

He rang off, and waited impatiently until a footman announced Miss Dorrington, and there entered an elderly lady in shabby black, with wispy grey hair, gold pince-nez, and an incongruously new silk scarf brightly striped with yellow, brown, and blue.

When the door was shut she moved as far away from it as possible and handed Lindsay a note.

"If you would just glance at some of our literature—" she said in a deprecating voice.

Lindsay tore open the note, which was in Garrett's scrawl. It ran:

"Dear Lin, we have got a line on the Vulture through Manning. This makes those two girls of yours very important witnesses, as we shall have to rely on them to establish Manning's identity with Drayton. Do you know where Miss Rayne is? She left Paris yesterday with the Mersons, the people she had been staying with. They all arrived at Victoria at eight o'clock. The Mersons took the next train to Ealing. Miss Rayne was to have gone down to her uncle's place in Surrey—their car was waiting for her at Victoria. She never reached it. Miss Manning is also not to be found. Thurloe doesn't know where she is and is raising Cain. We've collected the picture you spoke of from her rooms. There were papers inside the back of it— marriage certificate of Marian Carr and Lee Abinger—birth certificates of two daughters, Marian Carr and Elsie Lee. So that's that. Communicate through Miss Dorrington."

The blow struck him speechless for the moment. He stared at the note in his hand. Miss Dorrington talked about "our pets"—about animal intelligence—about a bazaar she was hoping to get up—"but people are so terribly apathetic."

Lindsay got himself in hand. He must see Garrett, and at once. He said so, speaking low.

"I must see him, Miss Dorrington."

"Inadvisable, unless it is very urgent."

"It is very urgent."

"Then you had better come to my house. I will let him know."

She gave him the address and went away, leaving S.P.C.A. literature strewed upon the table.

Lindsay burst in upon Garrett an hour later. He found him rather snappy.

"A bit thick this, Lin, unless you've got something to justify it!"

"I think I have. Will you tell me everything you know about Marian?"

"Report first. I tell you we don't know anything about her—there's no more news. Tell me why you dragged me here."

Lindsay told him. Dilling's drunken babblings, the *kraits* in his room, his interview with Restow, all seemed a long time ago.

Garrett listened, with his sharp eyes fixed on Lindsay's face. After a cut and thrust of question and answer he walked to the end of the room and back.

"Well, you can call that a night!" he said. "Now, what do you want to know about that girl of yours?"

"I want to know where she is," said Lindsay grimly.

"So do I. I've been on to the Ealing police, and they've been on to the Mersons. The Mersons say she said good-bye to them as soon as they arrived at Victoria. They saw her go off with a porter and her luggage. We've found the porter. He says he missed her in the crowd and never saw her again."

"And the luggage?"

"Still at Victoria. The chauffeur waited till after the last boat train was in and then rang up the Raynes. They rang up the hotel in Paris, and then the police over here. They seem genuinely upset."

"And Elsie Manning?"

"Started for work as usual this morning and never arrived at the shop. She has probably gone off for the day, and will make us all look silly by walking in to tea." Garrett barked out his sharp laugh. "Well, that was quite an interesting bag you brought along. Well, we'll gather Ibrahim and we'll pull Dilling in. I don't suppose Dilling knows anything that'll be the slightest use, but we'll go through him with a toothcomb. We are watching the house in Blenheim Square. Drayton will be followed if he tries to get away. Well, I've got work to do if you haven't. I'll give you a free hand and you can ring up or come round any time now I take it there isn't much the Vulture don't know about you by now. Ware snakes—and keep your pecker up!"

In the room where they were talking the telephone bell rang sharply. Garrett lifted the receiver. His sandy hair bristled and he rapped out a hard,

"What's that?"

The telephone buzzed.

Garrett spoke again.

"Well, he's here if you want him. Here, Fothering—you're wanted."

The telephone buzzed again. As Lindsay put the receiver to his ear, the buzzing resolved itself into words.

"Mr Trevor—"

"Trevor Fothering," corrected Lindsay.

Along the line came Drayton's voice, harsh and grating:

"Oh no."

There was a pause. Lindsay looked at Garrett, who nodded expressively and scrawled upon a bit of paper,

"I heard. No good bluffing. Get him to talk. Keep him talking."

"What is it?" said Lindsay.

"Nothing, unless I am speaking to Lindsay Trevor."

"And if you are?"

"Something that may interest him."

Lindsay's hand clenched.

"Trevor speaking," he said, and waited. The answer came slowly:

"In the matter of Marian Rayne—"

"Yes?"

"You would be interested to have her address?"

"I should."

"I sell things. I don't give them away."

"Yes?"

"I will sell you Marian's address for a pass out of England."

Lindsay looked round for Garrett, but the room was empty. He guessed that an attempt was being made to locate the place from which Drayton was speaking. It was for him to keep him talking.

"It's not for me to give passes," he said.

"Why not? You have friends, haven't you? Some of them are probably hunting me at this moment. If they catch me, it will be very unfortunate for Marian. I should think about that if I were you—I should think about getting that pass."

Lindsay felt a sudden rush of hope. Drayton must be hard pressed to ask for terms like this.

Drayton spoke again:

"Your friend Garrett could do a little thing like that for you easily. He has only to turn a blind eye, and it will all be very pleasant for everyone. It is a pity that I shall not be able to come to your wedding. I am afraid I shall be in France. Good-bye!" The line went dead.

Lindsay began to wonder. He wondered whether Drayton had been careless for once. He wondered why he was so anxious to convey an impression that he was in flight for France. He wondered whether he really knew where Marian was.

Chapter Thirty-Nine

MR. MERSON sat in the smoking-room of the Luxe. His large globular face wore a startled and offended expression. The little man with the clipped moustache who was leaning towards him raised a well kept hand and let it fall again upon his knee.

"You've got to take your orders like the rest of us," he said.

"That's a word I don't like," said Mr Merson.

The little man laughed.

"Do you suppose anyone cares whether you like it or not? I've got my orders, and Rayne has got his, and you've got yours, and that's all about it."

"I don't like it," said Mr Merson.

The little man swore without heat.

"If you don't like it, you can lump it." Then, briskly, "You've practically nothing to do. You cross by the afternoon boat. At Dover you send Rayne a wire telling him what time you get to Victoria and asking him to meet his niece. He will send his car and a chauffeur. You will say good-bye to the girl at Victoria. You understand? You say good-bye on the platform. What happens after that is no concern of yours. She goes off with her luggage and you take the next train to Ealing. Have you got that perfectly clear? You wire to Rayne—and you say good-bye on the platform. Those are the two things that matter. It is all perfectly simple, and you are not involved in any way."

Mr Merson's large face took on an uncomfortable expression.

"What is the idea?" he said.

The little man shrugged his shoulders.

"That's not your affair. The less you know the better."

Mr Merson looked still more uncomfortable.

"I couldn't be a party to her coming to any harm."

"Who said she was coming to any harm?" He swore again. "If you don't know by now that it's better to do what you're told without asking questions—well, you're liable to get a jolt. I suppose you wouldn't like that business about the Keeling Oil shares to leak out in your local paper. I suppose you have a local paper?"

Mr Merson's discomfort became firmly centred upon himself. He gave no further trouble.

When Marian Rayne looked back upon the journey afterwards, she tried to remember whether there had been anything which might have aroused her suspicions, but she could discover nothing. Mrs Merson fussed as usual over the luggage, and Mr Merson maintained his accustomed air of stolid boredom. He expected to be bored when he travelled, and he was bored. Paris bored him to extinction. Marian wondered what could possibly have taken him there. She would have been very much surprised to hear that it was herself and her affairs.

Between Dover and Victoria she dozed a little. The relief from sorrow and strain, and the joy of returning to England now that Lin was there filled her thoughts. Her light sleep was full of happy images.

She waked with a start to the bustle and confusion of arrival. It appeared that the Mersons wanted to say good-bye to her, to be free to attend to their luggage, and catch their train. Mrs Merson kissed her. Mr Merson touched her hand and let it fall again.

"Your uncle is sending the car," he said. "You'll find it outside." He did not look at her as he spoke, and the heavy gloom of his manner was intensified.

She was glad to turn away and move with the moving crowd. She had her dressing-case in her hand, and was looking about for the porter who was to bring up the rest of her luggage, when a chauffeur approached her and touched his cap.

"I beg your pardon—are you Miss Rayne?"

Marian said, "Yes."

"Mr Rayne has sent me to meet you."

Marian looked about her.

"I was expecting his own car," she said.

"He's had an accident with it, miss—coming up to meet you. Not hurt, he isn't, but a bit shook about, so he sent me along from the garage to meet you."

"Where is he?" said Marian quickly.

"At the Warminster Hotel—and he asked me to say would you come along at once."

"I'll come just as soon as I can get hold of my luggage."

"It's no distance, miss. I can run you up and come back for the luggage. He's a bit shook about, and wanting his dinner and not liking to begin without you."

Marian thought the man's manner a little familiar.

"I'd like to take my luggage with me," she said.

"I'll come straight back for it."

She hesitated.

The man dropped his voice.

"He's hurt a bit more than I said. I should come quick if I was you."

Why hadn't he said so at once? Suppose Uncle Robert was badly hurt.

She followed the man to the car, questioning him as she went. It seemed that he had not seen Mr Rayne himself.

"They took him off to the hotel, and the boss told me to go and meet the young lady and bring her along as sharp as I could."

As they drove away, she reassured herself. If Uncle Robert had been badly hurt, he would have been taken to a hospital. She began to feel that she had allowed herself to be frightened unnecessarily. She ought not to have left her luggage like that. There was something odd about the man wanting her to leave it. What had happened to Maitland, Uncle Robert's chauffeur? Uncle Robert never drove the Bentley himself.

She put her head out of the window and spoke to the driver.

"Was the chauffeur hurt?"

"All smashed up," he said laconically.

She drew back in horror. The man had a wife and children.

She had not noticed which way they turned, but now, as she stared out of the near window, she saw a lighted tram go by. That must mean they were in the Vauxhall Road. But what hotel was there in this neighbourhood that Uncle Robert would be likely to go to? She had never heard of the Warminster Hotel. Insistently there came the pressure of the thought, "I oughtn't to have left my luggage like that."

She leaned out of the window again and spoke her thought aloud:

"I oughtn't to have left my luggage like that. Will you please turn round and go back?"

"We're nearly there."

"Is the hotel down this way?"

"I'm cutting up through Vincent Square."

"Please go back. I would rather get my luggage first."

They were held up for the moment behind a van. The man turned his head.

"'Tisn't worth going back, miss—honest it isn't," he said with so much of the manner of the respectful servant that Marian, unaccustomed to authority, sat back again.

As she did so, some trick of the light gave her the man's face in the driving-mirror, with a look upon it that turned her cold. She couldn't have described the look, but it was wholly evil. He had deceived her, and he was gloating over it. She felt frightened, and weak, and very cold. And then suddenly a despairing courage blazed up in her. She tried the handle of the door on the left, but before she could get it open the car was moving again and next moment had turned off from the broad lighted road.

Marian struggled with the handle. She was quite determined now that she would not go on. At the worst, she could go back to Victoria, pick up her luggage, and take a taxi to the Warminster Hotel. Could she? The car was now going so fast that it was madness to think of jumping out, but she had turned the handle and next time they slowed down she would risk it. She sat on the edge of the seat, holding her dressing-case in one hand and the door in the other, her foot all ready to take the step.

Her opportunity came when a car came out of a side street just in front of them. Both drivers braked sharply to avoid a collision, and in a moment Marian was on the pavement. She had the presence of mind to shut the door noiselessly behind her. Then she picked up her feet and ran down the side street.

It was so dark that it was like running into a tunnel. She put out her hand in front of her and ran, keeping to the middle of the street. She had run into a lamppost once as a child, and the instinct to shield her face sprang from that old memory. The dressing-case dragged heavily at her left arm and shoulder.

Suddenly on her right a point of light showed against the dark—a candle flame high up at an uncurtained window, not in her street, but in a narrow alley running out of it on the right. She would never have seen the alley if someone had not showed the light.

She turned and ran up the alley, and as she did so, she heard a car coming down the street behind her. The little point of candle light went out before she reached the house where it had showed. Marian went on running, and listened with straining ears for the sound of footsteps behind her. She judged the alley too narrow to take a car.

No footsteps came.

The alley came out into a wider street. Presently she stopped running. She did not want to attract attention, and she wanted time to think. She was in a well lighted road and felt safer. She put her dressing-case down for a moment, stretched her arm, and then went on again. She did not know what to do.

Under a lamp she looked at her watch. The last train to Oakshot had gone. She might get a train to Guildford and drive from there, but it was a long way. She shrank from the idea of the seven mile drive alone. She felt shaken, and she wanted to get into touch with Lindsay and tell him what had happened. This on the surface. Underneath, a shrinking dread of what might have been behind this attempt to carry her off. The Mersons' decision to cross had been hastily taken. Who knew about it? The Mersons themselves and—the Raynes. Who knew that she was arriving at Victoria, and when? Again the Mersons, and the Raynes.

She didn't want to go down to Oakshot. She wanted to get clear away from these people who took orders from Drayton, and she wanted to keep away. But she hadn't enough money to go to an hotel. She remembered with something like panic that her purse contained about twenty francs and an English sixpence. There were plenty of people in town who would take her in, but there was not one of them who would not at once ring up the Raynes and tell them where she was. Her heart smote her hard; but stronger than anything else was the growing instinct to hide.

Her thoughts turned to her unknown sister. Lindsay had refused to give her Elsie's address, but she knew that she worked in a hat-shop. After a little hesitation Lindsay had given her the name of the hatshop. What was the good of that? The shop would have closed hours ago, and besides, she had no idea where it was.

She walked on slowly. It was not raining, but the road was dark and wet, and round every street-lamp a pool of spilled light made the pavement shine. At a crossing she went up to the policeman on duty and asked where she was. She had lost all sense of direction and had no idea what street she was in. When he said "Victoria Street," it was just as if a blind went up. Lin's flat—she could go to Lin's flat—it was quite close—Poole would take her in.

She hurried across the road, found the turning, and in five minutes she was standing at the door of the flat listening to the sharp buzz of the bell and wondering with a sudden cold fright whether there would be anyone there to let her in. Suppose the flat had been given up...No, there hadn't been time since Lindsay's official death—but the flat might have been shut up and Poole paid off. As the thought went through her mind, she became aware of how cold and tired she was. She leaned against the jamb, and felt it waver. The floor moved under her feet. From a long way off she heard footsteps coming towards her. They did not seem to come any nearer.

She let go of her dressing-case because she could not hold it any longer. It fell, and the sound that it made in falling seemed far away. Then the door opened, and a bright light shone in her face.

Chapter Forty

POOLE OPENED the door.

The first thing he saw was a hand clinging to the jamb. Then the light fell on Miss Marian Rayne.

Poole had a very methodical mind. Even as he opened the door, he received and arranged a number of impressions. He perceived with approval that Miss Rayne was dressed in black. Broken engagement, or no broken engagement, he would have thought very little of her if she had been wearing colours so soon after Lindsay Trevor's death. Her pallor and the shadows under her eyes also satisfied his sense of propriety. Something human and fierce behind the conventional Poole was humanly and fiercely glad that the girl who had turned Lindsay down should look so shocked and ill. All this in a flash. Then a second set of impressions. Her stockings were splashed with mud—her hat awry—the hand that gripped the jamb was shaking. He arranged these impressions too. She had had a fright—she had been running.

He said aloud in his most expressionless voice,

"Good evening, miss."

Marian's wavering glance went past him. She knew that he was there, but she could only see a blur in a changing mist, and she could not hear what he said because of the singing in her ears. Her hand dropped from the jamb. She took a faltering step forward and would have fallen if he had not caught her. When the mist receded she was on the sofa in Lindsay's sitting-room, with Poole in the middle of the room regarding her doubtfully.

"I'm sorry," she said. "I—I've had a fright."

"Yes, miss."

He looked very disapproving. She didn't think that Poole had ever approved of her. Now, of course, he must disapprove most dreadfully.

Her faintness had passed, but Poole and his disapproval still seemed rather far away.

"I haven't any money," she said, "and I've missed the last train—and—do you think I could stay here to-night?"

"I don't know, I'm sure, miss," said Poole.

Marian wondered suddenly how much he knew. Did he know that Lindsay was alive?

A little colour came into her face.

"I think—Mr Trevor—would wish me to stay—" she began.

The fierce, human Poole who adored Lindsay Trevor experienced a furious resentment—" She that had chucked him over like an old glove! And what for? Tell me that! When there isn't one of the whole blinking female sect good enough for him to wipe his boots on! She to come here, throwing faints, and going red in the face when she says his name!"

Aloud he said, in his most wooden manner,

"I can't say, I'm sure."

Marian leaned forward, her colour deepening.

"Poole," she said, "do you know that he's alive?"

Poole stood to take the shock of it, as he would have stood to take the shock of a bomb. It took all his self-control. But whilst the real Poole exulted and rioted, the conventional Poole preserved a perfectly expression-less face. He repeated his last remark mechanically and in just the same voice:

"I can't say, I'm sure, miss."

Marian jumped up.

"But he is! He's alive! Isn't it—isn't it wonderful? He's alive, but he's in danger. It's—it's a job—it's a very dangerous job. Oh, Poole—did you know all the time?"

Poole became aware that he was gripping the edge of the table. He took his hand away quickly, looked at it as if he expected to find something sticking to the palm, and said, "If you'll excuse me, miss—it's not my place to talk about Mr Trevor's affairs."

"You *did* know?" said Marian. "He told you?"

"Begging your pardon, miss, Mr Trevor never told me anything neither for nor against."

The conventional Poole had for the moment been thrust aside. The other Poole desired once and for all to make it clear that he was not dependent for his knowledge upon being *told* things.

"But you knew!"

"Well, it stands to reason, miss. Mr Trevor didn't need to tell me when he was going on a job, and he knew that he didn't need to tell me."

A little sparkle of triumph came into Marian's eyes.

"I saw him—yesterday," she said, and had to stop to think before she said *yesterday*, because it seemed a long time ago.

Poole's heart leapt. Poole's face showed nothing.

"Can I get you anything, miss?" he said with cold civility.

Marian woke next morning in Lindsay's little guest room—a very mannish apartment, with Lindsay's books over the mantelshelf, Lindsay's spare boots in rows along the wall, and Lindsay's clothes hanging inside the wardrobe. She had not expected to sleep, but she had slept dreamlessly for hours. Last night she had not known what she was going to do, but this morning she knew. She was going to find her sister. If she went to Santa's and walked up and down on the opposite side of the road, she would be able to catch Elsie on her way to work. She paused here to consider that Lindsay had told her not to try and see Elsie. But Lin didn't know that someone had tried to carry her off last night. She couldn't go home. She must get into touch with Lin and ask him what she was to do. Elsie would know how she could do this without endangering Lin. She couldn't go to him direct, but she must let him know what had happened.

It occurred to her with a stab that what had happened to her might have happened to Elsie too. Lin had thought Elsie in danger. Why, anything might be happening to Elsie, now whilst she lay in bed. She dressed quickly, and then remembered that Elsie would not *go* to work before nine.

At a quarter to nine she was walking slowly past the shop with *Santa* in a gold scrawl on the upper part of the plate glass window. The window itself contained three bare pegs and a strip of green and gold brocade. She had found the address quite easily by looking in the telephone directory.

A little farther down on the other side of the road was a paper shop. She went over to it and bought a *Daily Mail*. A tall fair girl came along the street and Marian's heart began to beat. She hadn't thought till now that there might be other girls at Santa's, and that she would not know Elsie if she saw her. She walked across, crushing the paper under her arm. No—this wasn't Elsie. She felt sure that this wasn't Elsie. She recalled Lindsay's description and passed by. The girl opened the shop door and went in.

Marian walked to the corner of the street and then turned quickly lest Elsie should come from the opposite direction and she should miss her.

As she stood looking down the grey street, a girl came past—a girl in a black coat and a small black hat. Marian looked at her eagerly and saw brown eyes, a bright colour, a round face. She touched the girl's arm and said, "Are you Elsie?"

The girl stopped.

"I'm Elsie Manning."

"Elsie—I'm Marian," said Marian.

Elsie turned to face her. The brown eyes fixed a clear searching look upon her face. Then she said,

"You're very like—Mother."

"Am I?"

They stood looking at each other. Then with a start Elsie caught at Marian and hurried her back round the corner.

"Let's come somewhere where we can talk."

Chapter Forty-One

POOLE ENDURED the arrival of a second young lady with self-control. Mr Trevor would doubtless wish Miss Rayne and Miss Rayne's friend to be provided with lunch, and in due course he went out to do the necessary shopping.

The sisters, who had not met since they were babies, and met now under the shadow of a very pressing danger, had everything to say to one another and very little time to say it in. Neither kept anything back, and each felt an extraordinary relief.

After an hour's talk Elsie produced a plan. She would find Jimmy Thurloe, and Jimmy should get into touch with Lindsay.

"You see, my dear, they'll all be tearing their hair thinking you've been kidnapped. Why, by this time, I expect, they're looking for me too. I shouldn't wonder if Jimmy's paper hadn't got headlines out already." She paused, frowning. "We don't want to do anything to queer Lindsay's pitch. It's all very difficult—but I'm bound to let Jimmy know I'm all right. I'll go and tidy up and *get* going."

She went into the bedroom.

Marian was just going to follow her, when the doorbell rang. Poole was still out. Marian went to the door and opened it. A very tall man stood on the threshold. He was well dressed and well set up. As he removed his hat, he showed dark hair cut close. He put his hand on the door, walked past Marian into the hall, and shut the door again.

"I think, my dear Marian, that we must have a little talk," he said in a harsh grating tone.

It was the voice alone that told Marian that this was Drayton. She looked at him with terrified incredulity. There was the great height—but Drayton stooped—and Drayton wore baggy clothes—and had bushy eyebrows and grey untidy hair. Yet this was Drayton's hand upon her shoulder.

He pushed her into the sitting-room and shut the door.

"We will have our talk before Mr Trevor's man comes back. I thought I should find you here."

"What do you want?" said Marian faintly.

What did he want? What did he know? He seemed to know everything. He knew Lindsay's name—he knew Poole had gone out. Did he know that Elsie was here? She stood, pale, with his hand on her, and looked at the cold, cruel eyes. Yes—these were Drayton's eyes—her father's eyes. She felt sick.

"I won't keep you," he said. "I'm not anxious to stay. I am in fact leaving England. I merely want an undertaking from you that you will hold your tongue. It is not much to ask from a daughter."

She tried to speak, and failed. There was a dreadful force in his look.

All at once she felt she could bear his touch no longer. She wrenched away from it and stood back, breathing hard.

Drayton lifted his smooth black brows. She watched him, fascinated. This wasn't Drayton at all. This was a much younger man, good-looking in a hard well-featured way. There was no likeness to the man who had terrified her at Blenheim Square. Only the cold force of his look and the harsh grating tones of his voice were Drayton's; yet when he spoke again, it was in a new voice—a voice that went easily with this new personality—a cold, well-bred voice rather lacking in tone.

"I am leaving England, probably for good. Before I go you will take an oath—" He paused and regarded her ironically. "I suppose an oath means some thing to you?" Then, as she made no answer, he dropped to the old grating note. "Does it?"

The question struck her like a blow.

She said, "Yes," and gave back a pace.

"If you took an oath, you would keep it?"

"Yes."

"Then you will take one now."

She went back another step, and felt the wall. What was he going to ask her to swear?

"You will swear never to identify me."

She said, "How?" in a whisper.

His eyebrows rose again.

"You have seen me as Drayton—and I was sufficiently indiscreet to let you know of my identity with Manning. These were confidences to a daughter. You will swear never to repeat them—never to give evidence against me—never to describe me as you see me now."

Marian let her head rest against the wall. If she promised—would he go away? Was it right for her to promise? Would it be right for her to give evidence against her own father? She felt sick and bewildered, and pushed by the man's commanding will.

And then all at once there was a little sound from the hall.

It was the click of a latchkey.

Marian made a startled movement. The door of the flat was opening. It must be Poole coming back.

With one stride Drayton was beside her, his lips against her ear.

"If you give me away, I shoot!"

Then there was the clap of the closing door, and Lindsay Trevor's voice calling:

"Poole!"

An awful expression of malignity broke the smooth surface of Drayton's features. For a moment he showed another face, and it was horrible. It warned, commanded, threatened. As Marian shrank, he left her.

On the side of the room behind the door that would surely open at any moment stood an oak press. Drayton reached it, opened the door, and vanished into the dark space. Marian caught a glimpse of golf clubs, and wondered whether they would come crashing down.

There was no noise at all. Drayton had moved without making any noise. The door closed silently upon him. Just before it shut, his hand showed at the opening. There was a revolver in it.

She stood still, and scarcely dared to breathe.

Drayton did not know that Elsie was in the flat. Did Elsie know that Drayton was here? Could she warn Lin what was happening?

What was going to happen?

For about five feet from the floor the press was of solid oak, but across its upper half there ran a row of small turned pillars with spaces in between. Through these spaces Drayton must be watching to see what she was going to do.

She stood against the wall, and knew what was going to happen. Lin would come into the room, and Drayton would shoot.

All this came to her in one terrifying flash. In the next she knew that if she had the courage to run for the door—now, at once—there was a chance that she might save Lin. She caught her breath and dragged herself from the wall. Drayton would shoot her. She wondered if the sound would be very loud in that little room. But perhaps she wouldn't hear it. She never thought that he might miss his aim.

She began to run. But she was too late; the door was flung open and Lindsay met her half way across the room.

"My darling child! What are you doing here?" he cried, and caught her in his arms.

Marian felt as if she had been trapped between two tides of violent emotion. There was fear—the sort of fear that stripped you of thought, courage, and self-control—and there was an irrational flood of joy and relief because Lin was there. She clung to him as if it was now that he had come to her from the dead, and, clinging, tried to put herself between him and the press.

His left arm tightened about her waist. His right hand gripped her arm with a steady warning pressure. His back was towards the press. His body screened her.

In that moment she knew that Elsie must have warned him. He knew that Drayton was here, and he was shielding her. But Drayton must not know. She must pretend—she must talk.

She said, "I came—"

And Lin said again, "My darling child!" And then "Where's Poole?"

And at that there came the click of Poole's key in the outer door.

At the first sound of it Lindsay swung her round and with all the momentum of the swing sent her flying across the space between them and the open door.

Poole, at the door of the flat, saw her come, her hands out in front of her, her feet stumbling and falling. She fell in a heap at his feet at the moment that the shot rang out.

Elsie Manning, half in and half out of the bedroom, screamed.

There was a second shot, and a shout and a splintering crash.

Poole took Miss Rayne in his stride and charged into the sitting-room. The doors of the press were open. A heaving struggling welter of legs, arms, and golf clubs met his view. He recognized Mr Trevor's legs in a pair of strange trousers, and Mr Trevor's voice calling his own name. The rest of the cupboard appeared to be full of a large and powerful man with a kick like a mule.

Poole got two kicks, and between the two another shot went off and smashed the window. There was a tinkle of glass, and then the sound of something snapping, and a sort of howl of mingled pain and rage. Then Mr Trevor's voice:

"Look out! I've broken his arm! Now, Drayton, you've had enough, haven't you? Chuck the revolver across the room! I've got him so that he'll break the other arm if he tries anything on."

They got him out of the cupboard, raging. Then suddenly he was silent and limp.

Lindsay called through the open door,

"Marian—are you all right?"

She said, "Yes."

He caught a glimpse of her with Elsie's arm round her, very white.

"One of you must telephone." He gave a number. "Say we've got him, and they must send along a doctor because his arm's broken."

The man who had called himself Drayton turned in the chair into which they had put him.

"My own daughters!" he said in a tone of great bitterness.

Lindsay saw Marian's face go whiter still.

"You know very well that they're not your daughters," he said. "You know very well that they are Lee Abinger's daughters."

Marian cried out, "Lin—is it true?"

"Absolutely. The papers were in the back of that picture of yours, Elsie. That's why your mother was pasting it up—you said it was the last thing she did. Well, it's set you free from the nightmare of thinking you belonged to this man. Your father was Lee Abinger, a brilliant young American artist. Elsie, will you get on to that number, please. Ask for Colonel Garrett. Say it's urgent."

The telephone was in the hall. As Elsie repeated her message, she heard, through the open door behind her, Lindsay say something to Poole in a low voice, but she could not have told what it was.

She kept on saying, "Yes, I must speak to Colonel Garrett. It's a very important message."

And then, at her elbow, Marian's voice, quick and frightened:

"Oh—he's fainted!"

Elsie turned her head. She could see Poole's wooden face and a bit of Lindsay's shoulder, and between them Drayton, all fallen forward and collapsed.

And then Garrett's voice snapped at her across the telephone:

"Well—what is it—what *is* it?"

Elsie turned back and said what she had been told to say.

"I'm speaking from Lindsay Trevor's flat—I'm speaking for him. Drayton's here—they've got him. He's got a broken arm. Lindsay says will you send a doctor?"

And just as Garrett rapped out a sharp "Why doesn't he speak to me himself? Tell him to come on the line!" pandemonium broke out in the room behind her. There was the crash of a falling chair—an exclamation from Lindsay—and a horrible hoarse roar.

She dropped the receiver, and saw through the open door Drayton, a towering, dishevelled figure with the revolver in his left hand. She was aware of Marian in the doorway, crying out. And then she herself was there too, looking into the room.

The chair on which Drayton had sat was overturned. Poole was on his hands and knees with a curious expression of surprise on his face. Lindsay, bent low, was charging across the room.

Drayton stood by the broken window. The revolver wavered in his hand. He fired at Lindsay and missed, stood for a second in his old stooped attitude as if he were hovering to strike, and then, before Lindsay reached him, he turned and dived crashing through the smashed window.

There was an awful silence—an awful sound—then silence again.

Into the silence there came the faint crackle of Garrett's voice from the deserted telephone.

Lindsay turned from what had been the window and crossed the room. He put his arm round Marian, and she clung to him with the tears running down her face.

Still holding her, he came through the hall and took up the receiver.

THE END

www.ingramcontent.com/pod-product-compliance
Lightning Source LLC
Chambersburg PA
CBHW070930190726
48292CB00004B/1173